THE IRISH IMBROGLIO

THE IRISH IMBROGLIO

Barry Fulton

Copyright © 2020 by Barry Fulton
All Rights Reserved
ISBN 979-8-64684-057-9
Independently Published
Benvenuto Press
Cover design by Davor Dramikanin
10 9 8 7 6 5 4 3 2 1

www.fultonpub.com

For Pippa

The warning lights are blinking red again.

—Dan Coats, former Director of National Intelligence

CONTENTS

Prologue

"Today, confronted with new threats that go well beyond terrorism, U.S. intelligence agencies face another moment of reckoning. From biotechnology and nanotechnology to quantum computing and artificial intelligence (AI), rapid technological change is giving U.S. adversaries new capabilities and eroding traditional U.S. intelligence advantages. The U.S. intelligence community must adapt to these shifts or risk failure as the nation's first line of defense." — Amy Zegart and Michael Morell, "Spies, Lies, and Algorithms," *Foreign Affairs*, May-June 2019.

"[The NSA's] early-warning centers have no ability to issue a warning to the president that would stop a cyberattack that takes down a regional or national power grid or to intercept a hypersonic cruise missile launched from Russia or China. The cyberattack can be detected only upon occurrence, and the hypersonic missile, only seconds or at best minutes before attack. And even if we could detect a missile flying at low altitudes at 20 times the speed of sound, we have no way of stopping it." — Glenn S. Gerstell, General Counsel of the National Security Agency, *New York Times*, September 10, 2019.

"Indeed, all the critical infrastructure that undergirds much of our lives, from the water we drink to the electricity that keeps the lights on, is at risk of being held hostage or decimated by hackers working on their own or at the behest of an adversarial nation. According to a study of the United States by the insurance company Lloyd's of London and the University of Cambridge's Centre for Risk Studies, if hackers were to take down the electric grid in just fifteen states and Washington, D.C., 93 million people would be without power . . . " — Susan Halpern, *New York Review of Books,* December 19, 2019.

"The COVID-19 pandemic foreshadows how a future bioweapons attack would unfold without proper preparation. Planning for a bioweapons attack is incredibly difficult— bioweapons can be delivered by states or terrorist groups, originate from existing agents or from scratch, and can be delivered in a number of different ways. While establishing a permanent military joint task force with appropriate funding is an achievable first step, combined efforts in deterrence, disruption, and defense are key in anticipating these variables of an attack and surviving it once unleashed." — Andrea Howard, "The Pandemic and America's Response to Future Bioweapons," *War on the Rocks*, May 1, 2020.

Chapter 1. Spooky Action

It began as a friendly call between two fishing buddies, but when Thomas Sebastian Scott heard, "the Bluefish are running," he understood there was no need for a rod and reel. "Meet you on the dock," he said, "tomorrow morning at seven," an agreed signal between two old colleagues.

By four a.m., he was traveling south on a rain-slick road. That would give him plenty of time to arrive before meeting with Hoople. Halfway to Fort Meade, traffic slowed to a complete stop.

Sirens interrupted the gentle patter of rain on the windshield. Firetrucks, ambulances, and police cars raced past on the shoulder. Scott turned the radio dial, but found only music, talk, and yesterday's news. He returned to his favorite jazz station and turned up the volume. "The Lion roars again," the announcer said, "with this vintage recording of *Ain't Misbehavin.*"

Traffic began to inch forward. Ten minutes later, he reached an overturned tractor-trailer smoldering from fire. Several nearby vehicles were still in flames.

Scott pulled off the road and stepped out of his car. The smell of diesel fuel and burning plastic hung in the air. He sniffed. A lingering odor of ammonia confirmed his hunch—all were signs of an explosive recipe favored by terrorists.

Walking toward a patrolman motioning traffic forward, Scott offered his assistance.

"Thanks, buddy, but we got it under control. Nothing *you* can do."

He thinks I'm some old duffer interfering with his work. "I'm a retired federal agent," Scott said, "trained in disaster assistance."

"Tell me how you could help," the patrolman said, "and I'll talk to the chief."

"This has all the markings of a terrorist attack. Cordon off the wreckage of the overturned semi and notify federal authorities immediately."

"Yeah, thanks, but we gotta move these bodies first."

Scott slowly returned to his car, walked by several charred bodies, and hyperventilated to maintain his composure. No way would he be able to decline Hoople's request now, regardless of how much he looked forward to his vacation to Northern Ireland and Austria.

The political divisions in the United States would be even wider tomorrow. Ignorance would lead to rumors. Jihadists or dark-skinned immigrants would be blamed. And if not, if it were a home-grown Timothy McVeigh or a Bible-quoting pastor, so what? It would be perceived as an attack on "us"—us who are trying to make America great again.

Scott had retired from the National Security Agency to a mountain village in West Virginia eight years earlier. He had envisioned a life of solitude and reflection. However, the phone call from Alex Hoople was the fourth time the agency had called him back for his cybersecurity expertise. He would insist on a long-planned personal visit to Northern Ireland and

Austria before accepting a new assignment—or perhaps have the good sense to decline. The young woman he had mentored, Rachel Sullivan, had the skills and temperament to succeed him.

A more cautious man would have driven to Fort Meade the day he received the call and rested overnight before his early-morning appointment. Of course, a more cautious man would not have chosen a career in espionage. Nearly seventy, standing just over six feet with a head full of silver-gray hair, he had the commanding presence of a military man despite a slight limp and an occasional stoop in his shoulders.

The impatient drive that had marked his career had not diminished. Puttering around the garden is restful, maybe even therapeutic, for those with an adrenalin deficit.

♦♦♦

Scott arrived at Fort Meade a few minutes before seven and met Alex Hoople in the parking lot.

"Welcome," Hoople said, "and thanks for driving down."

"Glad to be of service," Scott said, "and glad to be here. If I had left home thirty minutes earlier, you might have found me burnt to a crisp alongside the road."

"What do you mean?"

"A semi loaded with explosives—completely demolished, along with several cars in its path. A home-gown terrorist, I'm guessing."

Hoople cocked his head, waiting to hear more, when an eager young man caught his attention.

"Chief, you've heard . . . "

"About the explosion? Yeah, just now."

"The good news," he whispered to Hoople, "it's not on us. Nothing in the intercepts. Looks like it's domestic. Our liaison at Homeland Security agrees."

Scott continued walking with Hoople to his office.

"Imagine Washington indefinitely off the grid—cold, dark, and desolate," Hoople said. "Could happen tomorrow, or not for months, but it *will* happen unless we act."

Scott waited for Hoople to open his office door. He inserted his badge in the card reader, entered his digital passcode, and placed his thumb on a biometric scanner before the door obliged.

Twice the size of his former space, Hoople's new office came with his recent promotion.

Scott took note of a delicate miniature on the north wall: a sumptuous garden bracketed by beautiful calligraphy. *Shame I can't appreciate it now.*

He sat in one of the burgundy faux leather chairs that faced the artwork and closed his eyes to sharpen his focus.

"Coffee?" Hoople asked.

Scott nodded and opened his eyes.

"Sugar?"

"Yes, a little would be perfect."

Hoople took the chair beside Scott. "So, have you recovered from your Turkish adventure?"

"Completely healed," Scott said. "Never felt better. Even my limp has nearly disappeared." *Except when I'm alone recalling my life fading away in an ancient sanatorium.*

Hoople's expression soured. "My staff has been slashed. Even though he's recovered from his meltdown, our resident genius, Woody Woodward, is on the bench until his security clearance is restored. One of several reasons my hair is simultaneously thinning and graying."

"No surprise. The Feds always take it on the chin when a new administration comes to town."

"As a result," Hoople said, "we need you."

Scott grimaced. "Look, I've had a good run, but I'm getting too old for this. The next generation is not only capable, but better informed on the latest technologies. Rachel Sullivan's the best. And for tech savvy, no one's as good as Woody."

"Nor as crazy as Woody. You're right on Rachel, but she lacks confidence—and still needs your mentoring."

Hoople stood, walked to his desk, removed a single page from a folder, and returned to sit beside Scott. "It's from our new director, who's been schmoozing with the new CIA chief," Hoople said and began reading: "'I appreciate his past service and was moved by the strength of your appeal, but the decision is final. Mr. Scott is grounded.'"

He set the letter aside. "Period. That's it. Apparently, the station chief in Istanbul convinced the new team you were poaching on his territory. I explained that you succeeded despite the indifference of that lazy bastard, but to no avail." Hoople shrugged. "If Rachel hadn't rescued you, you'd be nothing more than a cold statistic in his missing persons ledger."

Scott smiled and raised his hands in a so-be-it gesture. "I'm not surprised nor particularly disappointed. As I may have told you," he said, "I *will* be traveling, not on your dime of course. First stop Belfast and then onward to Vienna to meet an Austrian friend. By dabbling in her genealogy, I've become interested in my own."

"Genealogy?" Hoople lifted an eyebrow. "That's new."

"After my parents died, I realized their life was a mystery to me. I didn't know what brought them to Pakistan, where they came from, or who they were. I've recently learned a little about my father's Irish roots, but only enough to arouse my curiosity. A genealogist in Belfast claims he can trace my family back five generations."

"Couldn't he provide that over the Internet?" Hoople asked.

"Maybe, if I insisted, but he's old school, wants to meet face-to-face. And a few days in Belfast will be relaxing."

Hoople scooted his chair closer to Scott, removed his glasses, and ran his fingers through his hair. His craggy face showed concern, maybe alarm. He shifted his weight in the chair and leaned toward Scott. "Before you run off, let me explain. Even if you can't travel overseas for us, we need you here. And if our intelligence is accurate, we need you more than ever. The entire government is focused on limiting the penetration of our computer networks by hostile governments—Russia, Iran, North Korea. It's taken a while, but our politicians are beginning to understand. Undermining Facebook and Twitter through misleading and malicious information is an existential threat to our democracy. So, we've increased our monitoring to identify and quarantine the bad actors."

Scott nodded. "I get it. Your staff has been decimated and refocused on social media. Still, you have the best forensic cyber analysts in the federal government."

"Yes, we still deliver," Hoople replied, "but we're stretched too thin to give enough attention to other threats, including adequate surveillance of potential cyberattacks on our nuclear reactors. For example, our analysts have found unusual activity around a nuclear power plant on the western shore of the Chesapeake Bay."

"Calvert Cliffs?"

"Exactly, and not more than fifty miles from Washington."

"Hmm, I seem to recall some press attention to lax security there a few years ago. And isn't the Russian *dacha* that Obama closed nearby?"

"Good memory," Hoople said, "but your cartography skills aren't up to snuff. The Russian compound is on the *eastern* shore of the Chesapeake, miles away from Calvert Cliffs."

"Seems my knowledge of the Chesapeake isn't much better than the little I know about nuclear-reactor security," Scott said, "but I promise to read in when I get back. By then, maybe Woodward will have his clearance restored."

"Maybe. Who knows? I thought the guy deserved a commendation for single-handedly destabilizing Iran's Revolutionary Guard, but our security guys didn't see it that way. He spends his days here in the library, undoubtedly doing research on cold fusion or some other esoteric topic."

"I'll spend the afternoon reviewing the files and stop by to see Woody on my way out," Scott said, "and if you'll direct me to Rachel's new office, I'll drop by there as well."

"Skip the office visit," Hoople said, "and drive directly to Molloy's Irish Pub. Woody and Rachel will be waiting to treat you to a Guinness. They insisted on seeing you over happy hour—and, as far as I know, have no idea you're on your way to Ireland, unless Woody managed to bug your West Virginia home."

♦♦♦

Molloy's looked like the real thing, a dive bar in yesterday's strip mall. A neon sign advertised Schlitz, and the voice of Waylon Jennings came from a tinny speaker on the wall. Rachel and Woody were nowhere in sight.

Why hadn't he heard from Rachel in the past month? Had returning from their Turkish assignment to her analyst duties been a letdown? Although blessed with beauty and brains, she didn't easily make friends. She had once remarked that people avoided her because she was deaf. Their problem, he thought, as she was easy to talk to if you looked at her straight on—and more engaging than most.

Scott took the only empty seat at the bar, ordered a draft Guinness, and checked his cell phone. A text from Rachel apologized for her delay.

> **<Waiting for Woody who may have wandered off the reservation again.>**

An unshaven guy, who must have begun happy hour much earlier, turned to Scott and said: "Hey, I wasn't minding my manners. Should have introduced myself when you sat down. Guessin' you're new here. Name's Mulligan, not my real name, but that's what everyone calls me. Started as a kid. What's yours, if you don't mind me askin'?"

"Thomas," he replied, "Thomas Scott. My friends call me Scott."

"Another Irishman, I'd reckon," he said with a sneer, "and dressed to kill. What brings you to this lowlife place? But first, here, help yourself to these chips." He pushed the basket toward Scott. "They're actually French fries, but the Irish call 'em chips. When I come in here, I always ask the gal at the bar for an order of fish and chips, and tell her to forget the fucking fish. And she brings me half a bucket of these by-god Irish chips." He laughed and took another drink. "Tell me again, what'd you say you do? Or forgive me for asking if you just came from a funeral, or a hanging, or somethin' real serious."

Before Scott could answer, the guy waved his hand and said, "Colleen, bring this gentleman another glass of what he's drinking. And, Mr. Scott, as you may have guessed, her name ain't really Colleen." He leaned forward and lowered his voice. "We all have our little secrets here."

"Thanks, Mulligan," Scott said. *How do I get out of this?*

"Not every day a stranger buys me a beer."

"Stranger? No way, my man. As I said, Mulligan's my name. And sitting here in this Irish pub is my game. That's not original. Heard that from some wiseass years ago, but it rhymes, so what the hell? And you, Mr. Scott, with your thousand-dollar suit, let me guess. A lawyer? Or just an ordinary guy trying to impress some woman?" He lifted his beer in a salute. "Probably half your age, maybe recently divorced, and not a clue that you're just another randy old bastard trying to get in her pants."

Scott's muscles tensed. He pushed his stool away from the bar.

The door opened. Heads turned. Rachel stood in the doorway, alone. She looked across the crowd, stepped forward, looked again, and then spotted Scott at the bar.

He stood as she approached, then heard his companion say, "Just as I suspected."

She walked toward Scott, her smile widening and her pace increasing. Arms extended for a hug, held long enough to convince Mulligan he was spot on.

"Mr. Scott," he said with a wink, "I trust you'll introduce me to your, ah, niece."

Scott ignored him. "Rachel, so good to see you. Let's find a table."

"What?" she said.

Scott looked directly at her so she could read his lips, "I said we'll find a table, so Mulligan here can enjoy his drink in peace."

"Mulligan?" she said. "Mulligan! Something about that name intrigues me." She paused.

Scott knew better than to interrupt her thinking.

"I remember now: 'Stately, plump Buck Mulligan, came from the stairhead with' . . . ah, a mirror, a razor, and a bowl —I think. Not perfect, but it's close. Just showing off, I guess. Anyway, nice to meet you Mr. Mulligan. My name's Rachel. Rachel Sullivan."

"My pleasure, Miss Sullivan. I've heard so many good things about you from my dear friend, Mr. Scott, who I presume is your *favorite* uncle."

Rachel turned to Scott and quietly asked, "What did he say? I don't understand."

Scott replied by mouthing the words, "Nothing but the ravings of an old drunk."

The two made their way to a table in the far corner of the pub. Mulligan followed, carrying the beer he had ordered for Scott, and with an exaggerated formality, thanked the couple for adding dignity and grace to a local hangout for an assortment of drunks and ne'er-do-wells. "Ms. Sullivan, before I return to the bar, my compliments on your stunning outfit. You do us Irishmen proud."

As Mulligan walked away, Scott said, "He's right, every eye was on you when you arrived."

She was wearing a soft leather biker jacket with a rich chocolate patina, a textured celadon blouse accented by a multi-colored silk scarf, high-waisted designer jeans, and an oversized silver bracelet. With a headful of curls and a beguiling smile, she defied the stereotype of an intelligence analyst. Her gracious walk and toned body did not offer a clue.

She apologized for being late and for arriving alone, contrary to plans.

"Woody's missing," she said, "for reasons only he can explain. He'd suggested we arrive early, but I couldn't find him. Wasn't in the library. Nor in the makeshift office they gave him while he waits for his security clearance. Wasn't in the cafeteria. Nowhere. So, here I am, alone. Marvelous to see you."

"Rachel, you look absolutely radiant."

"Thanks. Reflects my feelings. Top of the world. You may have heard, I got a promotion, a bonus, and . . . "

"Rachel, I want all the details, but let's get you started with something to drink. A beer, glass of wine, what's your pleasure?"

"I'm going to surprise you and order a Bushmills Irish whiskey, on the rocks."

"Well, I am surprised. Good choice." Scott placed the order with the waitress, then turned back to Rachel. "Any other surprises?"

"Yes, a wonderful one. A boyfriend. A serious boyfriend. A month ago, we went on a ski trip to Park City, Utah. Absolutely glorious. Powder snow every day for a week. Wonderful food in a stunning lodge. And he's already planning a vacation for us in Thailand—a few days in Bangkok and then to a resort at a coastal city called Pattaya."

Scott looked across the table at a woman in her mid-thirties who, by her glowing eyes and joyous tone was clearly infatuated. Or possessed by evil spirits.

"He visits practically every weekend," Rachel continued as the waitress brought her drink. "Works in finance for Goldman-Sachs in Manhattan."

"After a harrying start to the day, your news has lifted my spirits. Here's to you," he said, lifting his glass.

"Thanks! I haven't been so upbeat since you and I had our adventures in Italy and Turkey."

"Go on. Tell me more."

"Well, he's a few years younger than me, about six inches taller, slim, athletic." She winked. "And, most important, single."

"If my math is right and my memory still intact," Scott said, "that makes him about thirty-three, six foot-two, and the answer to every gal's prayers. Right? Perfect in every way and rich enough to escort you around the world."

"And that's not all. He's a wine connoisseur and my tutor on the varieties of Scotch and Irish whiskeys, also bourbon. You wouldn't believe what he's taught me." She sipped her whiskey with a smile.

Scott understood she wanted his approval. Something was amiss, however. Had his starry-eyed colleague been blinded by her newfound Prince Charming? *Or am I overreacting, maybe due to some latent jealousy?*

The waitress asked if they wanted another round. Scott shook his head and asked for the check. Rachel looked at her watch and suggested one more. He had a two-hour drive ahead of him but decided not to interrupt her celebratory mood.

"Your turn," she said. "What's happening in Berkeley Springs? And how's your Austrian lady friend?"

"The town's as quiet as a Zen monastery. I'm reading, writing, and tending to my garden. The daffodils are in full bloom, and the redbuds are beginning to break out. And the perfumed letters I receive from Austria make my day." Rachel laughed. Scott continued. "I see less and less of Berkeley Springs' infamous hard-drinking attorney, Spencer Cobb, who's commuting back and forth to Washington defending several former administration officials. And my best friend, Sean— Father McManus—continues to pray for my soul. Maybe I'll surprise him and show up for Mass some Sunday morning.

"Rachel, you haven't mentioned your work. From what Hoople said, I'd guess you've been working overtime."

"Yes," she explained, "with the Nuclear Regulatory Commission. We're assessing cyberthreats to nuclear power plants close to Washington. Anyone could look at a map and see there are several close by, including Calvert Cliffs and the Peach Bottom Nuclear Station southeast of Harrisburg.

"I'll tell you what's scary," she said, her smile fading. "Do you know there are nearly six million people living within fifty miles of the Peach Bottom reactor—including the entire population of Baltimore and the outer suburbs of Washington?"

Scott was about to respond when the pub erupted in applause. A young couple, obviously known to the regulars, walked to a low stage made from shipping pallets, tuned their instruments, adjusted the mike, and began playing *Whiskey in the Jar*. The woman's fingers moved across the strings of a well-worn guitar like hot lightning, as Scott heard someone say. And her partner matched her pace as he brought his fiddle to life. When she began to sing with a voice that must have been nurtured in the Emerald Isle, she was greeted with more applause and cheers. "Thank ye," she said, confirming her Irish roots.

Rachel looked toward the door and waved. A long-haired, bearded man with pink Elton John glasses waved back and headed toward their table.

"Someone you know?" Scott asked.

"And someone you know, too," she said.

Memory fading. Eyesight dimming. Neurons misfiring. Something missing. Not a guy I know.

Rachel laughed. "Appears that an introduction is in order. Scott, this is my good friend, the agency's foremost bad boy, Dr. Zachary Woodward."

"Woody," Scott stared. "My god, I couldn't have picked you out of a police lineup."

"Which is exactly where the security guys want me," Woody said. "Trust you're still hanging out in West Virginia, strumming your banjo and entertaining your friends with hoary old spy stories."

"Except when he comes here to entertain us or heads off to Ireland to reconnoiter with his ancestors," Rachel said.

"So sorry to be late. Wasn't paying attention to time. Spent the afternoon with a physicist at the National Institute of Standards and Technology."

Scott stared, still trying to connect the full-bearded, long-haired image before him with the man he had known before, the man who had been the object of his search in Turkey. Woody had angrily stalked off the NSA compound, made his way to Istanbul, and disappeared from sight to wage his one-man war against the Iranian Revolutionary Guard. After his erratic behavior became evident, he had disclosed he was being treated for dissociative identity disorder, better known as multiple personality disorder.

"You're pondering," Woody said to Scott, "who is this guy, exactly? Which of his many personalities has joined us? Well, we're all here: code writer, story teller, amateur actor, and certified nut case. Twenty-five years with the NSA and three years beyond a half century on this earth. And feeling better than I can remember. The doc taught me how to live with all my favorite personalities and ignore the others. And what about you, Scott? You're looking like a new man."

Scott grinned. "I've pledged to stay away from Turkish sanatoriums, to visit Austria more often, and avoid Irish pubs dressed like a two-bit lawyer to avoid discussions with people like the oversized guy at the bar."

"The guy with the cowboy boots?" Woody asked.

"That's Mulligan. We're buddies. He's an engineer with a degree in fluid dynamics and, as you may have guessed, a serious alcoholic. When he's sober, you'd best not sit down with him to a friendly game of Texas Hold 'Em, unless you'd like to lighten your wallet."

More cheering from the crowd as the fiddle player stepped to the mike and began a plaintive interpretation of the *Darling Girl from Clare*.

"Listen, you two," Woody said, "if you're not feeling this music, you're not living right. Remind me, Scott, what's the name of *your* darling in Austria? And Rachel, dear, the New York Casanova who's reduced you to a mass of jittering Jell-O, are you ready to reveal his name?"

"Woody," she said with a smile, "with all the free time you have, I thought you'd have found out by now. I'll give you a hint. Not Casanova, more like a Supernova."

"A transient astronomical event," Woodward replied with a smile. "Will fade away in a few months."

"That's *not* what I meant, and you know it. End of inquiry. Now, before we're all too far gone to focus, what were you doing at NIST?"

Over the music and the din of the crowd, Woodward said, "I met with one of the scientists who exploited the phenomenon of quantum non-locality with a loophole-free Bell test to build a random-number generator. An extraordinary development, the first time certifiably random numbers can be generated."

"A loophole-free Bell test?" Rachel exclaimed. "Are you kidding? We've been generating random numbers for decades. Is this new method more random, or what?"

Woodward pushed his chair back, threw up his hands, and continued his explanation—slower and louder.

"The new discovery uses quantum mechanics to ensure the random numbers cannot be predicted, unlike the best approximations available today. The method draws on an earlier NIST experiment that confirmed what Einstein called 'spooky action at a distance' by generating digital bits by photons."

"Spooky action?" Rachel said. "Isn't the real threat carelessness or an enemy insider? There've been fifty-six documented accidents at nuclear power plants in the United States. Whole communities are at risk because of carelessness. And that doesn't even include the potential for cyberattacks on control systems in nuclear reactors. *Stuxnet* shut down hundreds of Iranian centrifuges by introducing malicious code to gain control of their systems. Why shouldn't we expect the same thing to happen here, with or without better random numbers? We'll know it when a cooling system is flooded or radiation released."

"Or when a whole city loses power and goes black," Woodward added.

The amplified music stuttered, the spotlight on the two musicians flickered, and within seconds, the whole place went dark.

"Speak of the devil," Scott said.

"What's happening?" Rachel asked.

Scott turned on his cell phone light, shone it on his face so Rachel could read his lips, and replied, "I'd guess a power outage. I heard thunder, so a nearby transformer may have been hit by lighting."

"Or terrorists may have knocked off a nuclear power plant, right?"

"True enough," Scott said, "especially after the disaster on I-70, although I suspect the terrorists accidentally blew up the truck carrying the explosives. If we could count on their stupidity, we wouldn't have to worry."

Not worry? Impossible. The nation's vulnerable to a cataclysmic power outage.

Woodward appeared to be deep in thought and then said in a whisper that only Scott could hear, "I'm relatively certain that digital security can be profoundly improved with cryptography based on the spooky action of quantum particles."

Molloy's Irish Pub wasn't alone. The landscape was dark as far as they could see, interrupted only by the headlights of passing vehicles. Minutes passed, candles were lit, and the crowd began to thin. The Irish musicians were concluding their set with a melancholy version of "Danny Boy," when Scott stood and offered to follow Rachel home in the darkness.

"Thanks, but it's just a few miles away," she said. "Take care on your drive back to West Virginia. And thanks for being my mentor—and my best friend."

"Rachel," he said, "what a delight to sense your joy. Must be true love."

"Hmm. That's what he says, but it's still a little early . . ."

Walking to her car, she turned and waved goodbye. As she drove away, Scott recognized her previous infatuation with him had ended. Their bond now one of professional respect.

Scott sat quietly in his car before departing for home, toying again with the idea of calling it quits.

I lay in that godforsaken Turkish sanatorium for weeks. Drugged and left to die, I'd be dead if Rachel hadn't found me. My leg's nearly healed, but not so sure about my mind. PTSD? Nah, not me.

Heavy cloud cover and a light drizzle contributed to the gloom that surrounded the landscape—and to his dark mood. It would be well past midnight before arriving home in Berkeley Springs.

Chapter 2. West Virginia BBQ

Scott returned to NSA headquarters the following morning.

"Where've you been?" Hoople asked, striking the pose of an impatient boss. "Can't recall you ever showing up late before."

"Sorry, but I got a late start when the alarm at the Red Roof Inn failed me. When I finally arrived, one of your guards pulled me aside. Said my keycard had expired and called a supervisor. If they hadn't taken my cell phone, I'd have called. Ten, fifteen minutes later an officious guy shows up. Tells one of the guards to escort me to your office. As you might expect, I also received a stern warning to update my keycard." Scott grinned. "The good news, they didn't conduct a full body search."

Alex didn't crack a smile. His only failing: no sense of humor.

"My fault for not warning you," Hoople said. "Security's tighter than ever. Glad I caught you last night before you left for home."

"I stayed longer than planned because of the power outage. Hadn't been on the road more than fifteen or twenty minutes when I got your call. You saved me a late-night drive to West Virginia."

The power was back on, but I was fading after being up for twenty hours.

"I spoke with my counterpart at Homeland Security after you left yesterday," Hoople said. "And we've also heard from our cousins across the pond. So, I need to brief you before you take off on your Irish boondoggle."

"I'm scheduled to depart day after tomorrow," Scott said, "but could postpone if you insist."

"Remind me. How long will you be away?"

"Two weeks in Belfast and a third in Austria."

"Three weeks? Look, it's not urgent, but . . . we need your skills. Still assembling the Bluefish task force. Should be complete in a week or two. I'd like you to head up the team, mostly cybersmart youngsters who need a veteran to guide them. And before you ask, the answer is yes: Rachel will be a member."

"With Rachel on the team, not sure you need me. But, I could change plans—a week in Belfast, another in Vienna. I'll be back here in two weeks, ready to roll."

Hoople nodded, smiled in agreement.

Scott stood and stretched. "If you were to offer me an espresso, I promise to stay wide awake for your brief."

Hoople walked to the coffeemaker and began to talk as he ground the beans.

"We know a little more about the tractor trailer explosion, but . . . "

"As a near eyewitness," Scott said, "I'd still call it a failed amateur operation."

"You're right," Hoople said. "It carried a couple hundred kilos of ammonium nitrate fuel oil, stable and harmless unless it's ignited. It could've been detonated by the brakes catching fire or by a malfunctioning timer. Clearly the work of amateurs. The truck was stolen from a shipping depot in Secaucus."

After starting the espresso machine, he took a seat beside Scott.

"There's nothing in the intercepts," Hoople continued. "Nothing our analysts have found relates the truck explosion to the nuclear power plant threat. The FBI investigation won't be complete for weeks, but it has all the markings of domestic terrorism. From the DNA on a charred body part, they're trying to identify the driver."

"Hmm," Scott muttered, "any speculation on the target?"

Hoople stood and paced. "Heading south, fifty miles north of Washington. The target? No one knows, but that's not the reason I called you back."

He walked to a work table beneath the windows of his office and motioned Scott to join him. "I have a summary of the intercepts through eight o'clock last night. Calvert Cliffs is just one of several nuclear facilities mentioned. Planning is actively underway."

He passed Scott the papers.

"The locations are all familiar, all on the East Coast," Scott said, scanning them.

"And all feeding into the power grid serving New York and Washington."

"And the source?"

"Our friends in MI6 tentatively identified the signature as the Russia-based APT28, also known as Fancy Bear."

"I can't run off to Ireland with this in front of us," Scott said.

"We have droves of people to analyze the intercepts. Until you have a team to lead, there's nothing to do. Enjoy

Ireland and Austria, and get back here well rested."

Scott nodded. "I'll be here in two weeks, rested and ready. Earlier, if necessary." He headed to the door. "Top of the morning to you, Alex," he said as he left.

"They don't actually say that in Ireland," Alex shouted after him.

Scott shook his head as he headed down the corridor. *No sense of humor, but given the situation, I shouldn't blame him.*

♦♦♦

Driving home, Scott passed the site of the explosion. The remains of the truck had been removed. Nothing left but blackened grass and skid marks—a reminder of the nine innocent people who lost their lives.

Thirty minutes earlier and I might have been among them. The carnage from international terrorism would dwarf this. No more second thoughts. I'm in the whole way.

Scott turned on the radio. Not a word about the explosion—already yesterday's story on a Top 40 station. When a fast-talking DJ introduced rap artist Diddy, Scott turned it off. The music he had heard the day before reminded him of a simpler time.

Thanks to Siri, within several seconds he was listening to Willie "The Lion" Smith, the stride piano player he heard when he first arrived in the States. The oom-pah rhythm arguing with a beguiling melody spoke to him.

I wonder if it hadn't scrambled the orderly neurons of my brain—inviting a life of chaos and dissonance.

♦♦♦

Mid-afternoon, Scott reached Berkeley Springs. First stop: St. Anne's rectory, next to a Gothic-styled, stone church with a classic central tower. He bounded from the car, walked to the entrance, and knocked. Father Sean McManus welcomed him with a beatific smile, befitting his role as the village priest.

"Looks like Kierkegaard missed you," Sean said, as Scott's seven-pound Papillion yelped and spun in circles to welcome him home.

"Thanks for taking care of him. I wouldn't trust him to anyone else."

They walked in together to a living room that hadn't changed in decades. Flowered wallpaper, a sagging davenport, mismatched chairs, and a roll-top desk. A brass chandelier with two burned-out bulbs was the main source of light due to the heavy drapery that blocked the sun.

Sean and Scott had met nearly fifty years earlier as first-year seminary students. They had restored their acquaintance when Scott moved from New York to this West Virginia village after his retirement. Sean had lived in Berkeley Springs for years, ministering to his parishioners and anyone who needed a friend or a prayer. At over two hundred and fifty pounds, he insisted it was no sin to eat lavishly and laugh joyfully.

"Not your first visitor today, am I?" Scott said.

"Hard to disguise such a pungent smell," Sean said with a chuckle. "My Polish neighbor brought me another offering of stuffed cabbage rolls. 'Fresh from the oven,' she said, not thirty minutes ago. God bless her, although even Kierkegaard turned up his nose."

Sean motioned Scott to sit down. The dog leaped on his lap. A twenty-one-inch Motorola TV sat silently in the corner of the living room, showing the toothy smile of a network newscaster. When a video of the bombed semi appeared, Sean turned up the sound. In mid-sentence, Scott heard the words "Islamic terrorist."

"Assume you know all about it," Sean said. "People here blame it on Islam. The Syrian woman we sponsored is terrified. Says a neighbor told her to go back home."

"I can assure you," Scott said, "no one knows who detonated the bomb. A Muslim terrorist? A right-wing patriot obsessed by pedophiles in pizza shops? Not a shred of evidence yet."

Sean turned down the TV and sat on the sofa facing Scott.

"Nine people killed in the explosion and three million Muslims suspected by their neighbors," Sean said, shaking his head. "Haven't we learned anything since the Crusades?"

"Wait. You've always been the optimist. What happened?"

"Trying not to lose my faith. Wondering what to say at Mass when I see those frightened and accusing eyes looking back at me."

"You may want to mention my childhood friend from Pakistan," Scott said. "Abdul Jinnah attended middle school with me in Rawalpindi. We were born three days apart, he a devout Muslim and I a devout Christian. Yet, we were spiritual twins. 'Love thy neighbor as thyself,' I had learned. And Abdul was taught, 'Not one of you is a believer until he loves for his brother what he loves for himself.'"

Scott leaned forward, emphasizing each word as he continued.

"Abdul is now a neurosurgeon in Karachi. I've read of his skill and devotion to others. He saves Muslim brains—also Christian brains, Hindu brains, atheist brains. Yet many would consider him a threat, a potential terrorist. Ignorance is the enemy."

"I'm sure the Church would welcome you as a priest," Sean said. "Isn't it about time to stop risking your life on foreign missions?"

"That's ended," Scott said. "My visit to Ireland is pure pleasure."

Sean sighed. "A few more trips, and Kierkegaard won't remember you. The little guy may never return home. He's become very fond of a scoop of vanilla ice cream after dinner—which we enjoy together."

"Ice cream? Well, never mind, he looks great. Hope you haven't forgotten my barbeque tomorrow evening."

"Of course not, although I trust you appreciate partying on a Saturday night will interrupt my preparation of the Sunday morning homily."

"Ahh," Scott said, "don't overlook the value of spending an evening with confirmed sinners. The experience will give your sermon such a punch that the collection plate will be overflowing."

Sean chuckled as Scott scooped up Kierkegaard, thanked Sean for dog sitting, and waved goodbye.

◆◆◆

Scott stood in the kitchen Saturday evening chopping onions, his eyes watering, when Sean surprised him by arriving early with a loaf of bread and a bottle of wine. "I've brought emergency rations in case your barbeque is burnt to a crisp. Assume you've invited the whole community, slaughtered a pig, and added seven secret ingredients to the sauce."

"Nothing fancy, Sean," Scott said, "ribs, baked beans, and a fresh salad. The ribs are marinating and the salad will be ready when I add these onions and a little olive oil."

Scott poured a glass of bourbon for each of them before they walked outside.

"We better get our share before Spencer shows up. Although Mrs. Cobb may act as a *limiteur de vitesse* on his taste for spirits."

"Surprised he's in town," Sean said. "Spends most of his time in Washington defending politicians who he says are not ordinary crooks. I'm sure they'll all go free, even if Cobb can barely stand when he's defending them."

"Father," Scott asked, "do I detect a hint of non-Christian charity? Didn't Jesus pal around with crooks?"

"Touché, I meant to compliment Cobb for his skill . . ."

"Uh-huh," Scott laughed. "I must have missed the nuance."

"As I was saying . . . for his skill in saving these crooked politicians from prison and guiding them away from sin. Why, the lot of them may turn up at Sunday service to seek salvation."

"Fair enough, but keep your eye on the collection plate."

Billy Birdsong, the unheralded painter and sculptor who had moved back to Berkeley Springs from New York City, arrived next. "Too loud, too fast, too busy," he had said about New York when he returned home. He wore pink Bermuda shorts, an embroidered white Barong shirt, and flipflops covered with glitter. He greeted Scott and handed him a foil-wrapped gift.

"Mr. Scott," Billy said quietly, "your invitation came as quite a surprise. I don't think we ever met, but Uncle Roy told me you were some kind of government spy." He smiled. "I said if that were true, you couldn't admit it. Guess we'll never know for sure. Anyway, this little painting is my homage to you for keeping us safe."

"Thanks, Billy," Scott said. He removed the gold foil to reveal a figure in profile, partially hidden in the twilight shadows of the giant oak outside his home. The face obscured, but the body clearly his, capturing his lank figure, even suggesting his gimpy leg.

"Perfect," Sean said with a gleam in his eye. "Why, I'd recognize you if it were on a wanted poster in the post office."

"You're amazing," Scott said, looking at Billy. "You and Felicity have put Berkeley Springs on the map. We'll soon be nosing out Santa Fe as the second finest arts center in the country."

"I'm flattered, but guess you haven't heard about Felicity, though."

"No, not a word. Is she okay? I'm expecting her this evening."

"Isn't going to happen," Billy said, shaking his head. "She's given up painting for meditation and activation."

"Stopped painting?" Scott said. "I can't believe it."

"She's becomes obsessed with the Shawnee Indians. They lived here for centuries until they were driven out by white settlers. She petitioned the Interior Department to grant them their rights for the few descendants who still live along the Pennsylvania border."

Billy moved closer to Scott and Sean. He lowered his voice. "Felicity does *not* have an ounce of Indian blood. Acts like it, though. Says she can speak the Shawnee language. Between us, I think she's just making it up. Told me she sits for hours and hours to meditate. Also said she's pushed Vlad Petrov, her 'evil Russian stalker,' out of her mind. Claims she feels free for the first time in years."

A late-model Cadillac roared down the driveway and screeched to a stop. Scott and his friends stopped talking, waiting for Spencer Cobb and Mrs. Cobb to emerge. A few minutes later, Spencer opened his door and walked toward the house.

"The missus," he said, "prefers to stay in the car with the engine running and the AC cranking out cold air. In her memorable words, 'It's too goddam hot to sit on the porch and get eaten by bugs.' Pardon my language, Father, but it's the goddam truth. Exactly what she said.

"So, I told her, fine, just sit there like some Grand Poohbah while I party with my friends. Sorry about that, Scott. Anyway, congratulations for whatever it is we're celebrating. And if you have some lemonade or something non-alcoholic, I'll offer it to her. But first, didn't you offer a taste of your favorite bourbon?"

Before Scott could respond, Mrs. Cobb was out of the car, rushing toward the house. "Billy, Billy!" she exclaimed. "If I knew you were coming, I'd've been here the minute we arrived. Isn't a day goes by I don't marvel at the paintings you did of my little darlin'. Tell you the truth, why, it looks better 'an him. Poochie's been to the vet so many times. Got allergies like me, some kind of worms, an' rheumatism. I don't know if he's long for this world, but he'll be with me forever with those paintings."

"Thank you, Mrs. Cobb, I'm so . . . "

"Never mind, Billy, I'm the one to be doing the thanking. And I'll be thanking you for the next one as well."

"Another one? I've already done three."

"No, no. Not my sweet little schnauzer. I need one—just one, not three—of Spencer. Never can tell when I'll need a painting to remember him by. If he's not on the train to Washington, he's out with the boys drinking whiskey like it's spring water." She shook her head. "His liver must be crying out for help."

Spencer raised his hands in mock surrender. "Okay, okay. You win. Lemonade for me as well." He turned to Scott and said, "Let's be sure it isn't straight lemonade. Too much acid can ruin a man's gut."

Scott invited everyone to find a seat on the porch. When he returned with drinks, he said, "I guess we're all here, just the five of us. I intended to invite my neighbors, Grace and Luther, but they left town to greet their new grandson. And my Washington colleague, Rachel Sullivan, called a few hours ago to regret. Her New York boyfriend surprised her showing up for the weekend."

"You didn't tell us the occasion," Spencer said. "Your birthday or the silver anniversary of your divorce?"

"Neither, it's my bon voyage party for my trip to Belfast to explore my Irish roots."

"Ireland is so quaint," said Mrs. Cobb. "All those funny town names."

Scott nodded.

Father McManus raised his bourbon. "Still a wee bit suspicious about your so-called personal trip, I prepared this little limerick to reflect my doubts."

To Ireland, my friend Thomas O'Scott,
DNA proof is what he had sought.
But I say blimey,
This man's a limey.
It's a fact, or so I had thought.

Laughing, Scott said, "Sean, I have some late-breaking news for you. You don't have to be named McManus to be Irish."

Sean winked. "No, but it sure helps. Do you know seventeen percent of the population in Northern Ireland was named McManus in the nineteenth century. Scott? Perhaps a few got lost on their way home to Edinburgh after a night on the high seas." He turned. "Speaking of lost, look who's coming down the driveway. And after Billy said she wouldn't join us."

"Felicity?" Billy said. "She's here?"

"Looks like it." Scott rose.

Felicity drove up the gravel driveway to the edge of the porch where the others had assembled, slammed on the brakes, and jumped out of her classic cardinal-red Ford pickup. Wearing jeans and a white boatneck sweater, she said, "Sorry I'm late. Should've skipped it, but I wanted . . . actually, I *need* a hug. It's just not *fair*."

Her eyes were red and swollen.

"What's wrong?" Scott asked. *After Billy's story, I'm surprised she isn't dressed in buckskin and beads.*

"My brother's in a hospital in Frederick with third-degree burns. They just called, said I couldn't visit till tomorrow, but they let me talk to him for a few minutes. He was caught in an explosion two days ago. But he was lucky. Others were killed."

Father McManus, glancing at Scott, took Felicity's hand. "What happened?" he asked.

Felicity wiped a tear from her cheek. "He was driving from Pittsburgh to Richmond to meet an old Army buddy. Remembers a flash and nothing more, until he woke up in the hospital. Apparently, a truck blew up."

Billy embraced her.

"Could I get you a drink to calm your nerves?" Scott asked.

"Thanks, but I brought this thermos of sassafras tea, a common drink among the Shawnee."

"Any friend of Billy's is a friend of mine," Mrs. Cobb said. "Come over here and sit with me on the swing. Tell me all about your dear brother."

As they chatted, Scott excused himself and walked to the back of the house. Spencer Cobb followed him.

"This grill's big enough to roast a whole hog," Cobb said. "Were you expecting another twenty guests?"

"No, my colleague Rachel's the only one missing. I had the grill shipped from Argentina, where they use real wood to flavor the meat. Charcoal briquettes provide about as much flavor as propane gas."

"Listen. I followed you back here for a reason," Cobb said softly. "I have a prominent Washington client, a name you might recognize, who appears to be in trouble, all because of certain financial transactions in Northern Ireland."

"Uh-huh," Scott said, as he struck a match to the kindling.

"He has a colleague in Belfast named Viktor, a currency trader who's made my client a little money. More than a little, I guess. Enough to interest the FBI."

"Yeah? If I can get this wood to actually catch fire, we're going to have a serious barbecue."

"I'm confident your so-called vacation in Belfast is cover for some top-secret investigation." He ran a hand through his hair and blew out a gusty sigh. "Hell, you may even be heading there to investigate my client."

Scott focused on the small flame. "Spencer, the only investigation I'm doing in Ireland concerns my family tree."

"You expect me to believe that? Well, in case you run into Viktor, anything you might learn would be a great help to me."

"Because he's a legitimate currency trader?" Scott continued to fan the flames.

"Legit? Absolutely. Apparently trades every day. Euros and pounds, pairs and pips. Takes his commission and deposits the balance in my client's account."

Scott stepped back and smiled. "Look, we finally have a real fire. Seasoned oak from a tree that fell here last year."

Cobb leaned toward the grill, then nodded to Scott.

"Look at that flame, Spencer. Beautiful! We'll soon have some hot glowing coals to offer the ribs a flavor you won't forget."

"So, can I count on you?"

"To look for a guy named Viktor? Not a chance, unless his last name is Scott. Espionage is out. Genealogy is in."

Chapter 3. Enigmas and Puzzles

He looked straight ahead, without moving, so I could see only his profile. Maybe flying toward Dublin on Aer Lingus had influenced my perception, but he seemed to be a dead ringer for James Joyce, at least from the pictures of the thin-faced Irish novelist with the gold-rimmed glasses and mustache. Before my vacation was truncated, I had planned a brief Dublin stop to visit Martello Tower in nearby Sandycove, the setting for the opening pages of *Ulysses*. That would have to wait for another time.

He'll surely turn when drinks are served, I thought, so I could confirm my impression. I would have spoken to him, but his stillness suggested he might be sleeping. I felt a temptation to address him as Mr. Joyce and ask directions to Sweny's Pharmacy. I didn't, of course. Why make a fool of myself? On the other hand, I could have sought his attention by softly repeating the word "mrkgnao," the Joycean transcription of the sound more commonly represented as "meow."

It's unlikely I would return to *Ulysses* if the story were set any time except 1904, which happens to be the year of my father's birth. He wasn't born in Ireland, but his father, my grandfather, was born there in 1875. Forty years later, the 1916 proclamation led to the partition of Ireland and independence from Great Britain for most of the island. Northern Ireland, bitterly divided between Protestants and Catholics, remained part of Great Britain. I mention this because in my brief introduction to genealogy I learned my grandfather was born in what is now Northern Ireland in the seaside city of Carrickfergus.

As my parents were Protestant missionaries in Pakistan, my grandfather was probably born to a Protestant family. That remained to be confirmed through my research in Northern Ireland.

I glanced over again at my comatose seatmate. Eyes closed. Motionless. Silent. Maybe deep in thought. No business of mine, but impossible to quell my curiosity. We could have traded stories. I would have told him about my Irish grandfather who emigrated to America. He may have been a laborer working in the nearby shipyards, where the Titanic was later built.

I hoped to find my grandfather's story during my stay in Belfast. Then, I planned to return to Vienna to see Fredrica Wolf, or as I know her, Princess Fredrica. I had suggested visiting her home in St. Wolfgang, but she insisted we meet in Vienna.

She suggested attending Bellini's tragic opera *Norma* at the State Opera House. I was less enthusiastic. Would rather attend the *Volksoper* for something lighter. What was I thinking? Second-guessing this wonderful woman? For the first time in years I'm traveling without an assignment. And the first time in decades an enchanting woman would be waiting to greet me. So, when Norma rushes into the flames at the end of the opera, so what? It's only make-believe. I would be thrilled to enjoy the music and Fredrica's company.

I opened my eyes when I heard a pleasant female voice. My travel companion showed signs of life. He turned slightly to his left to respond to the attendant offering drinks. He spoke softly but firmly, ordering a Guinness stout. It was an opportunity to introduce myself. I asked for a Bushmills on the rocks.

"Greetings," I said, "Thomas Scott."

"Monsieur, it is my pleasure to meet you. Do I detect an American accent?"

"Yes, indeed."

His profile had not misled me—a perfect resemblance to James Joyce.

"Visiting Dublin?" he asked. "Bushmills is a fine choice of spirits. I've also come to enjoy the simpler pleasure of Guinness stout. It's no secret I used to drink absinthe, some say to excess. That, monsieur, is poppycock."

"And you? Returning home from America?" I asked.

"Yes, exhausted after a fortnight in New York. Busy every evening, but what energy—a city teeming with the poetry of movement, with the lyricism of discourse. And you can't walk more than a city block without discovering another Irish bar. And you, Thomas, what brings you to my city?"

"Tourism," I replied. "I'll grab a bus to Belfast as soon as we land."

"Belfast? A backward and quiescent town compared to the lively streets of Dublin, where 'bells clang, backers shout, drunkards bawl, whores screech, and foghorns hoot.'"

He waved the flight attendant over and said he wanted to join me in a Bushmills. "Make it a double, neat, and another for my friend Thomas."

"Thank you," I said. "And you are?"

"Jim," he said. "My friends call me Jim."

I had expected that. Still, I felt disoriented. Wide awake, for sure, but his look, his language, his name . . .

Jim sampled the whiskey, nodded approvingly, and

rubbed his mustache with the forefingers of both hands. He looked at me with amusement. "Your expression," he said, "reveals your curiosity. About me, I would say. Am I right?"

"Well, yes, you look familiar," I said.

"Hardly the first time I've heard that. You may have noticed a resemblance to Ireland's greatest writer, James Joyce."

"Yes, from the moment I saw your profile—"

"Thomas, allow me to assure you the deceit is not in your eyes. I *am* James Joyce." He lifted the whiskey to his lips and finished it in one gulp.

I took a deep breath, considering how to respond, but before I could reply, he continued. "'Tell me, muse, of that man of many turns, who wandered far and wide.'"

That would be an accurate description of me, but surely it was a coincidence. "From *Ulysses*?"

"No, no," he said, "it's the opening line from Homer's *Odyssey*."

I nodded, again not sure how to respond. He continued, now with more emotion, undoubtedly aided by a Guinness stout and a double Bushmills.

"Belfast," he began. "You are searching, Thomas, walking the sad streets and forgotten alleys of this godforsaken town to discover ye self."

He was right, but how did he know? I had told him I planned to visit Belfast, nothing more.

"'Every life is in many days, day after day. We walk through ourselves, meeting robbers, ghosts, giants, old men, young men, wives, widows, brothers-in-love, but always meeting ourselves.'"

I shifted my weight, looked away, decided to ignore this madman. Raised my glass, held it up to the window against the fading light, and then slowly sipped the whiskey.

My Irish grandfather may have enjoyed the very same treat. My companion interrupted my reverie with a smile and an unexpected warm greeting. "Thomas, Thomas, luck has blessed me this day to find myself so close to such an appreciative audience. Actors live for authenticity and adulation. There was a moment, a brief moment, when you suspended disbelief and said to yourself, 'By god, this is James Joyce.' But after that fleeting moment, you regained your senses and thought I belonged in an asylum.

"I confess," he said, his eyes twinkling. "I'm neither a dead writer nor a madman. I'm an actor, returning to Dublin after two weeks playing Joyce in New York's Public Theatre on Lafayette Street. And what an audience! They loved it. I love you Americans. Imagine a standing ovation and a review that would please my sainted mother—God bless her—if she were alive."

"Madman, yes, I had come around to that," I said. He had the look, the gestures, the language, even the voice as I had imagined it. I wished I had been in his New York audience. On reflection, a personal performance was even better, even if it left me a bit bewildered and uncomfortable."

"If theatre doesn't evoke discomfort, doesn't realign our prejudices, or challenge our beliefs, it has failed," he replied. "If I were standing, I'd take a bow and wait for your applause."

He had much in common with the real James Joyce: telling stories about Ireland until the attendant stopped offering drinks. Told me he would be performing at the Abbey Theatre in Dublin during a week-long Joyce festival followed by a two-week run in Vienna. As we were landing, I said I would try to catch his performance during my visit to Austria.

"Thomas, it would be my honor. After the curtain

closes, meet me backstage and we'll find some friendly bar to enjoy a stein or two of Austrian ale."

The plane pulled up. The pilot announced that air traffic control had placed us in a holding pattern. As we circled my companion excused himself and walked toward the back of the plane. When the plane eventually landed, we sat on the tarmac for nearly an hour while the pilot waited for a gate.

My companion had still not returned to his seat. Curious, I looked at the Public Theatre website and found no mention of a play about Joyce. And the Abbey Theatre site showed no plans for a Joyce Festival. I will think of him as I sit alone at a café in Vienna enjoying an Austrian ale. I will look again at his card, with the name James Joyce and this quote handwritten on the back: "Better pass boldly into that other world, in the full glory of some passion, than fade and wither dismally with age."

♦♦♦

Only half awake when he boarded the bus from the airport to Belfast, Scott felt alert enough to find a seat in an empty row for the two-hour trip.

Was I dreaming on the plane? Hallucinating? It seemed so damn real. Not a good sign.

He dozed on the bus, awakened when it stopped, stepped off, and walked the short distance to Benedicts of Belfast, a quirky hotel that appeared to date from the nineteenth century.

"Looks like it's been here forever," Scott said to the receptionist.

She laughed. "If twenty years is forever, why yes."

"Fooled again," he said with a shrug.

"The restaurant, bar, everything built with decorative artifacts salvaged from abandoned churches."

He took the elevator to the second floor, walked down a dark hallway to room 207, unpacked, showered, and shaved.

He rushed to hail a cab for his appointment with a genealogist named O'Malley. His office was on the third floor of a yellow brick building with a banner advertising "Flats to let."

Scott walked up the wooden stairs and knocked on the door.

O'Malley answered and motioned him inside. A lanky figure with a receding hairline and a severe face accented by frameless bifocal glasses, he offered Scott a chair in front of a battered desk covered with papers and photographs. Without a handshake or other pleasantry, O'Malley sat down and abruptly began.

"Mr. Scott, I've already initiated research on your behalf, fully aware ye wished to discuss my fees before engaging my services. And already, I've good news. Your namesake, one Thomas Scott, was born in Derry and emigrated to the States at the turn of the century."

"Mr. O'Malley," Scott said with a frown, "you shouldn't have started before we met."

"Oh, no? You gave me no choice when you decided to cut your visit short. I had to start immediately. Much more to be done, of course, in tracing your ancestry. I'm often able to find grandparents as far back as five generations. And if you've come from a noble family, we may be able to trace your lineage to the fifteenth century or earlier. Now, I must caution you, that is unusual. I've had only a few clients whose—"

"Before you continue, I must tell you my birth name is Franklin Lambert. I officially changed it to Thomas Sebastian Scott more than a decade ago. A death certificate was issued for Lambert because of a—misunderstanding. This must remain confidential between us. By whatever name, however, I am here today, very much alive."

I can't tell him any more. I can't tell anyone.

With a scowl, O'Malley rose from his desk, walked to a file cabinet, retrieved a file folder closed with an elastic band, returned to his desk, sat down, removed several pages from the file and tossed them on his desk in front of Scott.

"This research," he said, "is for the *real* Thomas Scott, if he should ever turn up."

O'Malley's posture and cold stare showed contempt. Scott remained impassive and waited for the genealogist to continue.

"I'll have to start over with Franklin Lambert," he said, "but first, tell me why you changed your name? And why didn't you tell me when we first corresponded? It would have saved me valuable time."

"Mr. O'Malley," Scott said, "which I trust is *your* birthname, I apologize for not informing you sooner, but some things are best conveyed in person. It's a matter of some delicacy."

"Give me two days," O'Malley snapped, "and then meet me here again. I'll get a fresh start, although I must warn you—Lambert is a Continental name, not typically Irish."

◆◆◆

With a day to kill before returning to O'Malley's, Scott took the *Game of Thrones* tour along the coast of Northern Ireland. The hotel desk clerk promised he would see some spectacular sights and likely meet a few stray cousins.

The tour guide, who had the only Irish accent on the bus, announced she'd been an extra in the last season. "Practically everyone in town has been in scenes with as many as three hundred costumed performers," she said. "By some kind of digital magic, the crowd grows to three thousand on the screen."

On the crowded tour bus, Scott sat next to an Italian journalist who told him it was her first visit to Northern Ireland.

"I'm here on assignment," she said, "to interview an actor with a key role in the last season of *Game of Thrones.* Taking the tour for background."

"So, when will you do the interview?" Scott asked.

"Tomorrow at the Fitzgerald Hotel. That's where many cast members are staying for a reunion. He's a big name in Italy, probably unknown in the States—Maurizio Ruzzene, a rugged, tough-looking guy."

"And you? Also well-known in Italy?"

She laughed. "Yes, by my parents, my brother, my best friend, and a few people who look at bylines in *Panorama* magazine."

Scott raised one eyebrow and smirked. "*Specializzato in politica e donne nude.*"

"What a pleasant surprise! You speak Italian. But you're also dating yourself, for it's now rare to see a nude cover."

"That's a change," Scott said. "When I lived in Rome years ago, the managing editor could count on more sales if the cover included a story about the CIA, a picture of a naked model, or preferably both!"

The bus stopped to allow a walk through the Dark Hedges, represented in the TV production as the Kings Road. "The brooding beech trees were planted by the Stuart family in the eighteenth century to impress visitors as they approached Gracehill House," the guide recounted. It was one stop of many, including the Cushendun Caves and the Giant's Causeway.

After eight hours on and off the bus, Scott had a new best friend, Laura Caputo. In her mid-thirties with a beguiling smile, she had shoulder-length full black hair that glistened next to her pale skin. She wore a perfume so subtle the fragrance was masked by a disagreeable odor when they were on the bus.

She was as tall as he and could easily outpace him. Although in relatively good shape, he had to push himself to keep up as they walked to the Carrick-A-Rede Rope Bridge, suspended a hundred feet above a threatening bed of rocks in shallow water.

"Your English, I mean your American English, is perfect," Scott said when they returned to the bus.

"Thanks. I lived with my aunt in Brooklyn for a year when I studied journalism at Columbia."

"Not far from my apartment years ago, close to a Manhattan landmark, McSorley's Old Ale House. My former wife still runs an antique shop in the neighborhood where she lives with her partner, Monica."

"The Old Ale House," she said. "Mostly an older crowd when I was in New York. Guess I'd fit in now."

They sat in comfortable silence until the bus stopped in front of Benedicts Hotel. Laura turned to Scott. "Are you also staying here?"

"Yes," he replied. "I was looking for something different. It certainly lives up to its reputation. And you?"

"Likewise. A friend recommended it, assured me I would be pampered by the staff and delighted by the bar, although I haven't had the pleasure yet."

Scott suggested dinner and a drink. She accepted and proposed they meet after her interview with the Italian actor at the Fitzgerald Hotel. "Let's say six o'clock tomorrow."

◆ ◆ ◆

Laura Caputo was sitting alone at the bar when Scott arrived.

"Hello, Tom," she said with a smile that appeared forced.

"Tom? Correct, but remember my friends call me Scott," he said as he sat down. "And if you don't mind me saying so, you look like you just lost your best friend."

"Forgive me. I've been here for the last hour, brooding and drinking. Stood up by that bastard Ruzzene. I flew here from Rome to interview him, scheduled a photographer, hired a room—and he shows up with some underage girl from the cast, says he's sorry but has a conflict."

"Oh. Did you—"

"The last I saw of him he was walking toward the elevator with his hand on her ass. My editor will be pissed if I can't reschedule the interview in the next twenty-four hours."

"Not the first time a man was distracted by a young woman," Scott said.

"Distracted! He's in his forties, and she's a child. I sit here nursing this drink, beating up on myself for failing to get the interview, while the great Ruzzene is three floors above us fucking some teenage groupie."

"Let's walk across the street and enjoy dinner at Belfast's oldest restaurant, the Crown Liquor Saloon. It'll give you a chance to cool off, and we can swap stories of life in Rome."

◆◆◆

The following day Scott returned to O'Malley's office. As abrupt as before but without the sour look, O'Malley pointed again to the chair in front of his desk.

"Here it is, my Lambert file," he began as he removed several pages and began reading. "Patrick Lambert, born in

Carrickfergus in 1875, employed as a cooper by a company that supplied barrels to Bushmills Distillery in County Antrim."

"My grandfather, right?"

"Exactly, but I bet you knew that before we met," O'Malley said. "And you knew he emigrated to New York, where your father was born. But did you know your father had six half-brothers, all born in Northern Ireland? I can't guess how many cousins you'll find here."

"I did notice a family resemblance among a few old guys," Scott said.

"Not sure if he looked like you, but I did discover one ancestor who may surprise you. According to a diary entry, he was the black sheep of the family."

"If you find only one blackguard in my family, I'd be pleased," Scott said. "I've suspected there was some calamitous event that shaped my father's faith. Had such an impact that he moved to Pakistan to save souls."

O'Malley adjusted his glasses and sorted through the sheaf of papers he held.

"Your great-grandfather rose to the rank of sergeant in the Carrickfergus Municipal Police Force. According to an account in *The Morning Post* dated June 1893, he was charged with the murder of a young woman who had returned to Belfast after receiving her baccalaureate from Trinity College in Dublin."

"A police sergeant charged with murder?" Scott said.

"Listen," O'Malley said impatiently, "I'm not finished. She had been celebrating her graduation in a local tavern, drinking too much, talking too loudly, when great-granddad happened by, making his nightly rounds. What happened next is in dispute. Did he arrest her for disorderly conduct? Did he offer to assist her home? Witnesses under oath at the trial had sharply conflicting stories."

"Trial? Don't keep me in suspense. Was he convicted?"

O'Malley offered a sardonic smile.

Scott was hooked. Who can resist a family scandal separated by a few generations? Murderers, horse thieves, bootleggers, deserters, pirates—romantic scoundrels all.

"Mr. Scott, he was not only *charged* with murder. He was *convicted* of murder. And, as reported in the press, 'hanged by the neck until dead.'"

Scott took a deep breath.

"Despite contradictory evidence, he was convicted by public opinion and for his alleged contempt for Jonathan Swift's pseudonymously published pamphlets known as *Drapier's Letters*. They were regarded by the government as seditious."

"Hanged because of Jonathan Swift?" Scott asked incredulously.

"Well, not exactly. The young woman, after a few drinks, insisted on reading aloud—or shouting—from one of the passages in the third pamphlet that many believed to be treasonous. The prosecution convinced the jury that your great-grandfather, an officer of the law and supporter of the Crown, was so incensed by her drunken disrespect for authority that he murdered her in an uncontrollable rage."

"Whoa? I'm dumbfounded. A cop kills an innocent young woman because she read Swift's words aloud? I'm . . . I'm trying to understand. And you? You sit there with a smug look enjoying my distress."

"Just reporting the facts."

"Mr. O'Malley, if he had been convicted on such spurious evidence, no wonder my grandfather left the country."

"I was about to tell you," O'Malley quickly responded,

"he left within a few weeks for America, promising his wife and children they would join him soon. His wife died within months and the children were sent to an orphanage. Your grandfather remarried in America, and a year later your father was born. I haven't had time to discover what became of the children in the orphanage. Undoubtedly some of their descendants are still alive."

"My great-grandfather a convicted criminal?" Scott looked at his hands. "That can't be true. The research must be faulty." He stood and took a few steps toward the door of the office but stopped and returned to the chair.

"I intended to march out of here," Scott said, "but it's not your fault. Twelve men convicted him, and a judge sentenced him for a crime he did not commit."

"Mr. Scott, I recognize your disappointment, but in fairness, I found nothing to suggest his innocence."

"Sometimes it takes a hunch—and memory. As a kid, maybe six or seven, I heard my father praying for the hundreds of thousands of innocents who had died during partition, when Pakistan had been carved out of India. All based on religious differences. As a child of missionary parents who taught peace and love, it struck me as odd. 'Hindus and Muslims,' I said, 'why aren't they like Christians?' He explained Christians, too, can be violent. He was quiet for a long time and said that's why my grandfather came to America, to flee the religious bigotry that had led to the death of my great-grandfather. I had forgotten the story but not the tears that flowed when he told it. It was the only time I saw my father cry."

"A hunch, you say?" O'Malley smiled. "Perhaps you should have consulted a mystic who would tell you what you want to hear. The facts do not lie. However—"

"Yes, but isn't—"

"Before you interrupted, I was beginning to tell you I would look further in the state archives and church records to see if there's anything to support your belief," O'Malley said.

"Good," Scott replied. "Draw up a contract or letter with the terms of your research. I'll give you a partial payment now and the balance when you finish. I'll be departing day after tomorrow, so you can send me your conclusions."

"Since you're leaving so soon, I'll work overtime and complete it today. The report will be ready tomorrow morning. I prefer cash, pounds or Euros, even dollars. And payment in full. In the meantime, there's something I discovered that you should know—the poor man who hanged from the gallows was your namesake, Franklin Lambert. Take good care and avoid women celebrating in an Irish bar."

Chapter 4. A Night to Remember

Scott might have been studying an ornate altarpiece in a nineteenth century church. Instead, he sat alone in the rococo bar of Benedicts of Belfast mindlessly focusing on a bottle of Chartreuse displayed among spirits from around the world. He knew it was French, but couldn't imagine the occasion when someone would order this greenish liqueur. Wasn't it a favorite of Gatsby? He guessed it belonged in the same class as the Italian artichoke-based drink called Cynar.

Could the antique altarpiece featured in the bar offer a clue? The monks from some obscure order might have carved it in another century, maybe at the time great-grandfather hanged from the gallows in Carrickfergus.

Scott looked at his watch. Ten more minutes and he would walk away. Stood up by a woman he thought he had charmed. The bartender asked if he would like another Bushmills.

"No thanks," he said. Then, hoping Laura would show, he changed his mind. "Wait, on second thought, I've nothing better to do."

I should've stayed in the States. Nothing but grief from O'Malley. Now stood up by the only agreeable person I've met.

Even if Laura was a no-show, eavesdropping on the

two women seated on the stools immediately to his left proved more interesting than retreating to his room. The plump woman in the tight-fitting bunny suit planned to be married the following day. Now at her bachelorette party waiting for the others to arrive, she had confessed to her best friend that she wasn't ready to be a housewife.

"He's a good man," she said, "but runs with a rough crowd. His best pal's in the Maghaberry Prison for knifing some fuckin' fleg. Had it comin' to him, I'd say. My guy would've done the same thing, so what's that make me? A bride just waitin' to see my man behind bars. And you knew his other so-called best friend. Shot dead by his wife for inviting some whore home. When she arrived, all tarted up, his old lady took his gun, pointed at his head, and pulled the trigger. Said she didn't know it was loaded."

Scott quietly rooted for the gal in the retro bunny costume, hoping she'd have the same good sense the next morning when she sobered up.

Good sense, huh? Who am I to judge? Nearly seventy years old and still living alone.

Absorbed in the drama playing out to his left, Scott turned at the slight tap on the shoulder.

"Hope I didn't keep you waiting," Laura said.

"Oh, no. Not at all. I've been sitting here enjoying my new Irish friends," Scott said as he stood and glanced at the women to his left.

The prospective bride turned. "My friend has to take a piss and probably won't be back for ages, so I'll move over and your woman can sit right here."

"Thanks so much," Scott said. Bunny gal moved and Laura took her place at the bar.

"Good to see you," Laura said. "I was on the phone

with my *avvocato*, my lawyer, you would say. He's representing me in a suit against my employer."

"So, Italy has joined the #MeToo generation?" Scott asked. "Before you answer, I've another urgent question. What are you drinking?"

"I'll have what she's having. I mean whatever the girl in the bunny costume is drinking. Maybe it will help pick me up after being beaten down by my publisher."

"He's already on your case?"

"No, no. It's not about the interview. We've been at odds for many months. And to answer your other question, I was a #MeToo gal long before the term existed. Ever since some creep put his hand down my jeans on a New York subway. He hasn't forgotten it either. All it took was a ninety-decibel warning for him to get his wanking hands off my ass. He slinked away at the next stop to the sound of applause from the other women on the train."

The bartender overheard the conversation and offered her a house specialty called the Bramble. "Made with gin, crème de cassis, fresh lemon, and mixed berries. It's on us for your troubles and a cracking good story."

"My kind of place," Laura said. "Maybe a little fruity for my taste, but if it moves me halfway into her upbeat space, I'll drink them all evening."

"And I'm here to serve you till midnight," the bartender said. "The minute you entered wearing those dangling earrings my attention was guaranteed. Even in this dim light, the sapphire stones glisten."

Scott ordered another Bushmills and said he would do his best to match her. "One for one, fermented grain versus alcoholic fruit salad. Or how would you say it in Italian— *macedonia correcto?*"

"Good try," she replied, "but no one would serve such a concoction in Rome. Maybe I'll introduce it when I win the suit against my publisher. It's not what you think. Never put his chubby paws on me, never an inappropriate word, never a lurid glance."

"And you're suing him for misrepresenting Italian manhood by being such a saint?"

"No, not at all. I'm suing him to get my job back. I'm officially on administrative leave and have been for the past six months. Not formally fired, but worse—because until the investigation ends, I'm stuck doing nothing."

"Except reporting on Italian TV stars."

"Not even that," she said. "I'm doing this on my own time at my own expense to convince him I'm indispensable."

Bunny gal took her friend's hand and bounced to a small dance space as the heavy metal music began. Scott and Laura both turned to watch—along with everyone else sitting at the bar. She was enjoying her last night as a single woman, with moves that looked like a honeymoon rehearsal. After trying to keep up, her companion sat down and left bunny gal alone. Her moves were surprisingly smooth—all curves, all sex. A wardrobe malfunction elicited an outburst of applause. Without missing a beat, she readjusted her bodice and continued.

Laura smiled at Scott and said, "Maybe her bunny suit's just a tad too small."

"Or maybe it's exactly what she intended on the eve of her marriage to Mr. Lowlife."

"Her fiancé?" Laura asked. "Who is it?"

"Couldn't help eavesdropping before you arrived. She's engaged to some guy who already has prison painted on his forehead," Scott said.

"Shouldn't we warn her against it?" Laura asked. "With

moves like hers, many respectable men would surely love to meet her. With a little encouragement, she may walk away before she finds herself among a long list of abused spouses."

"I agree," Scott said, "but afraid I'm not very good at counseling women. I married a wonderful woman who left me for another wonderful woman. Later I fell in love with the woman who saved my life, but she eventually ran off to save the world. And now, I'm courting—is that the right term in this age—an Austrian widow whom I barely know."

"I should know better than to advise anyone. My last love is slowly dying in an Italian prison. Says he can't live without me, but—"

"Let's have another drink before we're both overtaken by heartache," Scott said.

"Good idea, but one fruity Bramble is enough. Make mine a bourbon to honor your American heritage."

Is she flirting with me? Not that I mind, but . . .

"From what I've heard," Laura continued, "every American is part Irish and eventually turns up here to find out if grandad was a banker or a butcher. Much easier to trace our roots in Italy. Most of us were born in the same house as generations of our ancestors."

The bartender set their drinks in front of them. "Yours is still on the house," he said to Laura.

She thanked him and continued talking to Scott, now ignoring bunny gal and her raucous admirers. "Mr. Scott of Irish blood, what do you do? From the way you dress, I can see you're a professional. From your occasional smile, I'd say neither an accountant nor a pathologist. From your spirit, I'd guess you were, as Shakespeare wrote, 'to the manor born' and arrived here piloting your own yacht."

"All true," he said with a smile. "My father was a

Rockefeller and my mother a Mellon. No yacht, but close. I sailed across the Atlantic in a birchbark canoe I built myself, something I learned from a native American uncle who slipped into bed with grandma when grandpa was busy counting all his money."

"Seriously, Mr. Thomas Sebastian Scott," she said," who exactly are you?"

"Since you insist on the truth, I'm a spy. My friends call me the James Bond of West Virginia where we drink bourbon only on special occasions. One taste of Morgan County moonshine, and you'd begin to describe grappa as a smooth libation."

Laura laughed. "Since you've finally come clean, so will I. My lover's in prison, as I said. He'll probably die there. If I hadn't engaged a good attorney, I'd be there with him. We were both charged with a conspiracy to cover up a crime. He was a Vatican cleric, a monsignor well known in Rome."

"You're confessing to a life of crime?" Scott said with a raised eyebrow.

"Not exactly. My beat included the Vatican, notoriously unavailable to journalists. When I met Monsignor Polanski, I sensed his regret in choosing a vocation that denied him the company of women. I liked him. And before long, we were meeting in a friend's apartment. I'm not a whore, but in a way he paid me with stories of Vatican intrigue. Who's up? Who's down? For nearly ten years, my reporting for *Panorama* magazine was the envy of every reporter who covered the Vatican."

"Journalists are the unsung heroes and heroines of our age," Scott said.

"Unsung, but not undiscovered. Some bastard discovered our liaison and blackmailed him. He had his reputation to protect as well as mine. He began to borrow—his word—money from the Vatican. Thousands, tens of thousands of Euros. When the blackmailer demanded even more, Polanski confessed. The story hit every Italian newspaper, every magazine except mine. And I was suspended. A journalist, a guy I know, wrote I had really been fucked."

"And now you're a freelancer?" Scott asked.

"Free is the operative word. If I can score an interview with this actor, I'll be back in print and back on *Panorama*'s payroll. *Game of Thrones*, known in Italy as *Il Trono di Spade*, was mandatory viewing. And this actor is the idol of every lonely Italian woman. He has the look, the body, that certain swagger—although I'm told he's dumb as an ox."

"Have you managed to reschedule the interview?"

"Not exactly, but I have a plan. I'll tell you in a few minutes. Don't go away."

Scott watched her walk away. To the restroom? To make a call? She didn't say. Her stride conveyed her strength, her determination, her confidence. In her heels, she towered over all the women and most of the men. Like many Italian women, she appeared ready to take charge.

What does she think of me? A harmless old man—or someone looking for a tryst with a woman half my age? I'll let her know it's the former by telling her about Fredrica.

Laura rounded the corner, disappeared from view. Minutes passed. Too many. Maybe she wouldn't return. Scott stared at the half-empty glass of Irish whiskey. Raised it to his lips for a sip, a small sip. Another sip. Usually drank cautiously. Not now. She had been gone for ten minutes. He ordered another. He knew she wouldn't return. The bartender knew better, poured two whiskeys, hers courtesy of Benedicts Bar.

"Hello," Laura said, surprising him when she returned,

"Did you miss me?"

"Can't you tell?" Scott said, standing up to welcome her back. "Convinced myself you had run away, disappeared into the night, left me to drink alone."

"I had to step outside to clear my head. Felt a little woozy, maybe that syrupy drink, a smoothie laced with hundred-proof gin. I am better now. The night air helped."

I don't get it. She looked the picture of health before she left.

"I see bunny gal is still dancing the night away. And if you don't mind, I'll take your seat so the pillar doesn't block my view."

"Of course," Scott said. "So glad you're feeling better. And looking forward to hearing how you'll get the interview with Mr. Italian Sex Idol."

"The elusive Maurizio Ruzzene? Well, I learned he has breakfast delivered to his third-floor suite at seven-fifteen. Who better to deliver it than me? The cast is tied up early tomorrow with a publicity shoot, but the next day will be perfect.

I'll wait in the hallway till the server arrives, offer my assistance with the tray, knock on his door, and greet him with a smile and a hot breakfast. At that hour, I'll probably find him in a robe or maybe *in uno stato naturale*. A quick photo, a few questions, and I have my story. If he doesn't have time for a full interview, I'll improvise the answers."

"A little risky, if you ask me," Scott said. "I'd feel uncomfortable if a stranger burst into my room uninvited."

"Maybe less so if she weren't a stranger. Remember, he met me yesterday when he blew me off for the scheduled interview. Even if he doesn't remember, I doubt he'll object to finding a woman in his bedroom."

Scott nodded, sipped his drink, trying to recall what had changed in her fifteen-minute absence. Makeup refreshed?

Maybe. Earrings? Yes. He remembered the sapphire gems in the silver earrings she had been wearing. Now, nothing.

Why does a woman remove her earrings before returning to the bar?

"You seem to be in a trance, Mr. Scott," she said with a laugh. "I don't usually do that to men."

"Thinking," he said, "about my good fortune in meeting you. And sensing some change since you took in the nighttime Irish air. And please stop calling me Mr. Scott."

"Scott, how does that sound? Maybe you *are* a spy. Or a reporter." She sighed and placed her hand on her stomach. "Afraid I'll have to abandon you. Still feeling queasy. And a little annoyed. Doubt if you noticed the guy sitting at the far end of the bar. Wearing a black T-shirt with a washed-out logo, maybe the Guinness harp. Slight tic in his left eye."

"Yeah, I noticed him," Scott said. "but didn't pay much attention. Might have been distracted by the gal spilling out of her bunny suit. So, who is he?"

"Surprised to see him here, a figure from my past. He followed me outside, reminded me, in his broken Italian, of my . . . uh, Vatican adventure."

"I saw him leave," Scott said.

"He asked who you were, asked if I had told you about Monsignor Polanski. And then suggested I warn you, in his words, 'a good fuck isn't worth time in an Irish prison.'"

"Laura, I wouldn't take that lightly. Sounds like a threat. He must have been following you."

"You may be right. His reputation isn't exactly . . . "

She stood, unexpectedly. "Must go now," she said, "to calm my nerves and my tummy. I may have overindulged."

"So sorry. Will I see you again?"

"How about breakfast tomorrow? I won't be practicing

my interview by slipping into your room, so let's meet in the restaurant on the first floor."

They exchanged three air kisses in the Italian fashion. She walked away, looked over her shoulder, and smiled. He paid the check, left, and strolled toward the university—to calm *his* nerves. He found walking therapeutic.

Young people were exiting a theatre across the street. Passing by earlier that day, he had seen the poster for a gorgeous standup comedienne with the slogan "More Than a Little Cheek." If the laughter of the crowd was a clue, it must have been a good show.

Scott walked toward an abandoned Gothic church standing in ruins, which from the faint glow of the street light looked like the perfect set for a creepy movie. He stopped to take a picture, evocative of a changing cityscape. It wasn't the only abandoned church in the city. He had been told the remaining churches were nearly empty on Sunday mornings, attended primarily by older women.

He continued toward the university whose new graduates had gathered the day before for pictures with their parents, proud to wear their graduation gowns and show their new degrees. Close to midnight, the campus was quiet.

Scott recalled his undergraduate studies at Fordham and his decision to become a priest. He had no regrets in leaving the seminary after one year. Looking back, he hadn't imagined he would spend his life, even risk his life, protecting his country in a profession shrouded in secrecy. At this stage of life, his visit to Northern Ireland had been obligatory—not only to explore his roots, but to satisfy his curiosity. Who was he, exactly?

Continuing his stroll, his thoughts returned to Benedicts Bar. He had enjoyed Laura's company and looked forward to seeing her at breakfast. Later, he would show up for another meeting with O'Malley. And someday he would return to Belfast to learn more about great-grandad—to see if the conviction was just.

Scott insisted he was *not* a descendant of a murderer. Or was he? Did his father know? Had he become a missionary to atone for the sins of his grandfather? No, no! His great-grandfather had been a distinguished poet whose rhymes were known by every Irish schoolchild. When classmates at Fordham had mocked his accent and called him Pakii, he invented a noble history. Over time he lived that history and would not easily abandon it, would not accept the possibility of carrying the DNA of a convicted murderer.

Scott passed the university, continued to the Botanic Gardens, now closed. A clear sky and a half moon provided a little light. He sat on the bench at the entrance and replayed the threatening words from the guy who had followed Laura outside.

His cellphone rang. "Are you still at the bar?" Laura asked in a halting voice. "Could you do me a big favor?"

"Of course, anything. What is it?"

"I need something to calm my stomach. Called the desk and got voicemail. Could you go across the street to the *farmacia* and get me something? Must have had one too many."

"Shouldn't you see a doctor?"

"No, no. I just need something to relieve the pain."

"Give me a few minutes," Scott said, "I'm not exactly at the hotel."

◆◆◆

No pharmacy in sight, but he found a packet of Alka-Seltzer at an all-night market, rushed back to the hotel, and reached the third floor within fifteen minutes. Out of breath, he knocked on Laura's door.

"Come in, it's open," she said in a sad whisper.

Scott found her lying on the bed, still in her clothes, with a wan smile. He took a glass from the bathroom, dropped in two tablets, filled it with water, and offered her the bubbling medication. She sat up, drank it, and muttered her thanks as she lay down.

"I'll be okay," she said, "after a little sleep. See you for breakfast—let's say nine instead of eight? *Grazie mille.*"

"Nine o'clock it is. Sleep well," Scott said as he left the room and closed the door.

I hate to leave her alone, but will look like a creep if I insist on staying.

Scott returned to his room, undressed, brushed his teeth, and checked his messages.

"Book an eighteen-day voyage to the Pacific." "Reduce your student debt." "Meet Russian girls." He deleted dozens of annoying emails. He saved one from Father Sean McManus, but first looked at a text from Fredrica.

<Just two more days. Can hardly wait. Meet you at the Hotel Grand, within walking distance of the Opera House and several good restaurants. Miss you.>

He would reply after reading Sean's email, which would inevitably include a limerick to bring him a smile.

He left Berkeley Springs to visit Belfast.

And then, Vienna, to renew memories past.

Where a sweet Austrian gal,

With a ravishing smile

Will ensure the visit is hardly his last.

Too tired to respond to Fredrica after all, he crawled in bed, turned over, and went to sleep.

◆◆◆

"Coffee?"

"Yes, thank you, black and hot. Nothing more till my companion arrives."

Nine o'clock, already noisy, as patrons of the hotel gathered for breakfast. Every footstep was accompanied by a creaking sound from the age-old oaken planks scavenged from abandoned buildings.

I'll be surprised if Laura's here by nine-thirty after last evening. We both had too much to drink.

At ten o'clock, he called her room, then her cell. No answer. Annoyed? No. Worried? A little. He ordered breakfast. Of course, eggs Benedict in a hotel so-named, along with sausage, bacon, and Irish soda bread. The waitress kidded him, told him waiting an hour or more for a bonnie Irish lass was not unusual and certainly worth his time. He felt the same about this bonnie Italian lass.

At eleven, Scott stood in front of the receptionist on the ground floor asking for assistance. "Laura Caputo is two hours late for breakfast. Would you kindly check on her?"

"Mr. Scott, I'll ring her room, but as I told ye, we can't go bursting in. The lady's entitled to her privacy. And if you don't mind me saying, she may well have decided not to join ye for breakfast. Wouldn't be the first time, Mr. Scott, that what began at nightfall turned sour by daylight."

"I have an appointment in half an hour, maybe ten minutes away by cab. So, I'll write her a note, apologize for running off, and see her when I return in a few hours."

"Afraid she'll be gone by then, Mr. Scott. Check out time is one o'clock. I think she's flying to Milan, maybe Rome, can't remember exactly. I do recall she's meeting her husband for some award ceremony. She told me he's a TV producer, a program about the lives of glamorous women."

"Okay," Scott said, perplexed by mention of a husband. He paused briefly. "Well, in that case, forget the note. When you see her, please tell her I missed her for breakfast and . . . and wish her well."

◆◆◆

Traffic was bad. The cabdriver was rude. Scott was impatient. He arrived a few minutes late, which O'Malley interpreted as a slight. "My time is valuable, Mr. Scott, so I charge even for the moments you are dawdling. You see, your file is on my desk, waiting to speak to you with its sad history of grieving women and tortured souls."

"Not sure that's what I need to hear at this moment, Mr. O'Malley, but go ahead. What more have you found besides my poor old great-grandfather convicted of murder?"

"The detail is so very important, Mr. Scott. You just said 'poor *old* great-grandfather.' If he hadn't been hanged for murderin' that poor girl, he might have lived to an old age, drawing his pension as a retired cop. But, he was in the prime of life when he dropped through the scaffolding, when he drew his last breath. And absent any conflicting information since our last meeting, I'd hold with the press report: the bugger had it coming. No reflection on his progeny of course."

Scott tuned out, looked away, listened to the steady rainfall. O'Malley continued babbling on, words that did not register. Scott thought of Laura. He should have remained at the hotel. Instead, he had come here to sit in front of this dreadful boor.

"Thank you," Scott said. "This is all very interesting, but I must go. Let's settle up now, and I'll take the folder with me and study it carefully."

"No, no, it doesn't work like that. I've barely begun. I

mean, I've spent endless hours already, but have not yet begun to unravel some of the complex relations I've discovered. For example, your great-grandfather's so-called father spent a year at sea before the child was born."

"Mr. O'Malley, I've learned quite enough. Please draw up the bill for your work and send it to the Benedicts Hotel." Scott stood, walked to the door, bounded down the stairs, hailed a cab, and returned to the hotel.

"Mr. Scott, you're back in time. She's still in her room. I think she had breakfast sent up. I expect she'll be down in a few minutes, so if you wait here you can see her off."

"Thanks, I'll wait." Professionally trained to appear calm in the worst of circumstances—even when he feared the worst—Scott invented a story to maintain his tranquil appearance.

Perhaps she stood me up for breakfast after learning I'm the great-grandson of a notorious Irish murderer. I must have inadvertently revealed that family secret last night after my fourth Irish whiskey.

Chapter 5. Crumlin Road Gaol

Scott sat quietly in the lobby waiting for Laura. The phone at the front desk broke the silence. "No, I told you before," the receptionist said, "there's no one registered here by that name." The phone rang again. "Good morning, Benedicts of Belfast. May I help you?" Her tone revealed her impatience.

Scott heard the elevator door opening. He turned his head to look. Bunny gal stepped out followed by her girlfriends from the night before. With bloodshot eyes and matching blazer, she walked by him toward the receptionist. He wanted to tell her to run away from a marriage destined for trouble. Too late for that, so he remained silent. He would never see her again.

In a few minutes, however, he would see Laura. He had been counting the days till he arrived in Vienna to meet Fredrica. Now he felt consumed with Laura, a woman he barely knew, a woman who had missed their breakfast date, a woman thirty years younger than he, a woman who might be a fugitive from Italian justice. His mind reeled.

Waiting in line at the reception, hotel guests were checking out, probably eager to reach the train station or airport. A middle-aged man wearing a long gray overcoat stepped out of line and approached the receptionist.

"I'm already running late," he shouted. "Why are you ignoring us? Do we have to call you on the phone to get your attention?"

The phone rang again. The receptionist did not look up. An ambulance stopped at the front of the hotel. Two men dressed in white rushed in and interrupted the angry guest. Scott could not hear their discussion. Medics? He saw them enter the elevator. He watched the light above the door. It stopped on the third floor.

Scott imagined them rushing down the hallway, past the florid wallpaper, turning the corner, and entering Laura's room. Were they here for Laura? Maybe she was still ill, seriously ill. Why hadn't he known? He caught the eye of the receptionist, who shook her head and lifted upturned hands.

Scott took the stairs to the third floor, faster than waiting for the elevator, and hurried toward Room 304. He knocked. No answer. Knocked again. Still no answer. The housekeeper, wheeling a cart with sheets and towels, stopped in front of the door and spoke to him in a language he didn't recognize. He shrugged. She opened the door. The room was empty. He paused to collect his thoughts as the housekeeper began to strip the bed.

Suddenly it came to him. Not 304. Laura had been in Room 314, in the next corridor. He rushed toward it. Turning the corner, he saw the two men entering the room. Two others stood nearby, one in uniform.

Shaken, he walked toward the room. The door stood open. He looked in.

The man in uniform, a Belfast cop, walked toward him and shut the door.

"Wait," Scott said, "what happened?"

"Sorry, mister, it's a private matter. Just a routine

investigation."

"We're friends. We spent the evening together."

"Wait here. My partner will want to talk to you."

Scott tried to appear calm—but his heart was racing, his blood pressure surging, his breathing accelerating. He should have insisted on calling a doctor, taken her to the ER. Did she drink too much? Hadn't he encouraged it?

The other man approached, flashed his badge, and identified himself as a detective.

"Are you a friend of the woman in 314?"

"Yes, but we just met."

"Are you a guest in the hotel?"

"Yes," Scott said. He looked away, conscious the inflection in his voice would have signaled a confession of guilt to a veteran investigator. He comforted himself believing this young rookie hadn't enough experience to be suspicious.

"May I see your identification?" the detective asked.

"Here's my driver's license," Scott said, removing it from his wallet.

"West Virginia? America?"

"Yes."

"Okay," the detective said. "And, uh, don't leave the hotel. Maybe, hmm, let me think. I know. Meet me in the lobby in half an hour. I have a few questions."

"Half an hour?" Scott said. "I can't wait. Tell me what happened. Is she being taken to the hospital?"

"I've nothing more to share. See you in thirty minutes."

As Scott walked to the stairs, he passed a stern-looking woman accompanied by a young man carrying a scarred valise with the faded name of the Royal Ulster Constabulary.

He returned to his room and began reconstructing the events of the previous evening, anticipating the questions he would be asked. What time did they meet? Did they talk to anyone else? How much did they drink? When did she leave? Had he seen her since she left the bar?

◆◆◆

Blond, mid-twenties, puffy face, an oval of innocence— Detective Sergeant Royal McGinty showed his ID again when they met in a quiet corner of the lobby. Scott guessed he had been named to reflect his Protestant roots.

"Mr. Scott," the young detective began, "how long have you known the woman in 314?"

"Just a few days. We met on the Game of Thrones tour. I helped her when she stumbled as we walked back to the bus from the Giants Causeway. Chatted for a few hours on the drive back to Belfast. Met her for dinner the next evening. And last night we had a few drinks at the Benedicts Bar."

"How many drinks did you have, Mr. Scott?" McGinty asked, as he wrote in his notebook. He didn't look up as he spoke.

"Four, I think."

"And Ms. Caputo, how many drinks?"

"She began with a house specialty, the Bramble, then a bourbon. And later a third, all on the house. Nothing more."

Writing, looking down at his pad, never looking up, McGinty continued, "You had four drinks, you said. How confident are you? Might it be reasonable to assume your memory was somewhat impaired after four drinks? Or maybe five? And did you have dinner? Were you drinking on an empty stomach?"

"Detective, you should know she was followed outside by a man who, in her words, 'made a crude threat in broken Italian.' She knew him, someone she met in Rome."

"Interesting story, Mr. Scott, but is there any reason I

should believe you, a man who may have been in a drunken stupor by the end of the evening?"

"It was a long evening—"

"I'm sure, Mr. Scott. How long exactly? When did you two leave the bar? Did she return to her room? Did you accompany her? Did you spend the night with her? Was she alive when you left? I need your best recollection, time and place, every detail."

He's a rookie, reading from his notes, and by his tone confirming what I've denied to myself. Laura is dead. McGinty's likely a homicide detective—and I'm a suspect.

The interview lasted nearly an hour. McGinty hadn't looked away from his report pad until he closed it, stood up, and instructed Scott to remain in Belfast for the next twenty-four hours.

"Is Laura dead?" Scott asked. "Has she been murdered? Am I a suspect?"

"Yes, she was found dead this morning. No, you're not a suspect. Not yet, not unless the coroner rules her death resulted from other than natural causes."

♦♦♦

Scott walked north on Great Victoria Street from Benedicts Hotel toward the Grand Opera House, slowly replaying events of the night before—their time together in the bar, her hurried departure, his assistance when she called. For thirty years he had investigated and solved international crimes, but never a murder. He wanted to see the body to confirm her death, to be sure this wasn't some sordid prank. He knew better, but hope clouded his thoughts. He remembered a vivacious woman determined to redeem herself.

He passed the Fitzgerald Hotel where she had intended to confront the Italian actor for the interview. He stopped in front of the grand Gothic structure on the opposite corner, the headquarters of Ireland's Presbyterian Churches. It was a hundred-and-thirty-foot-high reminder that Northern Ireland remained firmly within the United Kingdom, despite the yearning of Catholics to join the Republic.

Scott unfolded a paper map of the city to find directions to Falls Road. Twenty minutes later, he reached the iconic heart of the Catholic uprising during the Troubles. The stark murals of martyrs and terrorists are reminders that past sins are not easily forgiven. He felt an unexpected calmness until he stopped in front of the Bobby Sands mural. Painted on the side wall of the *Sinn Fein* headquarters, it included these haunting words: "Our revenge will be the laughter of our children."

Scott unfolded a map and headed toward the Protestant side of the divide. Surprised to find a twenty-five-foot wall separating it from the Catholic side, he turned and retraced his steps for several blocks and tried another route. He paused before a collage of hundreds of faces accompanied by the word "murdered" in red.

Passing a burly, unshaven man who gave him a threatening glare, Scott picked up his pace. The man followed him, caught up, and said, "Looking for someone? Lost?"

"Looking for Shankill Road," Scott said.

The man stared at him. Scott tensed, expecting trouble. After what seemed like minutes, the man spoke. "Go back two blocks, make a left turn, walk for half a mile, and then take another left."

"Thank you, much appreciated."

"Be careful," the man said. "Some of my neighbors get riled up when they see a stranger pokin' round."

Shankill Road was dressed with the Union Jack—flying

on poles, decorating the street, brightening ancient buildings. Storekeepers, residents, and most visitors were proud citizens of the United Kingdom. Their murals told a different story from those south of the religious divide.

Below a banner welcoming visitors to THE SHANKILL ROAD were the faces of three Protestant martyrs accompanied by these words:

You smug-faced crowds with kindling eye
Who cheer when soldier lads march by,
Sneak home and pray you'll never know
The hell where youth and laughter go.

Scott reread it several times and silently prayed. He later learned the words were from a poem by Siegfried Sassoon, a World War I English soldier, born to a Jewish father and a Catholic mother.

The street was quiet. He passed a woman walking a dog. She did not smile. He walked by a bar where two old men sat quietly together. They would have known others who died fighting for their families, their religion, their beliefs. He guessed great-grandfather was hanged in part for *his* religion. Surely, he could not have been guilty of murder. Scott was overcome with sadness as he walked back toward the hotel.

If I had called a doctor, Laura Caputo would still be alive.

Nausea, indigestion, heartburn—all signs of a heart attack. In retrospect he knew it. When it mattered, he had not. It took him a day to recall what he had known for years. It would be his eternal shame for not reacting. He has planned this vacation to recharge his batteries. Maybe they were approaching the end of their lifecycle.

Scott slowed down as he came closer to Benedicts Hotel. He felt drawn back to the bar but resisted the impulse. There would be no trace of Laura left. Her body would have been removed from the hotel for an autopsy. Again, he wondered what might have happened when the stranger threatened her. Nothing. He told himself she died in bed of a heart attack. He lay awake all night.

♦ ♦ ♦

He was the first to sit down for breakfast at Benedicts' first floor restaurant. Hot coffee appeared with a cheery greeting from a young waitress. "Seen ye here before, haven't I?" she said. "Guess ye heard the big news. Italian lady found dead in her bed. Cops all over the place. Someone said she was strangled. Don't know about you, but I find it kinda scary and kinda excitin' all at the same time."

Scott sat with his hands clutching the hot coffee cup. Strangled!

"Are you sure?"

"Could be just natural causes, they say, but I doubt it. Don't recall her myself, but the gal at reception said she was a real looker. And they're sayin' she was on the tear last night. Don't know anything, just what I hear, but let's get ye some breakfast, Mister . . . sorry, what was your name?"

"Scott, Thomas Scott. And I'll have bacon and eggs, soft boiled, and toast. Keep it simple." Heading to the kitchen, she looked back and flashed a big smile. His expression remained unchanged.

Waiting for her return, he briefly focused his thoughts on his Irish heritage. Carrickfergus was less than twenty kilometers away. He could be there within an hour. Better than sitting in the hotel brooding.

"Mr. Scott, I'm back," she said. "Since everyone's sleeping in, you get my full attention. Here, I'll warm up your coffee.

"Thanks, exactly what I need."

"And, forgive me, but I forgot to introduce myself. You could read it right here on this name tag, but at this hour of the morning, that's asking a lot. You can call me Eva, which is short for Evangeline. My mum told me I was the only baby girl in Carrickfergus with such a sweet name. I hope you like it."

"Evangeline. I agree, a beautiful name. And you were born in Carrickfergus?"

"Yes sir, I still live there."

"What a coincidence," Scott said. "It's my next stop, after breakfast."

"I bet you're gonna visit our famous castle. Overlooking the Belfast Lough, it's been there since the twelfth century. From our first day in school till graduation, we studied its history, starting with King John's siege in 1210. And this will surprise you. During what you Americans call the War of Independence, John Paul Jones defeated a Royal Navy ship within sight of the castle."

"I look forward to visiting it," Scott said, "but my real focus is on my ancestry."

She rolled her eyes. "Should've known. You wouldn't be the first, Mr. Scott. You Americans all want to prove you're Irish. Can't blame ye, of course. Now, excuse me a moment while I fetch your eggs."

She returned with his breakfast. "Irish soda bread, Mr. Scott. Hope it's not too dark for ye."

"Perfect," he said. "Maybe you could offer a little advice about Carrickfergus. I'm particularly interested in visiting the North Road Cemetery."

"That's a new one, Mr. Scott. I don't mean the graveyard. It's old as sin. I mean your interest is unusual. Not far from my home—just beyond the railway track, next to the old St. Nicholas Church. Headstones all weathered and the grounds a bit overgrown. Kids still sneak in at night trying to scare each other, particularly on Halloween."

"I'll be visiting in daylight, so I'm sure it'll be fine."

"Have to go now, Mr. Scott, to welcome the old couple who just came in. Also Americans, I think. Maybe Canadians. Not sure. Been here for a week, and he hasn't said a word except 'oatmeal.' She makes up for it by jabbering all the time."

◆◆◆

The gentle sound of the train was comforting. A few more stops in the Belfast suburbs and Scott would be in Carrickfergus searching for the ghosts of his ancestors. Nearly certain he would learn nothing about his ancestry in an Irish graveyard, still he couldn't overlook the slim chance he was wrong. He walked from the station down a street like a replica from the fifties. Gary's Menswear advertised a Gents Suit with a free shirt, free tie, and free shoes. Jacq's Bar offered Beers, Wines, Ales, and Spirits.

The castle's stately towers overlooked the bay as though it were still ready to defend the city. The North Road cemetery was less than half a kilometer away. Scott stood in front of the neo-Gothic Chapel of Rest before searching the grave markers for a family name. Several were made of cast iron, most conventional hand-carved fieldstones. The oldest marked the grave of a Master Mariner who died at sea in 1886.

Scott found no evidence of a gravesite for his great-grandfather despite the cemetery's acceptance of persons of all faiths. Convicted murderers may have been buried in some Irish potter's field.

On the return train, Scott planned the balance of his time in Belfast before flying to Vienna. First stop in the morning would be the Public Records Office of Northern Ireland and then a brief visit to Titanic Belfast, the city's major tourist attraction, located where the Titanic was designed, built, and launched in 1912. Or maybe he'd skip it. Not another reminder of death.

◆◆◆

The hotel receptionist greeted Scott and handed him a note requesting he call Detective Royal McGinty. After returning to his room, he called and waited on hold for several minutes with periodic reminders that the station was experiencing unusual call activity. Finally, McGinty came on the line.

"Mr. Scott, I've reviewed my notes from our interview and have a few more questions."

"Okay," Scott said, "anything I can do to help."

"We'd like you to come down to police headquarters tomorrow at nine o'clock."

"Afraid that won't work for me, Detective. Couldn't we just continue over the phone?"

"Impossible," McGinty said. "Meet me tomorrow at 60 Victoria Street and please bring your passport for positive identification." McGinty's telephone voice had more authority than the day before. It was a voice demanding compliance.

"Detective McGinty, why can't we complete this by phone. I'm as eager as you to learn the cause of Laura's death."

"We need your help, Mr. Scott. And we need it face-to-face. Nine o'clock sharp tomorrow morning."

He slept fitfully, trying to recall anything Laura may have said that would interest the police. She had threatened to burst into the actor's room at the Fitzgerald to conduct the interview. Her death curtailed that plan. And she felt threatened by the guy from the bar who approached her outside. He may already have been identified and interviewed.

◆◆◆

"Good morning. Coffee?" the waitress asked with a scowl.

"Yes, thank you," Scott said. "And a bowl of oatmeal if it can be hurried. I must leave in a few minutes for a meeting. And, if you see Evangeline, please give her my thanks for her guidance on Carrickfergus."

"It's her day off, but I'll tell her tomorrow. And I'll fetch your oatmeal when it's ready." As the waitress walked toward the kitchen, Scott noticed her body language matched the look on her face. Anger, fear? Maybe a rumor among the staff had connected him to the death of Laura Caputo.

After a short cab ride to the station, Scott identified himself and asked to see Detective McGinty. He left his passport to be copied and followed a young woman through a labyrinth of halls and doors.

"Here we are, Mr. Scott. I have to take your fingerprints. Not to worry, it's just a routine practice, particularly with foreigners. And this nasty ink will wash right off."

He had come to the station voluntarily, hardly expecting he would be treated like a criminal. He hesitated, then took a deep breath and complied.

After rolling his fingers on the ink pad, she led him to a windowless room and promised Detective McGinty would meet him in a few minutes. Scott kept looking at his watch, growing impatient as he sat alone for nearly thirty minutes. The door opened. Detective McGinty greeted him and introduced a colleague, Detective O'Rourke.

"Appreciate your cooperation, Mr. Scott. We have a few questions. But before we begin, my colleague will read you your rights."

"Why? Am I a suspect?" Scott asked.

McGinty tapped a pencil on his notepad. No reply. Signaled to O'Rourke to proceed.

"'You do not have to say anything. But it may—'"

"I asked if I were a suspect," Scott said, glaring at O'Rourke.

"I'll repeat the obligatory warning. 'You do not have to say anything. But it may harm your defense if you do not mention when questioned something which you later rely on in court. Anything you say may be given in evidence.'"

Scott sat upright. He had arrived at the station as a cooperative witness. He understood now: He *was* a suspect. McGinty was no longer the novice detective who had interviewed him before. He had the look of a man stalking his prey.

"Mr. Thomas Sebastian Scott, I'd like to review the answer you gave when I asked if you had accompanied Ms. Laura Caputo to her room. You said 'no.' Would you like to change your answer?"

"I have nothing to say until I engage a solicitor."

"Mr. Scott, is it true you're using a fake passport?"

Scott remained silent.

"Mr. Scott, is it true your real name is Franklin Lambert?"

Scott paused. It was his birthname, but his name had been changed by the NSA to provide him cover. It would be truthful to say his *real* name was *not* Franklin Lambert. An explanation would be in his interest—but the consequences of revealing this information on the public record could put his life in danger.

McGinty repeated the question. "Is it true your real name is Franklin Lambert?"

"As I told you, I have nothing to say until I engage a

solicitor."

"Mr. Scott, are you using prescription medication for severe pain?"

Scott said nothing.

McGinty conferred quietly with his colleague, then continued. "Mr. Scott, my colleague will present to you the torn packaging for a fentanyl transdermal patch. Do you recognize it?"

This is a new twist. I'm being framed.

"We recovered it from a waste basket in your hotel room," McGinty said. "Would you like to help yourself by answering if it's yours?"

"Even if we sit here all day, I won't answer without a solicitor, so let's wrap it up. I have to get back to the hotel, check out, and then go to the airport to take a flight to Vienna." It was the first time he had raised his voice. He stood.

"Sit down, Mr. Scott. You're not going anywhere. Not back to the hotel, not to the airport, nowhere until we complete our investigation."

Scott had toured the Crumlin Road Gaol, where prisoners were kept in twelve by seven foot cells until its closure in 1996. Now restored as a museum, he pictured himself as its lone occupant on public display as a warning to tourists.

He inhaled twice to calm his nerves and asked, "Detective McGinty, are you arresting me, charging me with a crime?"

"We're holding you for another twenty-four hours, after which you *may* be released. The genealogist you visited, a man named O'Malley, told us you traveled to Belfast with an alias or as he described it, a *nom de guerre*. A toxicology report has confirmed that Ms. Laura Caputo died of a fentanyl overdose. If your fingerprints match those on the glass found at her bedside, you will be charged with murder."

Chapter 6. Girl Can't Help It

"Your belt, shoelaces, and electronics," the guard said. "and no funny stuff 'cause after I give you a receipt, you gotta walk through a scanner to see if you're hiden' anything. Then, if you check out, I escort you upstairs to corridor D, show you your new home, tuck you in for the night, and lock your cell door to protect you from your neighbors. Some of 'um ain't the gentleman like you appear to be, if you get me drift."

"Just a second," Scott said as he removed his belt, "I have to let a friend know I'll be delayed."

"Sure, mate. Just be quick, okay?"

"Thanks."

Scott turned on his phone and sent a brief text to Fredrica.

<Held up in Ireland. Sorry, won't make it today. Update you when I can>

She responded immediately.

<I was so hoping to see you tonight. After several months anticipating your visit, another twenty-four hours should be tolerable. I'll sleep in, have a late breakfast at the hotel, and enjoy a Viennese shopping spree.>

It was the first time Scott would spend a night in jail, which he found tolerable despite the indignity. The metallic sound of the cell door closing was imprinted on his memory. He would clear up everything in the morning. Would have done it today if McGinty hadn't rushed off. He had turned down the offer of a public solicitor, confident he would be free the next day. If not, he would seek counsel from his West Virginia friend, Spencer Cobb. If necessary, he would ask his agency to contact MI6 to validate his bona fides. However, after being rescued in Istanbul the year before, his reputation within the NSA might be shattered, marking him as a man followed by trouble.

♦♦♦

Scott came awake with a start. Where was he? The morning twilight showed steel gray through the tiny glass-block window at ceiling height. For a second he lay still, listening to strange sounds around him. A truck rumbling outside. Low snores from prisoners in other cells. The heavy tread marked the passing of a guard in the dimly lit corridor. A flashlight beam swung briefly across his cot.

Suddenly the reality of it all sank in. They had actually locked him in a cell. Him! Had it been a mistake to pass on a public solicitor? He chewed his lip. He could spend the rest of his life double-guessing that decision.

Nothing to do about it now. He shoved the thin blanket off and sat up, swinging his bare feet to the cold tile floor. No point lying there.

After relieving himself in the tiny steel toilet, he splashed water on his face from the miniature sink, then paused. No towel. He shook his hands dry, then rubbed his chin and felt the grizzle of beard beginning. No razor, either, of course. Nothing he could use to hurt himself.

He wandered over to the floor-to-ceiling steel bars that separated him from the corridor. A faint *squeak-squeak-*

squeak sounded somewhere out there, slowly coming closer. He pressed his head against the bars to try to see. A guard was wheeling a trolley down the corridor, pausing in front of each cell just long enough to slide a small tray inside. Breakfast?

"Back three feet," the guard said, voice raspy, when he reached Scott's cell.

Scott did as instructed, and the guard slid a tray through a thin opening at floor level. Then, with a *squeak-squeak-squeak*, he pushed the trolley on to the next cell and delivered another meal.

Picking up the dented aluminum tray, Scott wandered back to his cot and sat to examine it. He found a medium-sized scone on a paper napkin, a pat of what looked like butter, and a paper cup half full of a dark liquid. He took a sip and grimaced. Bad coffee, black and tepid. Clearly, they spared no expense to feed prisoners here.

An hour later the guard who had met him the prior day appeared, unlocked the cell door, and escorted him through a corridor of catcalls and down the stairs. After returning his belt, shoelaces, and phone, the guard asked Scott to sign, and led him outside to a police van.

"Shall we hold the cell for ye?" the guard shouted as the van door was slammed shut.

◆◆◆

Driven back to the station, Scott was left in the same austere room as the day before. Without a shower or shave, he was sure he looked the part of a cold-blooded murderer.

"Good morning, Mr. Scott," McGinty began, with a triumphant sneer. "Let's make this quick. Our forensic expert has confirmed your prints are on the glass—the drinking glass—we recovered from the victim's bedside. Curious, isn't it, since you denied accompanying her when she left the bar?

"We have no further questions, although we're bound by department rules to give you an opportunity to explain why we should disregard this compelling evidence."

To ensure it's part of the record, I'll repeat what I said in the hotel lobby yesterday. Nothing more.

"Detective, I'll summarize what I already told you," Scott began, speaking politely, "Laura Caputo went to her room alone. I left the hotel and walked toward the university. Ten, fifteen minutes later my cell rang. Laura asked me to buy medication for an upset stomach. I stopped at a convenience store, purchased a package of Alka-Selzer, brought it to her room, dropped two tablets in a glass, and added water. I stood by while she sat up and drank it. At her request, I left her alone, stretched out on her bed, fully dressed."

"Very clever, Mr. Scott. A little different from what you said before, no? You must'a laid awake all night to invent that story. It would be credible if you had substituted fentanyl for Alka-Selzer."

"I have given you a complete and accurate—"

"The courts will decide that," McGinty said. "A hearing will be scheduled at a Magistrates' Court within a week. In the meantime, you're released on bail on the condition you remain within the city, wear an ankle bracelet, and report to this headquarters by phone each day before noon."

"This is all a misunderstanding," Scott said. "If you were to check with my employer, you would find I have a spotless record, that I am known for my integrity, that—"

"Mr. Scott, murder is a serious charge. Our London counterparts in MI6 have already contacted your agency. Their guarantee you would honor our conditions is the *only* reason you'll not be spending your time behind bars pending the Magistrate's hearing."

"Thank you," Scott said in a contrite voice that hid his frustration. He rubbed the stubble on his chin, a token of a night in jail.

"Thank them, not me," McGinty snarled. "My recommendation was overruled. The leniency of my superiors will not bring Laura Caputo back to life. Enjoy the next few weeks, Mr. Scott. They may be your last as a free man."

Papers to sign, warnings to hear, advice to absorb. Scott shuffled through the Belfast police bureaucracy following McGinty's assistant, whose communication consisted primarily of pointing and grunting. Scott eventually decided to break the silence.

"Sergeant O'Rourke, I appreciate the time you're taking to process me out of here."

"Uh-huh."

"You've worked with Detective McGinty for some time?"

"Maybe."

"Like your job?"

"Dealin' with fecking lowlife who gets sprung because of some British MI6 toady? Just like McGinty told me, you're talkin' bollocks."

♦♦♦

Finally released, Scott walked swiftly toward the hotel, head down, avoiding eye contact. How would he explain to the woman who was waiting for him in Vienna? And would she believe his story? Fredrica knew he travelled frequently, knew his work was shrouded in mystery. He hadn't confirmed her teasing that he must be a master spy. To reveal he had spent the night in jail and was out on bail would inevitably lead to a far different conclusion.

What could he say? What would she do? Attend the

opera alone? Remain in Vienna until he was free? Absolutely not. She would be on the train toward her home in St. Wolfgang. He imagined her anger—and her relief that he had been arrested before she became more involved.

His colleagues at the NSA would be more understanding. They knew him and had already vouched for him. There would nonetheless be an inquiry. He would be placed on administrative leave.

He picked up his pace as he came within sight of the hotel.

◆◆◆

"Mr. Scott," the receptionist said when he entered, "we can't extend your stay. Your effects have been inventoried and safely stored. No charge if removed within twenty-four hours."

"What? I'm sure you have vacancies. My floor's practically empty. I need to extend for a few more days, maybe a week."

"Afraid that won't be possible, Mr. Scott. You seem like a nice man, but you must understand the staff have been spooked by rumors about the unfortunate death. Not true, I'm sure. Still, we must be careful."

"Careful?" Scott said quietly as he stepped back from the counter. "Have you considered closing the bar? More suspects there than in my room."

"There are many fine hotels in Belfast," the receptionist said, ignoring his comment. "The Fitzgerald, for example, isn't but fifteen minutes from here."

His cellphone had been returned without a charge. And without his passport, he wouldn't be warmly greeted at the Fitzgerald. He smiled as he silently rehearsed an approach: *Hope you have a room for an American charged with murder. Afraid the peelers are holding my passport until a hearing before a magistrate. I don't have any identification, but I'm confident you can identify me by my picture in tomorrow's paper.*

Scott smiled. He had been in worse jams. He retrieved his luggage, settled his account, and headed toward the Fitzgerald. He walked briskly, head up, confidence returned. He would not be intimidated by these half-witted wankers. Next stop: Belfast Central Railway Station. Changed his shirt, shaved, and charged his phone. Three texts from Rachel Sullivan confirmed colleagues at Fort Meade knew of his arrest. The earliest expressed concern, the next worry, and the third panic.

> **<Scott, PLEASE respond. Received a cryptic message from UK counterpart. Positive reply sent immediately. Since then nothing except press report of American charged with murder of Italian journalist.>**

First things first. Scott called the Fitzgerald Hotel, a few minutes from the train station, and made a reservation. The required credit card would confirm his identification.

Next, he sent a text to Rachel explaining his predicament, thanking her for being concerned, and promising he would be free to return home within a week.

The text to Fredrica in Vienna would be more difficult. Best not to disclose the exact reason for his delay.

> **<Apologies, a hundred times over. When you inquired about my profession, I couldn't provide a satisfactory answer, compelled by my employer to reveal neither the nature of my work nor the corporation that employs me. That has not changed. I expected to depart Belfast yesterday, then today. For reasons completely beyond my control, I must remain here longer, up to a week. I'll make it right in the near future. Affectionately, Scott.>**

He hoped she would forgive his delay. Within minutes his phone beeped. It would be Fredrica, he thought, disappointed but understanding. It was not. It was another text from Rachel. Another surprise.

> **<My request to Dr. Hoople to assist in Belfast was denied. So, I scheduled personal leave, booked a flight, and will arrive tomorrow before noon. Where shall I meet you?>**

♦♦♦

Before answering, Scott walked to the Fitzgerald, explained he had misplaced his passport, and presented the copy he kept on his cellphone. That was enough for the young man at the desk to book him into room 419. After sleeping for ten hours he was awakened by a phone call from Rachel. She had arrived at the airport and would meet him at the hotel within an hour.

♦♦♦

He waited in an upscale restaurant in an upscale hotel in the heart of Belfast. The coffee was hot, but otherwise unexceptional. Scott imagined a review by the International Institute of Coffee Tasters: *Hotter but even less flavorful than day-old coffee served at the Belfast jail.* Rachel would arrive soon, full of questions, eager to help.

Scott appreciated her caring, but questioned her judgment. Operation Bluefish would continue without him, but without Rachel as well? He was in her debt, using her limited vacation to assist him. It was a signal—time to return to the West Virginia mountains, time to pass the baton.

"Yes, please, a refill would be perfect," Scott said to the young woman waiting tables. Her generous smile suggested she had no idea he was a man charged with murder. Fortunately, the story in *The Irish News* did not include his picture, although it all but convicted him of murdering the Italian journalist. Detective McGinty had spared neither the details of his investigation nor his personal view of Scott's certain guilt. The baby-faced detective appeared eager to bag his first culprit— bragging rights and a promotion to follow.

Scott checked the time. Rachel would arrive momentarily, certain of his innocence, but full of questions. She would assume her mentor would have a theory. He had ruled out suicide, impossible for this high-spirited Italian woman. No, Laura did not die by her own hand. What about the black-shirted guy who followed her outside? Was there a Vatican connection?

♦♦♦

Rachel dashed to Scott's table when she entered the dining room and offered a hug before he could stand. She was wearing a backpack and carrying a canvas tote bag. In her other hand she held a copy of *The Irish News*, folded to the account of Laura Caputo's murder with the name of the all-but-certain perpetrator circled. She held back tears. She assured him she knew he was innocent, that he had the complete support of his NSA colleagues.

I'm pleased she's here, but wish she weren't. Far more important for her to be at Fort Meade.

"Welcome, Rachel," Scott said, "you shouldn't have, although I'm grateful you've come. Thank you." He hesitated briefly to compose himself before continuing. "Who knows? And what are they saying?"

Rachel removed her backpack and sat facing Scott.

"Who knows?" Rachel repeated. "Everyone. Everyone at headquarters. When the legendary Thomas Sebastian Scott faces trouble, the entire agency feels the pain. Dr. Hoople said the headquarters building trembled."

"And my friends in West Virginia—Father McManus and Spencer Cobb? Do they know?"

"I think not," she said, "unless you told them. Berkeley Springs is a long way from Belfast."

Scott signaled the waitress for a menu and coffee for Rachel. Ten hours since she boarded the first leg of her flight at Dulles, she looked her usual fashionable self, dressed in Tory Burch bootcut jeans, a black silk turtleneck, and an embroidered crimson vest. She didn't respond when the waitress asked for her order.

"Look directly at Rachel," Scott said, "and repeat the question. She listens with her eyes."

The waitress paused briefly, took Scott's advice, smiled when she recognized Rachel's deadness, took her order, and headed toward the kitchen.

"Mr. Scott," Rachel said with a flourish, "as your agency's best friend, longtime admirer, substitute attorney, and private investigator, I have a few questions."

"Fire away, Ms. Sullivan," he said, extending his arms in a gesture of surrender.

"According to *The Irish News*, your fingerprints were found on the drinking glass, which suggests you were in her room. Is that correct?"

"Yes, just as you are acting as my substitute attorney, I was acting as her substitute nurse."

"And you were in her room how long?"

"Five minutes max."

"Not enough time to make love, but enough time to poison her. Correct?"

"Counselor, in my experience, poisoning generally takes longer than lovemaking, but that may be unique to me."

When the eggs and sausage arrived, they were both

laughing, the first time since Scott had bedded down at the city jail. She had convinced him the nuclear power plant investigation was on track, that her absence for a few days would make no difference.

"Woody's spending day and night reviewing intercepts," she said. "Not his job you know, but he's detected a pattern that's redirected our planning. Can't say more here."

"And Hoople, what's he think?"

"He keeps a close eye on Woody, but is delighted with his findings. Hoople's also asked him to mentor three cyber geniuses we're bringing on board. More on that later. Our focus now is on you."

Before they left the restaurant, they had a plan. They would visit Benedicts Bar, he in a simple disguise—dark glasses and a baseball cap. And she would play the role of a naïve American tourist. Their mission: find the identity of the guy Laura met on the night of her death.

"Real cloak and dagger stuff," Scott said, "May be the first time I'll be investigating a crime."

"That's what most people assume we do anyway, so we'll be the only ones surprised if it actually works."

◆◆◆

"Whiskey on the rocks," she said to the bartender. "Something Irish."

"We feature Bushmills, distilled just north of here. Jameson from the Republic is also popular. And we've several other fine Irish whiskeys: Clontarf, Kilbeggan—"

"Whoa. I'm an amateur. So, I'll begin with Bushmills."

"Good choice," Scott said, "same for me. Neat."

The two were sitting at the exact spot where Scott and Laura had been drinking three days before. Same bartender. Bunny gal missing, by now a new bride. Sparse crowd, no music.

"The guy that threatened her," Rachel said, "where was he sitting?"

"To your left, at the far end of the bar."

"Could you describe him?"

"Not really. Barely noticed him. Middle age, stocky, short hair like a buzz cut. That's about it."

"Ethnicity?" she asked.

"Don't know. Maybe Eastern Europe. Doubt he was Irish. Still trying to picture him. Black T-shirt. The kind that weightlifters wear to show their biceps. Also, Laura said he spoke Italian with a heavy accent."

Rachel raised her glass and said, "For a guy who doesn't pay attention, you *sure* pay attention. Practically enough for an APB."

"Looks like you're enjoying that Irish whiskey," Scott said. "How's it compare to Scotch and bourbon?"

"To tell you the truth, they all taste the same."

Rachel lifted the near-empty glass and sniffed. "No, I can't tell any difference."

"So, your taste buds aren't as well developed as your eye or your intuition."

"Give me time," she said. "How about another?"

They agreed that muscleman must have played a role in Laura's death, somehow providing the drug that killed her. Was she an addict? Did she meet him outside for a heroin fix and end up with some bad stuff laced with fentanyl?

"How did the fentanyl package get in your room?" Laura asked. "I assume you're not still treating your bum leg."

"No, it's practically healed. Even after the fracture, I didn't use any medication."

"So, someone's framed you."

"Yes, of course. The fentanyl package was never in my room. It's a complete setup. By the guy who followed Laura out of the bar? By the cops?"

"Shouldn't we ask the bartender if he knows our black-shirted suspect?" Rachel asked. "May be a regular. May have been tracking her, waiting for a chance to do the deed."

"Your idea, your ask," Scott said. "If he knows anything, there's a better chance he'll tell you than me, particularly if you offer your most ingratiating smile."

"In other words, I should flirt with him, render him helpless by my charms?"

"Shouldn't be a challenge. The way he's been eyeing you, I think he's already fallen in love."

Rachel shook her head. "Just like my New York boyfriend who can't resist proclaiming his eternal love."

"Sounds serious."

"Hmm. I thought so, but at times he seems so . . . so distant, distracted. Like a different person."

The quiet was interrupted when a group of young men burst in the front door and spread out at the tables behind the bar. From their boisterous behavior and loud laughter, Scott guessed it wasn't their first stop. They were here to celebrate. The bartender left the bar to take their orders. "Bring a pitcher of the black stuff for every table," the short red-faced guy shouted. "And introduce us to the floozie at the bar."

Rachel didn't hear a word. Scott wanted to respond, to protect his partner. But he remained calm while containing a smoldering anger.

"Before I talk to the bartender," Rachel said, "I need a story if I'm going to sweet talk him into giving up all his secrets. A bartender's a poor man's shrink and can't go blabbing to every gal who leads him on. I'll tell you whom we really need to sort this out, Woody's poker-playing buddy, guy who calls himself Mulligan."

"Mulligan?" Scott said with a look of disbelief. "That seedy old drunk we met at the pub down the road from headquarters? You gotta be kidding."

"No, and here's why. You'll admit that Woody's the smartest guy around. A little whacko at times, but he knows everything about everything. What you may *not* know is his reputation as a poker player. His friends won't play with him because he inevitably walks away with their money, their IOUs, their credit cards, and probably their pants."

"So I heard."

"Mulligan's the exception," Rachel continued. "Beats Woody three times out of four. And Woody claims the bastard probably lets him win the fourth just to suck him in for the next round. Says he could have bought his dream car, a new Alfa Romeo, for what he lost to Mulligan since he returned from Turkey."

"So, how could he help us?" Scott asked.

"Woody says the guy has a sixth sense or as he put it, 'he fucking defies logic.' Says it makes no difference if he's stone cold sober or roaring drunk."

"I remember him as an overbearing ass. What I most remember about that evening is you telling us about Mr. Perfect, your unnamed, rich-as-Midas heartthrob."

"Heartthrob? My dear Mr. Scott, you're revealing your age. Didn't that term go out with twenty-three skidoo?"

Scott tuned out as voices behind him were raised, scowled at the punk bragging about fucking his sister's best friend. His buddies cheered when he said she was an old-fashioned gal, still hadn't shaved her pussy.

Scott turned to Rachel to continue their conversation.

"What's the current term of art, Rachel? Your main squeeze?"

Laughing, she said, "Close, but you're still off by a few years. You can think of him as a dear friend. Too early to say what the future holds."

"Look forward to meeting him," Scott said, raising his glass.

"I'm sure you'll like him. Woody says even Mulligan approves, although neither of them even know his name."

"Sixth sense, again? Sorry, I'm a fact-based guy. Never bought in to Ouija boards, Tarot cards, or fortune tellers."

O'Malley would undoubtedly disagree. Despises my intuition and me as well.

"I suggest you alert Woody about a practice called 'edge-sorting,' a sophisticated type of cheating. A high stakes American gambler was found guilty by the Supreme Court in London of using that technique last year. Had to return ten million dollars to the casino. Maybe Woody can win back his Alfa."

The bartender busied himself by washing glasses, dusting bottles from the top shelf, and frequently glancing at Rachel. She acknowledged his presence and nursed her drink. Scott suggested it was time to find out what the bartender might know about his black-shirted patron. She agreed, said she had conjured up the perfect story. She took a long swallow, emptying her glass.

"Care for another?" the bartender asked.

"You could convince me," Rachel said, lowering her voice. "My dad's leaving in a few minutes, but the night is young, as we say in America."

"You've come to the right place, girl. Another whiskey on the rocks?"

"Yes, but first I have a question."

The bartender leaned in to listen over the braying laughter behind her.

"I'm trying to find a guy I met here the other night. Unpleasant at first, but he had a rustic charm. Accent, bulging biceps, shorter than you, close cut hair. I suspect he might be a regular here. Wore a black T-shirt with a washed-out logo. May have been the Guinness harp. Someone you recognize?"

"Yeah, I know him. Fecking lowlife. Brags he's Irish. If he's Irish, I'm a Mongolian sheepherder. Russian all the way. Comes in here couple times a week and then disappears for months. Claims to work for some Italian export company. Might be true if they export bullshit."

"Know his name?" Rachel asked.

"Take your choice. Calls himself Paddy when he's in his cups. Sometimes goes by Viktor. Says his Italian name is Vincenzo. Wouldn't believe a word the eejit says. I'm gonna pour you that Bushmills and then take care of the crowd behind ye. Nearly scuttered already, I'd say. Don't run away. I'll be back."

"Nice work, Rachel," Scott said. "If I were looking for a suspect, he'd be it. Must have known Laura or knew who she was. Practically threatened her. Did he follow her, or was it happenstance that he spotted her drinking with me? What was the motive? Or, to exercise my imagination, was I the target? Knock her off and shift the blame to me. Far-fetched, I know, but we mustn't rule out anything at this point."

"Scott, you told me you turned down the offer of a public solicitor. Not your best move. You need someone who knows his way around Belfast, who can engage an investigator to check out Viktor or Vincenzo or whoever he is. Maybe his export business is illicit drugs. Cops might already be watching him."

"You're right. First thing in the morning, I'll look for a solicitor. Maybe contact my friend Spencer Cobb who used to have a few British clients. Doubt if he's licensed to represent me here, but doesn't mean he can't help. And before you suggest it, the answer is no! I don't need Mulligan, even if Woody vouches for his other-worldly powers. One drunk on the case is enough."

♦ ♦ ♦

The bartender was back, grinning at Rachel, apparently waiting for the moment her "dad" would toddle off to bed.

He's sure the three fingers of whiskey he poured will cement the deal.

"Me again," the bartender said. "Afraid I forgot something, for which I offer my humble apology."

"Apology accepted," Rachel said, "but I can't guess what you forgot. You certainly didn't forget to fill this glass to the top with your best whiskey."

"My name! I forgot to tell you my name. I'm sure you're curious. It's Jimmy. Same as the fat guy at the other end of the bar. You can think of him as the Jimmy with the oversized arse, if you see what I mean. And me? I'm the Jimmy with the good looks and sexy smile."

He showed his pearly whites again and asked her name. Fortunately, he looked directly at her, so lip-reading was a cinch. She didn't miss a word.

"Me? I thought you'd never ask. It's Cinderella. And like your good-for-nothing friend Viktor, I have an Italian version as well. Think of me as the hauntingly beautiful *Cenerentola*—at least until midnight."

Scott excused himself to give Rachel time to work her magic without the appearance of eavesdropping. Opening the door between the bar and the hotel lobby, he looked back at Rachel and offered a thumbs up.

Riffing on Rachel's fantasy, the bartender said, "After you return to being a scullery maid when the clock strikes twelve, I am at your service, available to escort you to the castle of your dreams."

"To meet Viktor?" she asked, with a look that shouted innocence.

"What? Of course not. Why would you want to meet Viktor?"

"Jimmy, my dear Jimmy with the good looks, I like you—but first I must see Viktor again. And if not tonight, then tomorrow. It's about a promise he made. When that's settled, I'd love to see your castle, even if we have to travel in a chariot drawn by a team of Irish mice."

"Pardon me," Jimmy said, "I see a few of my hard-drinking customers are getting impatient." He walked toward the ever-louder party holding high their empty pitchers.

♦♦♦

Scott returned to the bar, eager to hear what Rachel had learned. He settled in, picked up his glass, and glanced up. Two men, standing in the doorway caught his attention. One tall, one short. One with short-cropped hair, the other with long hair. One dressed for a night on the town, the other wearing the clothes he slept in. They surveyed the room, they pointed, they whispered to each other. For a moment, Scott thought Viktor was back.

They walked toward him. Now closer, the short guy wasn't Viktor. They stopped beside Scott and Rachel.

"Are you Thomas Scott?" the tall guy asked.

"Who wants to know?" Scott replied defensively.

"My editor and my cameraman."

FLASH! FLASH! Ten times. A hundred times. It felt like a paparazzi convention. Scott shielded his eyes as the cameraman got closer. The close-up shot would spell guilty. Everyone in the bar was looking at Scott until the camera chose Rachel. Same drill, searching for the picture that would shout accomplice or maybe victim. Who were these intruders? When Scott heard the two speaking Italian, he knew. He would be featured in the next edition of *Panorama*. Maybe on the cover. He could almost write the caption: ACCUSED MURDERER ON THE PROWL.

Jimmy acted immediately to protect his favorite customer. Climbing on a stool and jumping over the bar, he pushed and dragged the cameraman away. "Annoying our customers, yous are. Keep acting the bollocks and you'll be enjoying a long Irish vacation."

"Wait, we have every—"

The other Jimmy— a little bigger, a little tougher— joined his partner. He said, "Got busted out of the peelers for breakin' me sergeant's ugly nose. A skill I'm eager to demonstrate, unless I see ye makin' for the door."

"Scott, what's this mean?" Rachel asked.

"With our faces on the cover of Italy's most popular weekly, I suspect we'll soon be known as the Bonnie and Clyde of Belfast."

Chapter 7. Roman Holiday

"Good morning Rachel, hope I didn't waken ye. Found the fecking Russian's name. It's Viktor. Full name—Viktor Sokolov. Bit of a *chancer*, me buddy tells me. Must be printin' his own money the way it flows. Cars, booze, women. Nothin' too good for the bloke. Then he disappears, weeks, months at a time. Says he flies to Rome for the Pope to hear his bleedin' confession."

Rachel felt the vibration, recognized Jimmy's number, and opened her phone. "Thank you," she said, "but I couldn't understand a word. I'm good at reading lips, but can't hear. If you would kindly repeat your message in a text, I'll respond." He did and she replied.

<Thank you, Jimmy. **Any hint about his income. Drugs? Trafficking? Blackmail?**>

Within seconds, he responded.

<**Lots of guesses, but no one knows. His money talks, but doesn't reveal secrets. Hope to see you at the bar tonight.**>

◆◆◆

Rachel and Scott had planned to meet for lunch at Robinson's Bistro, across from the Fitzgerald Hotel. When she walked in, he stood and motioned her to his table. From his posture and the sparkle in his eyes, she knew the cloud had lifted. "Scott, you've been transformed. I mean you no longer have the look of a man preparing for twenty years in jail. What happened?"

"Picked the name of a solicitor from the phone directory at random. She answered my call, said she could see me immediately. Fairly new, I doubt if she has many clients. Told her my story. Mentioned Viktor, our Russian suspect. Turns out she'd heard of him."

"What a coincidence," Rachel said.

"Exactly what I thought, but she said there weren't many rich Russians in Belfast. Known as Victor Sokolov, she said the cops keep a close eye on him."

"Bingo," Rachel said. "Same name Jimmy the bartender gave me an hour ago."

A young waitress stopped at their table with a friendly welcome and two menus.

"Bring us each a Guinness," Scott said to the waitress, "while we decide what to order."

"Take your time," she said, "the kitchen staff has barely just arrived." She smiled and sauntered away.

Scott turned back to Rachel and said, "My solicitor will do some informal checking and hire an investigator if she runs out of leads. She asked if I had any contacts in Rome who might ask around about Viktor."

"Rome? You did say Rome, didn't you?" Rachel asked wide-eyed.

I'd love to go back, even if just for a day. The women know how to dress, and the men show their appreciation.

"*Sì, Roma,*" Scott replied, with his best Italian accent.

"Just kidding. Heard you perfectly well. Wanted to hear it again. And if you don't have a Roman friend, you will by this time tomorrow. First stop: *Panorama* magazine. Second stop: the Vatican, to get a readout of Viktor's confessions from the Pope." She smiled.

"Wait a minute. Appreciate your offer, but you should be returning back to the agency."

"One more day won't matter," Rachel said with a wave of her hand. "By the time we leave the restaurant, I'll have booked my flight on Alitalia."

The waitress returned and asked if they had decided.

"Yes," Scott said, "I'll have the Irish stew."

"And since I'm in training to go to Rome," Rachel said, "I'll have your luncheon special, Spaghetti Carbonara."

I seldom ignore Scott's advice, but in my gut I know I'm right.

♦♦♦

"Do you have an appointment, miss?" asked the Marine Guard at the American Embassy on Rome's Via Veneto.

"No," Rachel answered, "but I'm sure they'll receive me with this identification."

"And your passport, please."

Two hours later she was still waiting. Mistake to arrive at lunchtime. She hoped they would eventually confirm her identification and invite her to speak with an analyst. Finally, she was greeted by a gray-haired older woman—no makeup, knee-length skirt, starched white blouse, proper shoes. Rachel recognized her as the proverbial assistant who keeps the unit running, who knows everything that can't be found in a computer database.

"Ms. Sullivan, please follow me," she said and led her through the turnstile to the elevator. "You will be meeting with one of our young analysts. New here, but with far more experience than his boyish appearance may suggest."

"And his name?" Rachel asked.

"His office is down this corridor. I'm sure he'll introduce himself."

Rachel was accompanied to a small windowless office where she sat alone in a straight back wooden chair.

She had deposited her cellphone in a locked box before entering this section of the Embassy. Minutes passed. Then more. She lost track of time. Her reserve of patience had its limits, but she would remain appreciative even if she had to wait till dark. They could have asked her to return the next day. Or the next week. Or never. No obligation by officers from another agency to put aside urgent work to see her. Her association with Scott, if recognized, would be reason enough for the station to turn down her request.

◆◆◆

"Ms. Sullivan, good afternoon. I'm Larry Gold. Six-hour time difference with Washington delayed a response. When your agency finally woke up, they vouched for you and asked we extend every courtesy. Tell me how we can help."

"A long story," she began. "A veteran NSA contractor, on holiday in Belfast, has been charged with murder. He's being hounded by a reporter for *Panorama* magazine."

"Laura Caputo! Sensational story here. And you're telling me the suspect works for your agency?"

"I'm telling you, Mr. Gold, the man they arrested without evidence works for my agency. The suspect, *my* suspect, is a man known in Belfast as Viktor Sokolov. As he travels to Rome frequently, the station may know him. Given his opulent lifestyle, I would guess he's involved in drugs or some other illicit activity."

Gold appeared to listen with an unblinking intensity. His poker face revealed nothing. His blond curls suggested a

California surfer, anything but a government spy. After a long pause, he repeated his first offer. "Tell me how we can help."

"A small request: I need to call my agency on a secure line. More importantly, would you see if you have anything on Viktor Sokolov. In the meantime, I'm on my way to see the editor of *Panorama* and then check in at my hotel."

After another delay, she reached Fort Meade and eventually Dr. Hoople through a secure text-like connection.

<You're in Rome? Not Belfast? Where's Scott? What the hell's going on?>

His surprise and suspicion were brokered by his curiosity. After explaining she had flown to Rome to help Scott's defense, Hoople cancelled her leave, placed her on duty status, and promised the full resources of the agency to assist her.

♦♦♦

Rachel turned down an offer by Gold for dinner, suggested a raincheck, and took a taxi to *Panorama*'s editorial offices. Another wait, and finally she was escorted to the opulent office of the editor. He greeted her as the cover girl he promised she would become next week.

"So, you are Mr. Scott's consort? Thank you for dropping in. Our photographer didn't get your name. Our caption genius gave me a dozen options. My favorite: 'Murder Suspect Eyes Another Victim.' The sound of the word in Italian, *omicidio*, is almost musical."

"I am neither his consort, nor a victim," Rachel replied sharply, "and because I'm deaf, I don't know much about music. I am here to investigate the crime. Thomas Scott is not a murderer. He, too, is a victim, guilty only of responding to Ms. Caputo's call for assistance."

"Who are you?" the editor asked.

"A Federal investigator, an American, and a colleague of Thomas Scott. Not my first time in Italy, nor the first time to assist in solving a crime in your country. Trust me, I will find Laura Caputo's murderer."

"You sound determined."

"Yes, absolutely. I've come here to ask your assistance: Save my picture for the cover of your magazine *until* the real killer is behind bars?"

The editor picked up the phone, said something Rachel couldn't follow, stood up from his desk, walked to the far side of the room, invited her to join him in one of the leather chairs underneath a reproduction of a nineteenth century painting of a nude woman.

"This magnificent painting is by French artist Jean Léon Gerome entitled *Truth Coming out of her Well to Shame Mankind.*"

Rachel barely followed as he gestured to the painting but quickly positioned herself to better read his lips as he continued.

"I don't know you," he said. "However, we're both seeking the truth. Would I be correct in assuming Laura said she'd been fired and working on a story to prove her worth?"

"Yes," Rachel replied. "She was trying to interview some famous Italian actor."

The door opened. A young woman arrived with a tray she placed before them. "Let us toast the occasion," the editor said, "to *la verità.*" They touched their glasses and tasted the reddish-orange cocktail. She puckered her lips.

"Bitter?" he asked. "We Italians call it a spritz, made with Prosecco, Aperol, and sparkling water."

"It's, ahh, bracing," Rachel said. "To the truth!"

"The truth: we did *not* fire her. She did *not* travel to Belfast to interview an Italian actor. That was her cover. She could have interviewed him here. She learned—I don't know how—the name of the man blackmailing her lover, the monsignor now withering away in prison."

Rachel held her breath, hoping to hear her detour to Rome would confirm her hunch.

"By chance, would the blackmailer's name be Viktor Sokolov?" she asked.

"She said that?" the editor exclaimed with a look of surprise.

"No, not as far as I know. But, he's the man *we* suspect murdered her."

"I'm impressed. He's the lowlife Laura was investigating. Calls himself Vincenzo here in Rome, but must be the same guy. Blackmail, murder, what else? What evidence do you have?"

"None," Rachel replied, "except he followed her out of the hotel the night of her murder and apparently threatened her. Throws money around like he won the Irish sweepstakes. Suggests to me he's involved in narcotics or trafficking. Or maybe he simply makes a killing, no pun intended, from blackmail."

Rachel promised to keep him informed. He promised to kill the cover story, but complained it would cut sales in half if he substituted a story about corruption in the Italian judiciary. On reflection, he told her a cover featuring the beach at Ostia Antica with sunbathers in various modes of undress would be nearly as good as a closeup of an alleged murderer propositioning his next victim.

♦♦♦

Fifteen-minute walk to the *Hotel Scalinata di Spagna*. The sun was out, the air was fresh, and the birds were singing. She imagined the latter, as her skills did not include reading birds' lips. Two for two—embassy analyst and magazine editor—both on the first day. Rome was her kind of place, until forcibly separated from her purse by a hand extended from a passing Vespa.

Rachel was left with the broken strap and a bruised arm. She ran toward the fleeing thieves, one driving, the other holding the stolen purse. Shouting at the top of her voice, running at the speed of adrenalin, two guys on an underpowered motor scooter were no match for Rachel. The driver ran away. The guy holding the purse lay flat on the street with Rachel holding him down. The crowd cheered. The cops arrived, cuffed the perp, and drove her to the station to make a statement. Bystanders later told the police she had tackled the pair on the Vespa while it was still in motion.

A beautiful day turned sour, she thought, until she began chatting with the detective who took her statement. "Didn't hear a thing," she said, "because I'm deaf. Enjoying the scenery until my purse was ripped from my arm. Thankful they left my arm behind. My money, my ID, my credit cards, my phone, my whole life was in the purse."

"Miss," the detective said, "you are a brave woman. And lucky, too, with only a few scrapes. You could have been seriously injured."

"Thank you," Rachel said, "but I had to have it back. I'm here from America to investigate a crime. Maybe you can help."

She reached in her purse for her passport and showed it to the detective.

"Official, I see. Would be my pleasure to assist. You helped us catch a man who maybe always is robbing tourists."

"By chance, have you ever heard of a Russian named Viktor Sokolov, known here as Vincenzo Sokolov?"

"No detective here who does not hear of him. One of the kingpins of Russian mafia. Lives off the goodwill and how-you-say gullible of Italians. Arrested once, but released after twenty-four hours for no evidence."

"Must be the man we're looking for," Rachel said.

"We know he promises star-struck women from Bulgaria careers in Italian cinema. And sure enough, they soon end up on film, but not the kind they write home about. Although deceitful, it's probably legal, unlike his other activities."

"Could you share a picture of Viktor from your files?"

"Yes, I'll give you a mug shot. And also offer a ride to wherever you're staying."

♦♦♦

Rachel's room at the *Hotel Scalinata di Spagna,* overlooking the Spanish Steps, was small but comfortable, a Roman treasure from an earlier time, updated with Wi-Fi and a flat screen TV. She browsed through her email, learned Scott was pleased with his choice of solicitor, except for her opposition to inviting Spencer Cobb to assist.

Rachel also read a brief text from her New York boyfriend, the first she had received since arriving overseas.

<Missing you since you abandoned the states to seek the company of an older man. Been wondering if you'd fly across the Atlantic if I were serving hard time. As always, with a kiss and a hug.>

She hoped he was joking, but the tone suggested otherwise. Jealousy or control? It didn't feel right. She felt even worse when she looked in the mirror to see her face as a patchwork of scrapes and bruises. She hurt all over.

♦♦♦

Unbruised and unbent, Scott sat on the edge of his bed

in the Fitzgerald Hotel checking his email. As soon as he began to read the message from his friend Sean McManus, he knew the news had made its way to West Virginia.

> *German chocolate or Angel Food,*
> *Take your pick. They're both so good.*
> *Look inside, you'll find a saw*
> *May not be kosher by Irish law,*
> *But promises freedom, as it should.*

His solicitor, whom he met for the second time a few minutes later, was confident her defense would persuade the magistrate to free Scott.

'I'm sure you're doing the right thing," Scott said, "but I'm also sure my friend Spencer could convince the court this shifty Russian did the deed."

"Hold your horses, Mr. Scott. The purpose of the hearing is to defend you, not to convict someone else. Sokolov may be the killer, but in so far as I know, the evidence against him falls well short of circumstantial. Wistful, fanciful won't do it, even if your golden-voiced friend is twice-blessed with the Irish gift of gab."

Scott sighed. He hesitated to admit his solicitor was right, but couldn't contest her reasoning. Maybe if great-grandfather had listened to *his* solicitor, he would have walked away a free man. No capital punishment in Ireland now, but twenty years in prison was not a compelling alternative.

"You're right," Scott said, "what's your plan?"

"You bought some medication for Laura at a nearby convenience store, right?"

"Yes, and took it to her room, dissolved two tablets in water, and handed it to her."

"Paid cash or credit card?"

"Credit card," Scott said. "Also bought an apple and a

box of mints."

"That takes us halfway," the solicitor said. "Any chance you still have the receipt?"

"Every chance. I'm a packrat. It's in my room at the Fitzgerald. Halfway you say. What's the other half? My honest face?"

"The other half is the empty wrapper for the fentanyl patch you carelessly left in your room."

Scott bristled. "I have never owned a fentanyl patch. Never even heard of fentanyl patches until the detective sprung it on me. I did *not* open a package in my room or anywhere else. Did *not* leave a wrapper behind. Found in my room? A complete fabrication. A total lie. It was a set up."

The solicitor nodded her approval. "I want to hear those exact words before the magistrate, spoken in the very same indignant voice. Your conviction will complement the evidence my investigator has found."

"Evidence?" Scott asked.

"We requested and received a copy of the torn fentanyl wrapper. It carries a twelve-digit alphanumeric code, identifying the date and place of manufacture. Our man then checked shipments with his sources. The batch from which it originated had been shipped to a pharmacy in Londonderry two years ago."

"You work fast," Scott said.

"If we can show you haven't been shopping at McCafferty's Chemist since then, we're in clover. As they're required to maintain a file of all prescriptions, I'm guessing they won't find one with your name. Am I correct? Even been to Londonderry?"

"Never," Scott said. "This is my first visit to Northern Ireland."

"If there's a scintilla of doubt in the eyes of the magistrate," the solicitor added, "I will ask him if he takes you as an eejit. If not, I will point out that no one planning a murder would be careless enough to leave in plain sight the evidence needed to convict him."

"I like your logic."

"And to make my point, I'll ask for an investigation of the smarmy detective who framed you. He undoubtedly thinks he's going to be promoted and moved to a corner office. I say he'll be dismissed and moved to the cell they've reserved for you."

Scott tilted his head, nodded in agreement, and broke into a smile. "Wouldn't that be sweet revenge!"

♦♦♦

Shortly after being convinced by his solicitor that an American lawyer would be of no assistance in Belfast, his phone rang. It was Spencer Cobb.

"News travels slowly to the West Virginia mountains, but once it gets here it spreads like the Black Death. Father McManus is leading a prayer vigil. And Sheriff Hightower is saying suspicion hangs over you like a raincloud at a Sunday School picnic. For my part, Scott, I don't give a rat's ass if you're guilty or innocent. I've defended both, with a perfect win record."

"Spencer, appreciate the call. I've a shrewd Irish solicitor who promises the magistrate will almost certainly dismiss the charges."

"Yeah, and as I recall, Al Gore 'almost' won Florida. Can't take the risk, Scott. Already have my reservation on a flight out of BWI. See you tomorrow morning, if you'll share your location. Rumor has it you've been sprung from jail and are living the life of Riley in some plush hotel."

"Wait" Scott said, "I appreciate the offer, but . . . "

"Not an offer, my good man, I shall be at your side defending you in the King's English—or Gaelic, if warranted."

Scott, fearing his solicitor's perfect defense would hardly be improved by Cobb's uninvited assistance, resolved to keep them apart. Maybe an invitation to tour a local distillery would do the trick. Or, perhaps he could help Rachel with her pursuit of Viktor Sokolov. Send him off to Rome and invite him to pursue leads there.

"I'm at the Fitzgerald Hotel," Scott said, "living on a strict diet of bread and water."

♦♦♦

Belfast was overcast, threatened by storm clouds in the distance. Scott's upbeat demeanor crashed after the call from Cobb, whom his solicitor had vetoed with the words, "too many solicitors give ye bad *craic*."

As much as he might enjoy seeing Cobb chatting over a few beers, Scott feared it would not end well with his take-charge buddy trying to use his expertise in American law in an Irish courtroom. To lessen his anxiety, Scott decided to defy the forecast predicting a storm by walking south toward the scene of his alleged crime and onward again to the Botanic Gardens. The museum there would provide a distraction.

Sensing he was being followed, Scott decided to test whether his paranoia was clouding his observational skills. He turned west on Hope Street, walked to Great Victoria Street, and waited in a doorway out of sight. Within minutes, the man Scott suspected of tailing him passed by, paused, looked both ways, shrugged his shoulders, and continued south toward the Holiday Inn.

Scott followed at a distance, spotted his tail entering the hotel, and rushed to catch up with him. The man stood in the center of the lobby looking befuddled and lost.

"Pardon me," Scott said approaching the young man, "do you happen to know how to get to the Botanic Gardens?"

"Yes, a beautiful spot, just beyond the university. I happen to be going that way myself if you'd care to join me. We'd need to cut over to University Boulevard and walk south for a kilometer or so."

"You know the place?" Scott asked.

"Like the back of my hand."

"Wonder if you'd share a little of its history. Trust you wouldn't mind if I turned on this little recorder on my phone, so I can share it with my friend."

"Sure, okay, but I may have exaggerated a bit," he said. "It goes back to the early nineteenth century when it was called the Royal Belfast Botanic Gardens. It has lots of plants—.and it's really big. If you're not too keen on looking at flowers, there's a museum with art and historical things. Very exciting."

Sensing his tail had exhausted his knowledge, Scott thanked him and asked where he worked. Still walking, looking straight ahead, the man said he worked for the government.

"The government," Scott responded. "Let me guess. I'd say you're about twenty-two, maybe twenty-three, relatively new at the job. Right?"

"Yes, close."

"Close? Let's see if I can get closer. I see you as a rookie with the Belfast Cops, working for Detective McGinty, sent to follow me. And, if you don't mind me saying so, you've just failed Suspect Tailing 101."

"I don't know what you're talking about."

"No? I bet McGinty will," Scott said. "I'm sure he'll be interested in a copy of this recording, harassing an innocent man enjoying an Irish vacation. He may even suggest disciplinary action for your botched surveillance."

The young man, wearing an expression of guilt, did not respond. The two continued walking toward the Botanic Gardens. Scott stopped in front of the Benedicts Hotel and spoke about being framed by Detective McGinty.

"That baby-faced prick sized me up as a man whose arrest would lead to a promotion. He surely knows I'm not the killer, but what difference does that make to a man without a conscience? Don't know what he'll think of this recording, but I'd say you'd have a more promising future with the Sanitation Department than the Police Department. On the other hand, tell me why McGinty is such a vindictive bastard, and I'll forget about the recording."

"Never heard that, and I have nothing more to say."

"Fair enough," Scott said, removed the phone from his pocket, and stopped the recording. "Now, may we continue? Tell me why I ended up in his crosshairs, why he had you tailing me."

"I don't know anything," the young cop said. "However, there are rumors. Gambling debts, they say. Had his arm in a cast until a few weeks ago. Some say it was broken by a not-so-friendly debt collector. I know for a fact he's been called in front of an internal review board. Don't know what happened, but I'd guess his future's as bleak as mine."

"Your future's already looking much better," Scott said, "and so is mine. We'd both feel even more confident if we knew a little more about McGinty's debts. And about his arm-breaking debt collector."

"Don't know much more except what I heard from one of me buddies, another rookie on the force. He said some Russian gangster gave McGinty another month to come up with fifty thousand quid or enjoy life with both legs in a cast."

Chapter 8. Touched with Fire

"Listen," **Scott said**. "I know you care, but . . . my solicitor insists there's no role for you." He was sitting across from Spencer Cobb in the restaurant of the Fitzgerald Hotel.

Cobb, who had arrived an hour earlier after an overnight flight stared at Scott and leaned across the table, his face revealing impatience.

"You *cannot* allow some fresh young Irish woman to defend you against a charge of murder," he said, lowering his voice. "This is Belfast, for god's sake, where crimes of passion are settled on the street between angry mobs."

"I don't need a history lesson," Scott said sharply.

"For all we know, your Detective McGinty may already have it wired. A trophy for him if his testimony leads to the conviction of a smug American found flirting with a young woman half his age. 'Your Honor,' he'll say, 'don't know what possessed him. Maybe lost his temper when she rejected his advances, maybe an accident when he spiked her drink with the wrong poison, or perhaps ruthlessly preplanned.'"

"You're forgetting my solicitor knows—"

"Oh yeah, your solicitor, Miss Naiveté, knows what? Newly minted in her profession, she blushes and asks the judge to consider her evidence, completely circumstantial, and proceeds to bury your future in archaic legal precedents. Probably even bring up your great-grandfather who she'll say was wrongly hanged for murder. Another young gal if I remember, right?"

The waiter stopped by their table and said, "Refills for both of yous?"

"Yes, please," Cobb said, "I need enough caffeine to keep me awake all day."

"No thanks, not for me," Scott replied. Then responding to Cobb, he said, "Your sarcasm won't help."

"Sorry, you're right. But you do seem a bit obsessed with granddaddy's hanging. Now, let's say the judge takes pity on your young solicitor, for her lame defense, and sentences you to twenty years instead of thirty. Twenty fucking years! Why, you wouldn't last half that in an Irish jail."

"Spencer, you have it all wrong. Laura was *not* half my age. My solicitor is *not* inexperienced. Her evidence is compelling. And, not to insult you, but she knows the legal system here far better than you."

"Yeah, she knows the system, I'm sure. She'll know exactly how to appeal when you're doing time."

Scott paused to curtail his mounting anger, then continued in an even voice. "A magistrate, Counselor, not a judge. Even if he doesn't dismiss the charges, he's not the one to pass sentence. In short, I have complete confidence in my solicitor and also in the fairness of the Northern Ireland judicial system."

"So, what the fuck am I doing here?" Cobb asked.

"A question you could answer better than me," Scott snapped, "although I don't mean to seem unappreciative."

"You've made a good start."

"Spencer," Scott said, "forgive my tone. Not used to

being charged with murder."

He's well intentioned, but will only make a bad situation worse.

"Uh-huh," Cobb said, "I hadn't appreciated how all this had affected you."

"I'll start over by thanking you. And suggesting you sit down with my solicitor and me to review our defense strategy before we stand in front of the magistrate. With your imagination, I'm sure you'll think of something that hasn't occurred to her."

"Fair enough. Tell me when and where," Cobb said.

I'll arrange the meeting with my solicitor but have to find something to keep him from annoying her.

"And after the meeting, perhaps you could fly to Rome to assist Rachel with her research on Viktor Sokolov."

"Viktor? Don't you recall? That's the name I asked you to investigate? My Washington client's in hot water because of occasional so-called gifts from a man named Viktor."

"Yes, you mentioned the name," Scott said. "No reason, however, to assume there's only one Viktor who operates in Belfast and Rome. However, if he's your man, you can help Rachel as well as your client."

"I flew here to help you, not to chase after Viktor."

Scott sighed. "Fair enough. Then, how about poking around to see what you can learn about my great-grandfather's conviction."

I should never have told him, but maybe this will be a distraction.

"And if I were to discover his hanging was just, should I conclude that murder runs in the family?"

"Don't tempt me," Scott said.

"Got it," Cobb replied. "You're not exactly in the mood for joking."

"Guess not. Concentrating on my defense, on a

meeting with my solicitor."

"Today? Tomorrow?"

"Tomorrow morning. Meet me here for breakfast at seven-thirty and we'll take a cab to her office."

Cobb stood and picked up his luggage. "Sounds like a plan. I'll check in, take a nap, and explore the city to get my bearings."

◆◆◆

Scott left the hotel to walk off his anxieties, to quell his doubts. First stop: The Cathedral Church of St. Anne on Donegall Street. At the entrance he read a brief history: construction began in 1899 on the site of the old parish church of St. Anne, dated to 1776. He stood motionless looking past the massive pillars toward the distant altar. His face revealed his fear.

"May I help," an old woman asked.

"Oh, yes," he said, regaining his composure. "Is this a Catholic Church?"

"Catholic Church? No. Neither Catholic nor a church. It's a Cathedral affiliated with the Church of Ireland, a Protestant cousin of the Anglican Church."

He thanked her and walked to the back of the empty cathedral where he sat alone. Raised as Protestant, converted to Catholic, and now neither, Scott bowed his head and silently prayed. He offered thanks for Rachel Sullivan and Spencer Cobb traveling to Belfast to assist in his defense. He prayed for wisdom by the magistrate and justice in the Irish courts.

Next stop: the nearby St. Patrick's Church with a spire that seemed to reach to the sky. Opened in 1877, it was the largest Roman Catholic church in the city. Quiet and nearly empty inside, it had often been the site of marches and demonstrations by the Loyalists. For the second time within an hour, Scott closed his eyes and prayed, this time for Belfast's hard-won peace after more than thirty-five hundred violent deaths during the thirty-year period of the Troubles.

He wandered for hours without a destination or a map, stopped briefly at a rundown pub for a bowl of Irish lamb stew and a Guinness, and continued walking.

What's happening to me? Charged with murder? Last night I dreamed I was standing on a scaffolding with crowds jeering. I shouted my name, cried my innocence, and then whimpered under my breath, "who am I."

Scott guessed he had walked for eight or ten miles before he asked directions to the Fitzgerald Hotel.

"Fitzgerald Hotel? You best hail a cab. It's down toward the city center, hours from here if you're walking."

"Much appreciated, thank you, but I've nothing better to do than continue my walk."

"Straight ahead to the light, and then take a right."

◆◆◆

Hours later, the streets crowded with rush-hour traffic, Scott was not yet back at the Fitzgerald, but found himself once again approaching Benedicts Hotel.

What pernicious force drew me back to the scene of the crime?

Unable to contain his curiosity, he cautiously opened the door to the bar. Still early for Belfast drinkers, it was nearly empty. Among the few, he spotted Spencer Cobb, apparently cured of jetlag. He was engaged in animated conversation with a woman wearing a blue sweatshirt with "West Virginia Mountaineers" emblazoned in gold. Scott did an about face before Spencer spotted him, walked to the Fitzgerald Hotel, and decided to call it a day.

Prior to turning in, he recharged his phone and found three texts, one reminding him of an upcoming dental appointment and the other two sent by Rachel. The first described a memorable Italian meal at *Osteria Margutta*, a short walk from the Spanish steps. She wrote she had enjoyed a dish called *Saltimbocca alla Romano* so delicious she had asked to speak to the chef.

> <Roberto, the chef, was so attentive. Maybe all Italian men are like that, but he seemed special. I felt like Audrey Hepburn in *Roman Holiday*, but unlike her did not visit his apartment.>

Her next text, sent a few hours later, included Roberto's description of the dish.

> <Il saltimbocca e preparato con carne di vitello, rivestita con prosciutto crudo e salvia, marinato nel vino bianco.>

Scott read it a second time and a third, still failing to understand why she had forwarded an Italian description of *Saltimbocca*. Rachel hadn't said a word about her investigation. Had she sent the text to say she was okay? Or did it have some subtle meaning concerning her progress? More likely, he thought, the text was sent after a second carafe of wine offered by Roberto. Scott recalled from the time he had lived in Rome that the literal meaning of *Saltimbocca* is "jumps in the mouth." That memory added nothing to his comprehension of her curious text.

◆◆◆

Scott and Cobb met the next morning for breakfast at the Fitzgerald Hotel. Cobb ordered the classic Ulster Fry consisting of Irish bacon, bangers, fried eggs, grilled tomatoes, baked beans, sautéed mushrooms, black pudding, and toasted brown bread.

"Is that all?" Scott asked. "Didn't you forget the bubble and squeak?"

"And you, sir, the same?" the waiter asked.

"No, thanks. Keep it simple—oatmeal and juice plus a large mug of strong coffee."

"While we're waiting, tell me a little about this woman who's going to keep you from meeting your granddaddy's fate," Cobb said.

"Clare Sheehan, mid-thirties I'd guess, graduated from Queen's University several blocks from Benedicts Hotel, studied law at Trinity College in Dublin. She spent two months living with relatives in New Jersey, commuting daily to Columbia Law School where she studied American Constitutional law."

◆◆◆

An hour later, the two men sat in a crowded reception room waiting to see Scott's solicitor. Cobb had dressed the part of a New York corporate attorney—starched white shirt, classic cufflinks, bespoke dark blue suit, and a Windsor-knotted tie. He told Scott the best defense against a government prosecutor was confidence augmented by a dazzling appearance.

At that moment, the receptionist nodded to Scott and motioned him toward Sheehan's sparsely furnished office. The morning sun streamed through the window behind her desk.

"Ms. Sheehan, as promised, this is my friend, Spencer Cobb, also from my mountain village in West Virginia. Spent his career in American courtrooms representing the rich-and-famous and occasionally the down-and-out when he suspected justice was at risk."

Rising to welcome him, Sheehan said, "Welcome to Belfast. Mr. Cobb. I hadn't expected a lawyer who looks ready to defend the Prime Minister before the Lord Chief Justice."

Cobb lowered his head and grazed her hand with a near kiss in the style of an upper-class European. "My honor, Solicitor Sheehan," he said.

With heels, she stood nearly his height. Her commanding presence, steel-gray eyes, and easy smile conveyed an air of quiet confidence. Cobb offered his assistance "to ensure this good man remains a free man."

"Thank you," she began, "I'm prepared to speak about Mr. Scott's distinguished career. And I'll show the drug that killed the unfortunate woman was bought from a small pharmacy in Londonderry long before he visited the Emerald Island.

"However, if I were the prosecutor, I would claim that means nothing. 'Who exactly bought the fentanyl? And what evidence do you have that he wasn't a supplier for Mr. Scott?' I would ask."

"And how would you answer those questions?" Cobb said.

"We have the name of the doctor who prescribed the fentanyl patch for a patient who suffered grievous injuries in an automobile accident. He died within a few weeks. His widow can't recall what happened to his medication. She said it was destroyed. My investigator is sure she was lying, believes she sold it to someone preying on opioid addicts."

"Still, that doesn't prove the killer drug didn't end up with Scott," Cobb said, cocking his head.

"No, but I would then remind the magistrate that drugs are frequently confiscated in a police raid and point to last year's scandal in a certain Belfast precinct concerning the absence of records or accountability. In short, I would suggest there is more reason to believe the fentanyl packaging was planted by a corrupt cop than by the accused. The wrapper had been wiped of fingerprints, hardly the behavior of a killer who would then leave it in plain sight to ensure his arrest."

Scott observed their verbal dance. *Cobb loves the limelight, but this shrewd Irish woman is confirming her competence and showing who's in charge.*

"Sounds like he'll walk away a free man," Cobb said. "I'm impressed. But for the pleasure of meeting you and sampling some Irish whiskey last evening, I should have stayed home."

"Since you're here, may I ask a wee favor?" Ms. Sheehan said, eager to find some role for Scott's friend. "I'm still working on a closing summary. Suggestions?"

"You may not know Scott was born to missionaries in Rawalpindi, studied briefly to become a priest, and dedicated his life to protecting civilization."

"I've done my research and interviewed my client, Mr. Cobb."

"Sorry, of course. I meant to suggest you speak of his character. If I were defending him, I would conclude by quoting one of America's finest Supreme Court Justices, Oliver Wendell Holmes. I would repeat his exact words from an 1884 speech: 'Through our great good fortune, in our youth our hearts were touched with fire. It was given to us to learn at the outset that life is a profound and passionate thing.'"

Cobb paused briefly and then proclaimed in his finest courtroom voice, "This is a man with a heart touched by fire, a man who could not take a life."

Recalling her seminar on the jurisprudence of Oliver Wendell Holmes at Columbia, she thanked Cobb. "This good man," she said, gesturing toward Scott, "will go free."

As Scott and Cobb stood to leave, Sheehan said, "Wait, I meant to tell you when you first arrived. Your hearing has been scheduled for tomorrow, much earlier than we estimated."

For the first time in days, Scott broke into a smile. "Great news, I already feel like a free man."

"Compliments on your work," Cobb said, with the satisfied look of a lawyer who had won another judgment.

♦♦♦

Back on the street, Scott said, "I should be using my time productively, but I'm still on the cusp of an anxiety attack. Walking's the only way I can relax. Yesterday, I briefly stopped feeling sorry for myself after seeing so many sad neighborhoods. Feeling the pain that still punishes the city is a reminder I'm not alone. Dreams have been crushed, beliefs shattered."

Cobb picked up his pace to keep up with Scott. "You find this relaxing?"

"Look around, and you'll see an army of old people who wonder how their tatted and vaping grandchildren will survive. Yet, there's a miracle here: the fragile peace is holding. Even with the current uncertainty, Catholics and Protestants will somehow forge a stronger future. And the anger and despair I've felt after being charged with murder will make me a stronger person. I'm in your debt for your unbending support."

"While you're pacing around town," Cobb said, "I expect to be chatting with a bonnie lass at the Public Records Office. My new best friend, Clare, called and made an introduction. Since we're on a roll, I'd like to see what evidence they used to convict your old granddaddy. If you're convinced he was railroaded, I'm damn sure you're right. If we can prove his innocence, we'll appeal for compensation. There's a precedent established by Lord Justice Rose in 1998 who awarded £725,000 to the family of Mahmood Hussein Mattan for his wrongful execution."

"Delighted, Spencer. I like your optimism. One question: how much will remain after your fee?"

"Should just about cover the cost of an Ulster Fry, hand delivered from Belfast to Berkeley Springs."

◆◆◆

The next morning, Scott deleted several hundred emails accumulated over the past two days. Disappointed to find nothing from Fredrica. He saved only one to read with care, sent by his agency colleague Alexander Hoople. It arrived unencrypted, but written with enough care to obscure its meaning from prying eyes.

> *No doubts here among your many friends of your innocence. Eager to have you back. Global warming continues to threaten the Chesapeake Bay. Crabbing may foretell an economic disaster. Your expertise in aquatic life is sorely missed. Godspeed. Alex.*

Scott responded immediately.

> *Concentrating on avoiding hanging. Back to water sports ASAP.*

Realizing it had been days since anything from Fredrica, he sent a short email.

> *I'm so eager to see you, to hear from you. I promise I can explain the delay. Please respond.*

◆◆◆

Spencer Cobb took a cab to the Titanic Museum and walked to the Public Records Office. Unlike the records it held from centuries past, its architecture complemented the twenty-first century design of the Titanic Museum.

Quiet and nearly empty, it was a retreat for scholars and genealogists. He had expected to be assisted by a tidy graying lady with helpful eyes and a serious face. Instead, a young woman with flowing red hair greeted him with the enthusiasm usually reserved for a long-lost friend, barely short of a hug and kiss. Holding an open book in one hand, she asked how she could help. Her name tag identified her as Bridgette Walsh. She said, "Your friend Clare suggested I pull out all the stops to help you."

"Thank you," Cobb said with a broad smile, "I'm here to find a murderer—"

Interrupting, she said, "Sorry to say I'm the only one here today and haven't killed anyone, not yet. Thought of it once, mind you. A young lad, American, I met on the *Costa del Sol* during holiday. Guessin' from your accent you're American too, but won't generalize from my brief holiday romance. Met him on the beach with some of his buddies and before long we were havin' a drink and . . . well, enough said. A long evening and a great week. Said nice things and made many promises."

"And then?" Cobb said with a tone that suggested he knew how the story would end.

"He returned to America and then nothing. Not a call, not an email, not a text, not a tweet. Bloody nothing. So, I tracked him down on Facebook and asked him about all the blarney he had thrown about. Had him cornered, so he had to say something. Told me I was a sweet girl, but confessed he wasn't serious. Thought I understood I was only an FWB."

"FWB?" Cobb asked.

"Guess your generation wouldn't know. Friend with benefits. Or to put it more succinctly, an FWB is a gal who offers a good fuck with no strings attached. It was a memorable week, so I shouldn't hold the bastard completely responsible for my heartache. Nonetheless, there are still occasions when murder comes to mind."

"I've come to learn about the short life of one Franklin Lambert of Carrickfergus, hanged for murder in 1893."

Bridgette's generous smile grew broader, conveying to him her interest in opening a cold case. She motioned him to follow to a bank of computers, sat down, and began typing.

"I assumed you would lead me to some dusty archive and leave me to climb up and down a ladder searching for a file marked Lambert," Cobb said.

"Or just send you down to Murderer's Row? Sorry, just kidding. If he's in our files, I'll find him in a jiffy in this nifty online index. With the luck of the Irish, as they say, the file will be digitized and I'll print out your very own copy."

"I'm stunned. Won't know what to do with the rest of my day."

"That's easy. Call it a holiday, Counselor, and find yourself an FWB. I could introduce you to my grandmother," she said.

"Very funny. My assumption you were an archivist has been shaken. Turns out you're a comedian," Cobb said.

"Not too far wrong. I've tried standup at a local pub. Got a few laughs—not many, but enough to be invited back after I got the *hang* of it. Yeah, I know that was bad. To tell the truth, I was only invited back once."

"You tell a good story," Cobb said. "Maybe you needed better material."

She looked up from the computer screen and said, "Wait, look what I found—the Last Will and Testament of Franklin Lambert dated 1893."

"Amazing," Cobb said. "Best you keep your day job."

Within a few minutes, he was sitting at a desk reading a copy of the hand-written will.

The bold cursive script reminded him of another age.

I, Franklin Andrew Lambert of Carrickfergus in the County of Antrim, being a condemned man but sound in mind, do hereby declare this to be my last will & testament & revoke all other wills.

I give and bequeath to Lorcan Crawford Knox
my right title and interest to the land where I
now reside along with all my chattel property.

There was still more in the document to be studied later, but Lambert's signature immediately caught Cobb's eye. As sergeant in the Municipal Police Force, Lambert would have signed his name on official documents thousands of times with a hurried distinctive signature. At the end of the will Cobb saw a signature rendered with such care it could hardly have been authentic.

Scott's insistence that great-granddad had been framed might easily be proven if Cobb could discover the relationship of Lorcan Crawford Knox to the man convicted of the crime.

◆◆◆

Expecting a call from Larry Gold, Rachel spent the day waiting. Nothing. Silence from the embassy. Lunch at a sidewalk café consisted of a salad and an Italian spritz—suffused by memories of Roberto. And interrupted by the guilt of her absence from the NSA. She happily returned that evening to *Osteria Margutta* when Roberto called with an invitation for a *cena speciale*. She found it wasn't only the dinner that was special.

◆◆◆

Raucous street sounds, men shouting, horns sounding. Rachel didn't hear a sound but awoke suddenly the following morning to blinding sunlight streaming through an open window. She blinked, rolled over, and briefly closed her eyes. Disoriented, she sat up in a small unfamiliar room with stark white walls, a high coffered ceiling, and a single broken-down chair. She had spent the night in Roberto's third-floor apartment after a sumptuous meal, a second carafe of wine, and a dangerous Italian nightcap called grappa. She remembered his tousled hair, his soft eyes, and deep voice. Would daylight reveal someone different from her dreamy memory of a Roman chef?

Her slacks and blouse were lying rumpled on the floor next to the chair, her bra thrown over its back. She pulled the covers over her head, refusing momentarily to face the day. Distracted from her Roman trip to investigate a crime by sleeping with a man she barely knew, her psyche screamed guilt. It was nearly ten o'clock, hours past her normal wakeup.

She finally bounded out of bed and opened the door to the bathroom. Wrong door! Roberto, wearing boxer shorts and a blue T-shirt, stood in front of a stove in the kitchen. With a smile as bright as the sun, he turned and waved. She was wearing a gold necklace.

"Fungi," he said. *"Sto facendo una frittata."*

"What? I don't understand," Rachel said. "Please look directly at me when you speak."

"Scusi, I forgot you have to see my lips. Happens every time I find a gorgeous woman standing naked in the doorway of my kitchen."

"Uh-huh," she said with a beguiling smile.

"Mushrooms," he said, pointing to the skillet. "I am making a frittata for our breakfast. First step is to sauté the mushrooms. Next, add some artichoke hearts and fresh tomatoes, stir for a few minutes, and . . . "

She walked closer. Touched the hem of his T-shirt and gently pulled it over his head.

He turned off the gas burner and suggested they postpone breakfast.

Hours later they enjoyed a spicy frittata, rustic bread

dipped in olive oil, and another bottle of red wine. He said it was Abruzzo's prize vintage from 2014. She said it was heavenly.

◆◆◆

"Postponed indefinitely? Did I hear you right?" Scott asked, speaking by phone with his solicitor after being awakened by her early call.

After a long silence, Ms. Sheehan said, "Yes, a total surprise to me. Before calling I spent a few hours at the Magistrates' Court. As you know, their role is to conduct a preliminary hearing to determine if there is enough evidence to bring the alleged crime to trial. If not, the case is dismissed. I felt certain you would walk free tomorrow."

"What changed?" he asked.

"Better we talk in person, my office in an hour."

Scott had answered his phone as he was finishing a light breakfast at the Fitzgerald Hotel and scrolling through his interminable annoying emails. He had time to finish his coffee and complete the purge of junk from his phone. His cup was being refilled when an audible ping from the phone signaled a new text. Rachel again. He still hadn't deciphered the meaning of her last text.

<Sorry Scott. Please ignore my text with the description of my classy Italian dinner. I meant to send it to myself as a memory of a glorious evening. Rome really is The Eternal City.>

Her welcome words confirmed he hadn't lost his edge in interpreting cryptic messages. It wasn't the first misdirected text he had received. It also inadvertently confirmed her eagerness to assist him had been temporarily shelved by her infatuation with Chef Roberto. It appeared the investigation of Viktor Sokolov was temporarily on hold.

◆ ◆ ◆

Walking briskly to his solicitor's office, Scott decided not to concern himself with Rachel's dalliance nor with Clare's warning about the delay. Another few days in Belfast would give him time to confirm his hunch that great-granddad wasn't a killer. Optimism had saved Scott from situations more precarious than a trumped-up charge by a crooked cop.

Clare's dour greeting suggested she did not share his optimism.

"Because of the press attention to the murder," she said, "the police have closed ranks to protect the detective who they insist has solved the case. With public trust in the balance, they're trying to demonstrate their competence."

"And the magistrate's going along with this?"

"For the moment. I have friends in the court who've quietly told me he's inclined to dismiss the charges, but is under enormous political pressure to advance it to a trial. Please don't ask me how I know. Belfast is a small town. People talk."

"Understood," Scott said. "What would it take to convince him to dismiss?"

"The prosecutor would inevitably show laboratory evidence that Laura died from a fentanyl overdose. The forensic labs here are beyond reproach. So, I must be able to advance a credible theory to show how and where she ingested this killer drug.

"The prosecution will assert you had the opportunity. I will argue that opportunity without motive should have no standing in a court of law. To demonstrate the weakness of the prosecution's case and thereby ensure your release, I must demonstrate the opportunity to spike her drink was also available to others. The challenge is to find the evidence, for which we must reexamine your evening at the Benedicts Bar.

Chapter 9. Noli Timere

Fleeing from Grendel, he awoke drenched in sweat. He was not afraid. Not of the monster slain by Beowulf. Not of Grendel's murderous mother. Not of the cop who had planted the evidence in his hotel room. *Thomas Sebastian Scott is not afraid.* He sat up on the edge of the bed, stood, and walked to the window. Overcast and drizzling, a perfect day for reflection. *I am not afraid.*

Scott had visited a used bookstore the day before and picked up a dog-eared book of poetry by Seamus Heaney. The bookseller, a fiftyish woman with an arthritic knee, said the price was fair for a book long out of print. Before he could respond, she offered a ten percent discount and said it included her favorite poem. She took the book from his hands, leafed through it, and began to read:

> *Terraced thousands died, shaking scythes at cannon.*
> *The hillsides blushed, soaked in our broken wave.*
> *They buried us without shroud or coffin*
> *And in August . . . the barley grew up out of our grave.*

She stopped, her eyes moist from a poem written on the fiftieth anniversary of the 1916 Easter uprising. Scott knew Seamus Heaney was a Nobel Laurate and learned from the bookseller he had been born in Northern Ireland in the village of Bellaghy thirty miles west of Belfast. The son of a cattle dealer, he was raised Catholic. He is remembered as the most important Irish poet since Yeats.

Chatting with the bookseller, Scott recalled that Heaney's reputation did not stop at poetry. He had translated *Beowulf* to universal acclaim. Among the sixty-some translations of this epic Danish poem, critics credited Heaney of uniquely capturing both the rhythm and narrative of tenth-century Anglo-Saxon speech. Beowulf, he mused to the bookseller, had twice prevailed in battle against monsters, but fifty years later lost his life to a dragon that terrorized his country. Scott recalled a few lines from the Heaney translation: *"He was sad at heart, unsettled yet ready, sensing his death."*

◆◆◆

Spencer Cobb, arriving at the Public Records Office, had left a message advising Scott not to expect him for breakfast. Bridgette had promised to continue the search for Scott's great-grandfather.

"Maidin mhaith," she said when he approached her desk.

"And that means . . . what? Stop pestering me with your bloody research?" Cobb asked, with a mischievous smile.

"No, no, not at all. It's Gaelic for good morning." She motioned him to the chair in front of her desk." And it's not only a good morning. It's a *great* morning. I've found exactly what you're looking for."

She handed him a folder and pointed to the two boxes on the floor. "We haven't indexed everything yet. There're thousands of documents our archivists are still examining. With a little help and a prayer to St. Patrick, I found these two nineteenth century boxes from Carrickfergus."

"Must have taken you hours," Cobb said, opening the folder.

"I found the boxes after you left yesterday, came in early this morning to sort through them, and the documents in your hand practically jumped out. I've made copies of Lambert's signature on numerous arrest and court documents up to the day *he* was arrested. You were absolutely right: the signature on the will is not his."

Cobb examined the documents. It did not take a handwriting expert to convince him of fraud. "I'm usually not at a loss for words," he said, "but I don't know how to thank you."

She tilted her head, smiled, and handed him another folder. "This folder," she announced, "contains the smoking gun." She pointed her index finger and raised her thumb. *"Bang!"*

Cobb opened the folder and found a photograph of a wedding party. The names of the bride and groom were written on the back in faded ink. The groom was identified as Lorcan Crawford Knox.

"I got it," Cobb said, "that's the son of a bitch named in Lambert's will. The man who got everything after grandpappy Lambert was hanged. Not sure, however, that it helps to prove his innocence."

"Not unless you consider the best man, pictured to the left of the groom—the solicitor who drew up the will and . . . "

"You're Ireland's answer to Miss Marple—sorry, I mean more like Miss Marple's granddaughter. Practically proves that Lambert's family was swindled out of their estate."

"That's not even the half of it," she said, bursting with pride. "Years later that very same man, the so-called *best* man and *respected* solicitor, was convicted of raping and murdering a young university graduate. The prosecutors charged him with another unsolved murder, also of a young woman. The second case never came to trial, nor did others that remained unsolved despite rumors the police believed he was a repeat killer. There is, I believe, sufficient evidence in these files to clear the good name of great-grandfather Lambert."

"I'm wondering if you'd be interested in—"

"Wait, that's not all," Bridgette said. "Also found a document showing his Baptism at St. Patrick's Church in 1877."

"Are you sure?" Cobb asked. "I understood he was raised Protestant."

"Yes, but he apparently converted the year of St. Patrick's consecration. He would have been just twenty-two, perhaps somewhat of a rebel, although that's only a guess. His family would have been displeased."

Cobb sputtered a word of thanks, stood up, shook her hand, and resisted a hug. "Yesterday I learned you were an accomplished researcher and an occasional stand-up comedian. Today I'm seeing you are also a criminal investigator and a fledgling lawyer. Have I missed anything?"

"Since you asked, yes, I'm also an amateur videographer."

"You make movies?" he exclaimed.

"Not exactly, just short riffs on life in Belfast. I call them DocuClips with a Twist. You can see a few of my early videos on YouTube, but they won't accept my latest. They don't pass their nipple barrier. Would you like to see an example?"

"I'm curious, but I'll resist," Cobb said.

"How about a video of my standup routine? You can see it on my phone, and I guarantee you there's not a hint of a boob, not even any cleavage."

As he nodded, she searched her phone. "Here, sit down

again and take a look," she said. "My friend shot the video at the Accidental Theatre on Shaftesbury Square, and I did the editing to make it look professional. Added the music, the credits, and even the applause. That's me in black, turtleneck and slacks."

He watched her walking to the small stage as the theatre echoed with applause.

"You're receiving quite a welcome," Cobb said.

"Thanks, but you're hearing the soundtrack I added."

Cobb continued watching as she began with a joke.

"What do you do if your girlfriend starts smoking?" Ignoring the guy who asked if she would be his girlfriend, she offered the punchline: "Slow down and use a lubricant."

More fake applause, enough for Carnegie Hall. Her next joke drew a little laughter, although it may have been too subtle for most of the drunks in her audience.

"How does a woman scare a gynecologist?" she asked, her eyes pleading for attention.

"By becoming a ventriloquist," she answered with a smile.

She tried a few classic jokes that didn't warrant even fake applause and ended with a story she admitted stealing from an old Joan Rivers video.

"Everybody talks about multiple orgasms. Multiple orgasms! I'm lucky if both sides of my toaster pop."

The screen went dark. The video ended. For the second time within an hour, Cobb was speechless. Finally, he said, "Tough crowd. I know the feeling. First time I argued a case before a jury, it went right over their heads. I like your humor and your delivery. Maybe with more practice, you—"

"Thanks, but I learned my lesson. I love humor, but I'm best behind the scenes. For example, I recently agreed to be a bridesmaid if my friend would allow me to videotape her bachelorette party. Not for prime time on her last night of freedom, her last night to flash her enormous boobs in public. Her party was held at the Benedicts Bar, across the street from the Accidental Theatre where I went down in flames."

Cobb stood, thanked Bridgette for her assistance, paused, and sat down again in front of her desk. "Benedicts Bar?" he asked, raising an eyebrow.

"Yeah, it's a classy hangout for my crowd. Also, for tourists who stay at the hotel."

"And from American lawyers who happen to be in the neighborhood. Stopped by the day I arrived to overcome jetlag. They say sunlight's the answer, although I'm living proof that sipping Irish whiskey in a dimly lit bar's a sure cure. Didn't see you there, so I'd guess you're not a regular."

"Right," she said, "I haven't been there since my friend's party. Still editing the video of her celebration. I have to cut out more than five hours of her carrying on, wearing a ridiculous bunny costume."

"And this the night before the wedding?" Cobb asked.

"Yes and no. The wedding was scheduled for the following day, but she called it off at the last minute. A woman murdered in the hotel that very night set her on edge. Got her thinking about her short-tempered fiancé who had threatened her on several occasions, beat her up once. She made the right decision."

"Bridgette," he said, raising his hands in a gesture of helplessness, "I've one more favor to ask. Could I borrow a copy of the video?"

"I'll send you a copy when I've completed the edit."

"Much appreciated, but I'd like the complete video of bunny gal's big night at Benedicts Bar."

"Some sort of Yankee pervert, are ye, looking to see those big bouncy tits? Just kidding. Be happy to burn a copy of the DVD for you. Stop back tomorrow for the whole show."

♦♦♦

Rachel returned to her hotel, nearly seventy-two hours after checking in. The desk clerk handed her a sealed envelope, personally delivered by a young man with blond curls. Within it she found a brief handwritten note, "Tried to reach you by phone. No luck. We have something that may interest you. Please drop by. Larry."

Larry? It took her only a few seconds to realize it came from Larry Gold, the intelligence analyst she had met at the Embassy. Earlier, he had offered a raincheck for dinner, but this was different. This was business.

She walked up one flight to her room, took a shower, dressed, hurried downstairs, and asked the desk clerk to call a taxi to take her to the Embassy. He told her it would take at least thirty minutes, maybe more depending on the traffic. A walk would take half that.

♦♦♦

Gold met her at the Embassy entrance and escorted her to his office. So nonchalant in his manner and so laid back in his appearance, he might have been a college kid on vacation visiting his hard-working father in Rome.

"Mid-afternoon," he said looking at his watch, "how about a cappuccino?"

"Thank you, Mr. Gold, that would be perfect," Rachel replied.

"Mr. Gold? That's so official. How about Larry? And you, Ms. Sullivan, how's Rome treating you?"

"With the exception of two guys on a Vespa who tried to lift my purse, it's been a delight."

"That was you? Rachel Sullivan? Astonishing!" he said, his soft voice rising. "*Il Messaggero* has a story in the style section about an unnamed American who they called Wonder Woman. Recovered her purse, practically destroyed the guy's scooter, and left him in the hands of the Carabinieri."

"A gal's gotta do what a gal's gotta do," she said.

"Too bad it wasn't your man Viktor Sokolov. My colleague has an exhaustive file on this creep. He would have been arrested many times over for smuggling, trafficking, blackmailing, you-name-it, everything but murder, if he had not been cooperating with AISE. That's short for *Agenzia Informatizoni e Securezza Estarna*, more-or-less Italy's version of the CIA."

"He's working for them?"

"No, not exactly, but they're protecting him because of his connection with an informant in the Kremlin, who allegedly provides valuable intelligence."

"And if he actually murdered Laura Caputo, would he be given a pass?"

"No," Gold said, shaking his head. "Absolutely not. Just as there are rules among thieves, there are agreements between spies and their recruits. Murder is murder. He would be off the street for good."

Gold's phone rang. He picked up, listened, and said, "Thanks, I'll be out in a second." He stood, excused himself, and left the office. Rachel waited. A minute later he returned with two cups of cappuccino.

"Freshly brewed from the *Bar Ludovisi,* courtesy of my assistant whose favor I'll return tomorrow. Before you take a sip, close your eyes and enjoy the aroma. One of the many reasons I love Rome."

She smelled the fresh brew, lifted the cup to her lips,

and gingerly tasted the foamy drink.

"Thank you, Larry. It's wonderful."

"My pleasure," he said, raising his cup. "I seem to recall you accepted a raincheck for an Italian dinner?"

She nodded.

"How about tonight?"

"I'd love to, but I'm in a bit of a rush," she said. "Need to pack this evening and . . ."

Negotiations followed. After she admitted that packing wouldn't take more than five minutes, he suggested *Armando al Pantheon*, a family run *trattoria*, for a taste of real Roman cooking. Sensing her reluctance, he assured her there were no strings attached. "It's only dinner I'm suggesting. No entangling alliances. I'm gay."

"Makes no difference to me," she said, shaking her head. "I'd be delighted to join you for dinner, but I'm not sure I'd be good company."

"Because you're exhausted, feeling sullen, becoming bored—"

"No, none of those. It's because of my colleague. I flew to Belfast when he was falsely accused of murder. Came here to help, but now I'm worried he'll be convicted."

"You're sure he's innocent?"

"Yes, absolutely. However, if his solicitor cannot convince a magistrate that someone else, namely Viktor Sokolov, poisoned that woman, Scott may spend the rest of his life in an Irish prison. And if Viktor is being protected by the state, nothing less than a witness to the murder will convict him."

◆◆◆

Rachel was waiting in the lobby of the *Hotel Scalinata di Spagna* when Gold arrived breathlessly, apologizing for being late. He walked with her to the restaurant, a few steps from the Pantheon.

"Would you like me to order for you?" he asked.

"Yes, please. Anything but mac and cheese."

He laughed. "I was thinking of SpaghettiOs."

They began with *Bruschetta al Tartufo Nero*, followed by *Pasta Puttanesca* with a carafe of the house red wine. She passed on a second course, but joined him for *Frutti di Bosco* for dessert.

"We'll stop at *Sant' Eustacchio* after dinner," he said, "for the finest coffee in all of Rome."

♦♦♦

Scott had overslept, missed his eight o'clock breakfast with Spencer Cobb. He lay in bed pondering the injustice of his situation. With no plans for the day, he was in no hurry to get up. The light drizzle he saw through the window did nothing to elevate his mood. He rolled over, sat up, checked his email. Nothing from Rachel. Nothing from colleagues at the NSA. Nothing from friends in Berkeley Springs. He was alone. His great-grandfather would have been alone when he stood in front of a crowd with a noose around his neck.

Another hour lying in bed, in and out of sleep. Sensing a low noise, he reached across the bed and picked up his phone.

"Scott, are you okay?" Cobb asked. "I've been calling repeatedly."

"What time is it?"

"Ten-thirty, which makes you two-and-a-half hours late for breakfast."

"Sorry," Scott said. "I'm in a bit of a funk. Had my phone on vibrate. Didn't hear a thing."

"Get up, get dressed, and meet me in the restaurant at

eleven. I'll be there with a gift from Bridgette."

Scott sat up in bed, rubbed the sleep from his eyes, and checked his phone. He opened a text from Rachel.

> **<Returning to Belfast tomorrow. Had a flight out today, but was persuaded by a certain Italian chef to stay over one more day. Promised to take me to the Rome Opera. Not my cup of tea, but he has a way with words.>**

♦♦♦

Too late for breakfast, two early for lunch, Scott and Cobb sat alone in the Fitzgerald restaurant. Neither spoke for several minutes. Finally, Cobb broke the silence. "As we'd say back home, you look like shit. As a world class imbiber of spirits, I'd say you're sporting a serious hangover."

"A hangover? No, after my daily walk yesterday, I had a light meal at a funky little restaurant called The Other Place near the Botanic Gardens. Nothing to drink stronger than water. I have this recurring image of my great-grandfather, hanging dead in front of a cheering crowd. I tell myself I'm not afraid, but then feel the rough rope tightening around *my* neck."

"The coffee will help some," Cobb said, "and what I learned yesterday at the Public Records Office is guaranteed to lift you out of your depression. Bridgette scoured through boxes of ancient documents, none yet indexed, and found the records that prove old granddaddy was framed. Every bit as innocent as you. We can pursue that later with the Irish authorities to seek official recognition of this grievous miscarriage of justice."

"Feeling better already," Scott said, "and even better if the coffee ever arrives."

"That takes care of the past. And this little polycarbonate disc may set you free, also courtesy of the lovely Bridgette Walsh. As you will see, it features you and a cast of hundreds, shot on the evening of Laura's death."

Cobb explained that the woman who found the evidence to clear great-granddaddy of murder was also an amateur videographer who shot bunny gal's bachelorette party at the Benedicts Bar.

"She's editing it down to ten minutes for YouTube to celebrate her friend's release from bondage. Her fiancé had showed up unexpectedly at the party at midnight, made a scene by loudly berating her for dancing with another man, and assuring her it would be the last time if she valued her life. She called off the wedding the following morning, in time to alert her friends to skip the ceremony."

"And this is the ten-minute version?" Scott asked.

"No, this is the footage of the entire evening, five hours she said. I looked at the first few minutes and could see a grainy image of you at the bar sitting beside some woman who I assume was the victim later that night."

Scott was about to return to his room to watch the video when the coffee finally arrived.

"They must have been waiting for a shipment from Sumatra," Scott said.

"You're sounding better already."

◆◆◆

Twenty minutes later they were looking at the video on Scott's computer, listening to the music and crowd noises. Most of the footage focused on the prospective bride and her bridesmaids. They laughed, drank, and danced. After a half hour or so, the video showed a close-up of Scott talking to the woman seated at his left who told him she would be in the wedding party the next day.

"If she'd listened to me," the woman said, "she'd never've gone out with that fecking creep, let alone marry him.

Look at her dancing, look at that smile. If she'd come to her senses, call off the wedding, and lose thirty pounds, every guy in town would be chasing her."

The camera moved away from the bar to focus on the honoree. As the camera revealed through a zoom shot, she wasn't in a hurry to correct her crowd-pleasing wardrobe malfunction. As the applause continued, her dancing became even more joyous.

"The trouble with the video," Cobb said, "is the poor lighting. With the exception of the close-up of you and the maid of honor, the images are so poor they wouldn't be admissible in a court of law."

"You also saw Laura, didn't you, sitting to my right?"

"Yes, obviously enjoying herself, but that's of no use in your defense. I thought the video may have provided a lifeline, but afraid my friend Bridgette is no more a videographer than I am."

"Spencer, let's not waste another minute. With decent bandwidth, I can send this to some friends in Maryland. They can use a little digital magic to bring out every detail. If there's anything suspicious on the video, they'll find it. I'll alert them to watch for the stocky guy at the end of the bar in a black T-shirt, the guy who threatened Laura."

◆◆◆

Cobb departed the hotel at 5:00 a.m. to catch a flight to Washington. He left a brief note for Scott.

> *Please give my appreciation and highest esteem to Clare. Send a bouquet to Bridgett. And keep an eye on Viktor. Wish I could stay to witness your victory dance, but the Deputy Attorney General insists I return immediately to help him save the Republic.*

Rachel texted that she had completed her Roman inquiry and was returning home by way of Belfast for a debrief. "If the flight's on time, I'll meet you at the Fitzgerald at about six this evening."

Alex Hoople confirmed the video had been received at the NSA. "Our analysts pulled an all-nighter and will be sending you the results by email within the hour."

Still nothing from Fredrica, no reply to a man described in the press as an accused killer.

And within moments, he received the email promised by Hoople with numerous attachments. Scott read it over and over.

> Our guys enhanced the footage to offer a clear view of the festivities. **Exhibit 1 (attached):** Several photos of the guy in the black T-shirt, known to authorities. **Exhibit 2 (a brief video):** Black T-shirt returns to the bar with the woman who had been sitting to your right, whom you identified as Laura. She appears to be enjoying their discussion, although it is inaudible. **Exhibit 3:** You and Laura on the dance floor. She is dancing and you are moving slowly in what our experts declined to identify as dancing. **Exhibit 4:** The bartender places drinks at your unoccupied positions at the bar (shot immediately after the dance sequence). **Exhibit 5:** Bartender looks left and right before adding an unidentified liquid to your drink. **Exhibit 6:** A blown-up photo of bartender's hand adding the liquid to your drink.

"My drink?" Scott said out loud to no one in particular. "No, no." He had been sitting there before his woeful attempt to dance. When they returned, Laura changed seats.

A limerick from Sean McManus briefly lifted his mood even higher.

> *I'll speak of an old sinner named Scott*
> *Whose future was not what he sought.*
> *So, I offered a prayer,*
> *For the judge to be fair.*
> *The charges I'm sure are for naught?*

◆ ◆ ◆

"Madam Solicitor," Scott said, after rushing to her office, "here it is. Exactly what we need to show my innocence."

"You're a different man, Mr. Scott. First time I've heard such enthusiasm. What do you have?"

"Five hours of video taken the night Laura was killed including a brief scene where the bartender is shown adding some substance, presumably poison, to her drink. And the video demonstrates it was intended for me, as Laura switched seats after returning to the bar. Look at these six exhibits and you'll see why I'm so excited."

"I'll need the original to present to the magistrate."

"Here's the DVD from which the analysis was conducted. You could obtain the original from the woman who shot it."

"That will take forever, but this may satisfy the magistrate. It should be enough to release you pending a trial. Trust you won't mind a brief return in a month or so."

◆ ◆ ◆

Scott walked back to the hotel, this time with a jaunty step and his head held high. By mid-afternoon, Solicitor Sheehan called to say he would be free to leave the next day, with his personal guarantee he would return as a witness when and if another party were charged.

She accompanied him to the magistrate's office to sign numerous forms and then to the police station to retrieve his passport.

"I enjoyed representing you, Mr. Scott," she said, "as well as meeting your colleague Spencer Cobb who apparently charmed my friend Bridgette at the records office. We shall be in touch if you're called as a witness."

"Thank you. You've saved my life. Please send your invoice to my West Virginia address."

Rachel was waiting in the lobby when he returned to the Fitzgerald. "Caught an early flight. Couldn't wait to see you," she said, standing and hugging him. "I've been so worried. Could hardly sleep last night."

"Thanks for stopping over. I should be returning with you to the States, but I *must* take a short detour by way of St. Wolfgang to explain to Fredrica why I was detained in Belfast."

"Scott, I still can't believe you're free. I knew you'd eventually prevail, but had no idea it would happen so quickly."

He told her about the video and the magic performed by the NSA techies in rescuing the images from the shadows, showing the adulteration of the drink was intended for him. The video also revealed that Viktor and Laura appeared to be friends.

Rachel told Scott of Viktor's Roman reputation as a con man, engaging in everything from trafficking to blackmail. However, the information he provided from his Moscow contacts shielded him from arrest.

"I still can't believe I'm free to leave."

"And I can't believe the murder was solved so quickly," Rachel said.

"Solved? I'm no longer a suspect, but it's hardly solved.

Although Jimmy the bartender has a police record, why he targeted me remains a mystery. My solicitor also discovered a possible link to a genealogist named O'Malley whom I'd engaged to assist in my ancestry research. I terminated him for . . . how shall I put it, for his unbearable rudeness. Let's say we didn't hit it off. After revealing my great-grandfather was hanged for murder in the nineteenth century, O'Malley insisted he deserved no less. I can't help but wonder if he hadn't discouraged further research because of my great-grandfather's estate that might be worth millions today."

"Your great-grandfather?" Rachel said, looking perplexed. "I must have missed something. Did you say he'd been hanged? And what about the estate?"

"Yes, he was hanged, but that's a story for another day," Scott said.

"And that's it?" she asked.

"Not exactly. They may be charging Jimmy the bartender. With what we know about Viktor, he may have put Jimmy up to it—through blackmail, bribe, some kind of threat. Why me? That remains a mystery."

"The Italians are protecting Viktor, but not from murder," Rachel said

"Something that still puzzles me," Scott mused. "When Laura left the bar to chat with Viktor, she was wearing dangling emerald earrings, probably worth a small fortune. They were gone when she returned fifteen minutes later. What could have happened to them? Another strike against Viktor, I'd say."

"Have you ever worn heavy earrings?"

"Not so far."

"Well then, Mr. Scott, you're talking to an expert. That's one mystery I *can* explain."

Chapter 10. A Ripple in the Chesapeake

Rachel took a cab directly from Dulles to the NSA. After several days in Rome, headquarters looked antiseptic. Carrying a tote bag and wearing a backpack, she proceeded directly to Dr. Hoople's office.

"Rachel, welcome back," Hoople said as he rose from his desk. "So happy you're here. Not sure Scott would have made it without you."

"Truth be told, while I was enjoying Rome, Scott's Irish solicitor did the heavy lifting to set him free, along with a little help from a West Virginia lawyer. And, of course the video analysis by our resident cyber geeks."

"So, you're saying your Roman visit was a vacation? On my tab, no less," Hoople said with a smile.

"Can't deny I enjoyed it, but also learned the primary suspect, Viktor Sokolov, is well known to the cops. Involved in drugs, trafficking, and a host of other crimes, but enjoys high-level protection. He's on the payroll of one of our Italian counterparts. I'll prepare a full report."

Tilting his head and nodding, Hoople said, "You've changed. Can't quite place it, but . . . "

"A blind spot for most men," she said, laughing. "It's my hair, the latest Italian fashion requiring a fistful of dollars and hours watching an Italian hairdresser talk with his hands while snipping off my curls. I had to look my best to attend my first ever opera."

She opened her backpack and removed a program from the Rome Opera, Beethoven's *Fidelio*."

"Not often performed," Hoople said. "And I'm a little surprised you like opera."

"Because I'm deaf? I can feel the music and love the costumes and sets. The Rome Opera provides simultaneous English-language text, so I didn't miss a word. Set in a dark prison, the story reminded me of Scott's near conviction."

"So, you would be Fidelio to Scott's Florestan, rescuing him from death."

"I would have, of course, but Clare Sheehan played the role perfectly—without having to spend prison time in disguise."

"And you saw Scott before you flew back?"

"Yes, I flew back to Belfast. He looked good and promised to return within a week—after a detour to Austria to see his sweetheart."

"Yes, he told me. I reminded him the agreed week in Belfast had already exceeded two. He said he had failed to anticipate being a murder suspect or being abandoned by his Austrian girlfriend. He told me he'd find her and be back next week."

"Let's hope," Rachel said. "He'll be a wreck if he can't locate her."

"I'm already late for a meeting," Hoople said, standing and putting on his jacket. "While I'm away, pull up a chair at my desk, log on to your TS account, and look for the file labeled CRIN-038. It shows that forty percent of all US critical infrastructure systems have been probed by a hostile state."

"Not surprised."

"In the time you've been away, we've monitored thousands of attempted cyberattacks on our nuclear power plants. The northeastern electrical grid was again threatened by malware comparable to the earlier HAVEX and BlackEnergy attacks."

Rachel shook her head and scowled. "I recall Homeland Security updating its analysis of the HAVEX trojan last year. And the BlackEnergy malware caused the 2015 power outage in Ukraine."

I shouldn't have said that, telling him what he knows better than me. Showing off to regain his trust after my Roman holiday.

Hoople looked over his shoulder as he left his office and said, "Old news. It's the latest that keeps me awake nights."

Rachel began reading the report:

EXECUTIVE SUMMARY

NSA's intrusion group repeated the process previously used to hack the Third Group of the People's Liberation Army. Within the past week, they successfully accessed the infrastructure of another prominent state actor. Reliance by the American energy sector on system control and data acquisition systems (SCADA) with Internet-interfaces controlling energy systems substantially increased their vulnerability for cyberattack. The number of attempted attacks in the past six months continued to accelerate. The Department of Energy's Office of Cybersecurity, Energy Security, and Emergency Response recently peer-reviewed some thirty DOE-funded projects to reduce vulnerability of America's energy delivery systems to cyberattacks. However, it will be years before they are fully executed.

The nineteen-page report confirmed the incursion at the Calvert Cliffs Nuclear Facility.

She was still sitting at his desk, eyes on the screen, when Hoople returned. "Guess that made your day," he said.

"Very sobering," Rachel replied as she logged out of his computer and stood. "Not the threat, which we all know well, but the urgency to address it. Ten days' absence seems like a lifetime in cybertime."

I had to go to Belfast to help Scott, but my trip to Rome was foolish. Selfish, even.

"Get some rest tonight and come in tomorrow prepared to help jump-start our task force. We'll include Scott as soon as he returns."

"And he'll head it, right?"

"You think? No doubts about his judgment? Or his confidence?"

"His judgment? Unimpaired, I'd say. Confidence? You know, a little beaten up, but he's a pro all the way. He'll be ready to take over the Chesapeake investigation when he returns, even if he doesn't locate Fredrica."

Hoople sat down and ran his hands through his thinning hair. "Maybe I should be questioning *your* judgment, Rachel. A man's charged with murder, spends a night in jail, loses his true love, fears he'll spend the rest of his days behind bars—and you say he's ready to lead a major investigation. Hero worship, pure and simple, Ms. Sullivan. I'll put him on the case, but not in charge, no way."

"Who's better to lead this?"

If Scott's lost standing with Hoople, so have I—the two of us ignoring the threat for personal pleasure.

"I have the ideal candidate, ready for the challenge, who'll draw on Scott's experience and wisdom."

"Woody?" Rachel asked. "You're telling me his security clearance has been reinstated?"

"I understand he'll have it back shortly and will join the team, but I never know when he's going to slip over the edge," Hoople said. "He's the most creative analyst here, but not the person to direct a complex operation."

"Then who—"

"Ms. Sullivan, I'm naming you as team lead of Operation Bluefish."

♦ ♦ ♦

"Mr. Scott, welcome back to the *Seeböcken* Hotel. We've upgraded you to a suite, no additional charge. The manager said to tell you he enjoyed your generous review of your visit last year."

"Thank you," Scott said, "it's my pleasure to return to St. Wolfgang. The view of the lake brings back fond memories."

Scott had called, texted, and emailed Fredrica. No response. She had reason enough to ignore his pleading, undoubtedly read he was a suspect in the murder of Laura Caputo. But, still, wasn't she curious? Hadn't their brief romance counted for something? He had flown to Vienna and taken the train to Salzburg, rented a car, and driven to St. Wolfgang to see her. She would answer the door, and he would explain. His presence would indicate his innocence.

During the long walk to her home, Scott rehearsed his explanation, imagined her smile, convinced himself that standing her up for their reunion in Vienna would be forgiven.

What if he was wrong? What if she knew nothing about his arrest? What if she's in trouble?

He paused briefly as he approached her home, a modest white stuccoed house in a quiet neighborhood. He stopped to admire the geraniums cascading from the window boxes, stepped forward, and softly knocked. No answer. Again, he knocked, now louder. No answer. The blinds were drawn.

"Hello! Fredrica?" She wasn't home. He would return.

Strolling through this storybook village, Scott recalled the pain he felt during his walks in Belfast, a city still coping with thirty-five hundred deaths during the Troubles. The cobblestone streets of St. Wolfgang, surrounded by mountains and water, elicited memories of a simpler time, of a harmony the Irish were unable to enjoy.

Hours later he returned to Fredrica's cottage. No lights, no answer. Still not home. He would return in the morning. She would be there.

♦♦♦

The sun was setting when Scott arrived back at the hotel, took the stairs to his room, and looked for an English-language station on the TV.

Nothing about a murder in Belfast. Thank God. No images of me. But when will I be free?

An hour later he sat alone in the hotel dining room, looking at the lake, studying the chalet-style structure of the interior, eavesdropping on an English-speaking couple to his right. She was complaining about her feet. He said no sensible person would wear heels on cobblestones. Then, silence.

"Good evening," the waiter said, "may I suggest a cocktail while you look at the menu?"

"Thanks, maybe a light white wine."

"I'd suggest a young Riesling with a note of peach."

"Perfect," Scott mumbled.

"A bottle?"

He paused. Maybe a bottle would ease his pain.

"No, thanks, a glass will be fine."

While he waited, he dialed Fredrica on his cell phone. No answer. No surprise.

I'm sure she's not avoiding me. She must be in trouble.

He studied the menu. Sausages, ham, veal. No appetite.

The waiter returned with the wine. Scott handed him the menu and asked, "Would you choose, please?"

"I recommend fresh char, often described as Alpine salmon, with boiled potatoes and a fresh green salad."

"Okay, good," Scott said, forcing a smile.

He closed his eyes, listened to laughter from a table across the room, and enjoyed the lake breeze through the open window next to his table. He felt at peace for a brief moment.

◆◆◆

Scott returned early the next morning planning to awaken Fredrica before she left for the day. Same routine. Knocked on the door. No answer. Knocked louder. No answer. On his second pass, just before noon, again no response. Maybe traveling or visiting friends. He tried her nearest neighbor. The door opened before he knocked. An elderly woman with a friendly face spoke rapidly in German. He didn't understand.

"Pardon me, I don't speak German. English?"

"I have some."

"Do you know when Ms. Wolf will return?"

Shaking her head, she said, "*Fräulein* Wolf in Munich. Visits *enkelkinder*. In English, little childs of child. Next month returning."

"Where? Location? Address in Munich?"

"*Nein. Ich Weiss es nicht.*"

"*Danke*," he said, with a stiff bow. "Thank you."

◆◆◆

Scott walked back toward the hotel, shoulders slumped, eyes down. Meandering through the backstreets of the village, he passed a travel bureau, resisted the temptation to inquire whether Fredrica had used their services to plan a trip. He paused in front of a small restaurant but continued on, hardly in a mood to join the laughter spilling through the door.

He stopped in the next block at a small shop with faded lettering on the door identifying it as an *Antiquarische Buchhandlung*, an Antiquarian Bookshop. Although he couldn't speak German, bookstores had a magnetic pull.

The owner looked up from a desk at the side of the door, nodded, and returned to sorting through a stack of old books, perhaps from a recent estate sale. With barely room to walk between the shelves, Scott found himself wandering through the children's section. Recalling a book his mother had read to him before he began school, he walked to the front of the store and asked the bookseller if he had a copy of *Little Red Riding Hood*.

After a long silence, the man said, *"Ich versteche nicht."*

Scott tried a second time and eventually drew a rough sketch of a little girl and a wolf.

"Rotkappchen und der Wolf!" the bookseller said and then motioned Scott to follow. He opened the door to a small office at the back of the store, climbed a ladder to a ten-foot high shelf, and retrieved a well-worn volume with numerous full-color prints.

"Sehr selten," he said.

When it became obvious Scott didn't understand, the man walked to the front of the store, consulted a dictionary, and said in English, "very rare." He then wrote €100 on a scrap of paper. Scott leafed through the book, shook his head, and thanked the man for his courtesy. The bookseller crossed out the number and substituted €80. Scott stopped and looked again. The Gothic drawing of the wolf baring his teeth was captivating. Worth the price. He bought the book.

When Scott returned to his hotel, he felt the fool for believing a woman named Wolf would have been waiting for him at her home, compounded by having paid a hundred dollars for a tattered children's book about a deceitful and ravenous wolf. Memories of childhood in Rawalpindi flooded his mind. *Have I come here to look for Fredrica? Or am I looking for the man I no longer recognize—for the man born in Pakistan as Franklin Lambert?*

♦♦♦

"How do you signal SOS in the middle of the Chesapeake?" Woodward asked with a mischievous gleam in his eye.

"You're doing fine, Woody—standing up, waving your hands, and shouting at the top of your lungs. If they weren't in school, the fish would surely come to our rescue."

"Very funny, Mulligan. You promised, practically swore you knew how to handle a motor boat. We've been drifting here for nearly an hour. If we have to be rescued by the Coast Guard, I'll never live it down at the agency."

"Maybe a little quiet would help. Meditation, or even a silent prayer. The outboard's a twelve-year old two-stroke Evinrude, usually very reliable. Give me a few minutes to fiddle with it before you return to panic mode. And for God's sake, sit down."

Woody began singing from *Guys and Dolls*: "Sit Down, You're Rockin' the Boat." Would an engineer like Mulligan have a clue about its origin? Woody was sure it would annoy him, so much the better for leaving them adrift.

"And the devil will drag you under . . . "

♦♦♦

Six hours earlier they had rented a boat at Fred's Marina on Solomons Island where the Patuxent River flows into the Chesapeake Bay. "I told you before we drove down here," Woody said, "I'm here for sightseeing."

"Sightseeing, my ass," Mulligan replied. "The last thing you'd do is spend half a day on the bay gazing at the clouds and breathing fresh air. Your high-powered binoculars and a five-hundred-millimeter telephoto lens on a high-end Nikon ain't the usual tourist trappings."

Twenty-five miles north of Solomons Island, they'd stopped to photograph Tom Clancy's Peregrine Bay estate. "You could have it for a cool six million bucks," Woody said.

"That's a little steep for me, unless you'd like to play a few more hands of Texas Hold 'Em. None of my business, but it'd be a swell retreat for you. Why, by just inhaling the atmosphere, you could be the next Jack Ryan, hunting the cybercrazy Russians screwing with our political system."

"You're full of surprises." Woody said. "Didn't know a guy who spends his time fixing AC systems gave a shit about politics."

"Oh yeah? You've known me for years, but continue to assume I'm some backwoods yokel, just out for a little sport on the bay. I couldn't help but notice you took a buncha snaps when we passed the Calvert Cliffs Nuclear Reactor. Any idiot would conclude you're conducting some kinda reconnaissance."

My shrink told me one of my personalities makes judgments on superficial clues. I know he has an advanced degree in fluid dynamics, but with a long-overdue haircut, three day's stubble, and a belly that begs for cantilever support, he's one sorry looking dude.

♦♦♦

Home after several hours in the office, Rachel felt a shiver of foreboding. The director had made a mistake by assigning her to lead the Bluefish team. How could she manage a veteran like Thomas Scott or a genius like Woody Woodward? Like asking a lieutenant to lead a company of colonels. She removed her backpack, slumped on the sofa, closed her eyes, and imagined her colleagues laughing at a thirty-five-year-old woman directing an operation against an army of foreign cyberspies.

She awoke well past midnight, confused for a second to find herself back in her apartment. She unpacked, charged her cell phone, sorted her accumulated mail, paid utility bills, and opened a can of tuna.

Her cell phone, recharged and reconnected, revealed hundreds of unread messages. She had turned off the cellular connection in Rome to avoid overseas charges. A text from her New York boyfriend suggested they go sailing from Annapolis when she returned. The next repeated the first, asked whether she had received it. The most recent, sent just hours before, had a tone of bewilderment.

> **<Where are you? Angry, lost, injured, kidnapped? Why haven't you responded?>**

She replied immediately.

> **<My apologies. Just returned. Delighted to go sailing. I don't know starboard from port or a jib from a jibe, but will do my best to be a good mate.>**

Rachel had barely slept, her body insisting on Roman time, already well past an early espresso to start the day. Still dark when she arrived at work, she began sorting through intercepts, draft reports, and completed analyses. No surprise the Russian FSB remained active in attempting to penetrate government and corporate networks. The Russian Internet

Research Agency continued its use of social media to disrupt American politics with methods subtle enough to fool even sophisticated media consumers.

More ominous was the activity of an elite unit of Russia's Ministry of Defense that had successfully targeted America's energy sector. A TS analysis concluded with a high level of confidence that critical elements of a major American power company had been mapped and assessed. Recognizing the weakest link in the chain of research, development, production, and deployment would allow the exploitation of vulnerabilities as well as the introduction of malware that would lie dormant until triggered.

The analysts recalled the Northeast Blackout of 1965 when thirty million people in the United States and Canada lost access to electricity. They suggested the thirteen hours it took for restoration would be dwarfed by a Russian cyberattack. "Imagine New York City off the power grid for weeks or months," the analysts wrote in conclusion.

Rachel looked up from her computer screen, saw the first hints of daylight, and headed for the cafeteria. Woody was usually the first person through the door, the first person to tap the coffee urn for twenty-four ounces of darkroast Arabica brew. He wasn't there. The government-designed cafeteria lighted by yesterday's flickering fluorescent, was practically empty.

She sat alone. Had Woody heard she would be heading Operation Bluefish and skipped the country again? Would Scott stay in Austria when he learned she'd been chosen to head the team?

She sent a text to her boyfriend.

<In case you didn't get my last text, I'm looking forward to sailing with you from Annapolis, the sooner the better. I miss you.>

She did not receive an immediate answer. Sipping her fresh-brewed American coffee, she remembered the espresso Chef Roberto had offered after a night in his apartment. She allowed herself a brief smile. It disappeared when the memory of a glorious Roman morning was overtaken by the reality of a Fort Meade morning in a cubicle pulsating with a vision of Russian cyberdominance.

Lights out, they'll report. Who's in charge? A young woman, standing alone against the Russian army and all Putin's horses and all Putin's men. I can't do it.

Rachel lingered in the cafeteria, refilling her coffee, nibbling at a blueberry muffin, checking her phone, and rehearsing another meeting with Hoople. She would ask to be reassigned to her previous duties as an analyst. She would retreat to the comfort of interpreting digital intercepts. She would tell Hoople she was not ready for the responsibility of battling an army of Russian cyberwarriors.

She was waiting at the door of his office when Hoople arrived. "Aren't you the early bird," he said. "Trust you're rested and ready to run."

"Not exactly," she said. "I need a few minutes of your time—"

"Sure, but not now. I have a meeting with the director in a few minutes and then a dental appointment. So, why don't you come by after lunch, say two o'clock."

♦♦♦

Scott recognized it was irrational, even perverse, to delay his flight to the United States. He had been told his return to the NSA was urgent, but he felt one more day wouldn't matter. He would text Fredrica, tell her he was staying overnight in Munich, and invite her to join him for dinner. Even if she wasn't eager to see him, an evening away from her grandchildren might overcome her resistance.

He arrived at the Hotel Laimer Hof, was offered a beer and a copy of the *Süddeutsche Zeitung* while his room was being prepared. With his rudimentary German, he recognized the meaning of the headline: CYBERANGRIFF AUF AMERIKANISCHES ATOMKRAFTWERK.

At his request, the young woman who had welcomed him readily agreed to translate the story:

"A nuclear reactor at the Indian Point Power Plant, twenty-five miles north of New York City, had malfunctioned. The plant manager reported one of the reactors closed down without warning and automatically restarted before any damage was done. Energy experts traced the unprecedented behavior to malicious code introduced to an outdated control system."

Scott suspected the Russians. The Chinese had the capability but not the motive, and the Iranians had the motive but not the capability. Kim Jong-un might have the capability but was still pursuing his bromance with the American president.

Twelve hours had passed since his text to Fredrica. Still no answer. He knew it had been a foolish idea. The left side of his brain had been attacked as surely as the attack on the nuclear reactor. While America burned, he fiddled in Munich.

♦♦♦

"By the light of the silvery moon, I want to spoon . . . " Woody sang, continuing to make fun of Mulligan's boating skills.

"You think this is funny?" Mulligan asked.

"No, what's funny is sitting in the middle of the

Chesapeake at midnight without a Marine Radio," Woodward said. "We couldn't call the Coast Guard if we were stranded here for days. And now you finally confess your cell phone doesn't have a charge. With all your bragging about patrolling the Mekong on a Navy LST, I had the impression you'd be better prepared for a little pleasure trip on a placid lake. Wouldn't surprise me to drift into the Atlantic before sunrise and find ourselves attacked by sharks."

"Yeah, along with giant squid and Russian submarines," Mulligan replied.

"Did I mention the temperature is dropping so fast that we risk dying of hypothermia?"

"Woody, my friend, or should I address you as Dr. Zachary Woodward, your book learnin' hasn't done much for your common sense or your appreciation of fluid dynamics and probability theory. Now an old blue-collar coot like me, who spends his time installing air conditioning systems, is a little more grounded. No need to be burdened with a Marine Radio when I have my wits about me and this bag with emergency supplies."

"Let me guess," Woodward said, "you've brought along a sextant, so we can navigate by the stars."

"Not exactly," Mulligan said as he opened the bag. "This bottle of Jack Daniels will help ward off the elements, and this flashlight will help us find our way when we sight land."

"Or signal for help when we wake up in the ocean," Woodward added.

"If you'd been paying attention, you'd have known we were drifting southeast, and if you'd open your eyes right now, you'd see we're in sight of land, drifting into a cove."

"Holy shit, Mulligan, you're not kidding. 'Tierra, Tierra,'

in the words of Columbus' alert watchman. We're safe, but where are we?"

"Just a guess, but from my recollection of the faded map on the wall of the marina, I'd say we're practically at Taylors Island Wildlife Management Area on the eastern side of the bay."

♦♦♦

When Alex Hoople returned to his office, he found Rachel waiting. Her urgent request to see him meant something was wrong. When disaster struck, she inevitably remained calm. What might have happened to give her the appearance of an anxiety attack?

"Come in," he said. "I hope you had a good night's sleep, but jetlag must still be taking its toll."

"Yes, maybe, but that's not my concern. I appreciate your trust in selecting me to head Operation Bluefish." She paused. He waited. "This is difficult," she continued, "hope you'll understand."

"Of course."

"I'm, ahh . . . okay, let me blurt it right out. You've made a mistake—"

"Hardly my first. I'm human, too," Hoople said.

"No, I don't mean that. Sorry. What I'm trying to say is this: I can't head the team. I don't have the qualifications, the experience, the seniority. I mean, there's too much at stake. When the lights go out, you and I will both be sitting in front of a congressional committee, by candlelight undoubtedly, explaining why I was given the responsibility to defend the country against a battalion of Russian cybersoldiers."

"Rachel, you'll have a team with as much experience and savvy as we have in this agency."

"I appreciate that, but . . . "

"And your team is one of many in an inter-agency task force with the Defense Department, Energy Department, and the CIA. Rachel, we wouldn't expect you, even with Scott and Woodward on your team, to defend the whole nation. Furthermore, that would be well outside of our bureaucratic lane. Our role is to detect cyberthreats and provide intelligence for network defense. Our mandate in Operation Bluefish is narrow, but critical."

Rachel's eyes focused on his lips. She understood the responsibility of her team would be leavened by experts from other agencies. Nonetheless, she shook her head. She was a patriot, knew what the nation deserved. She wasn't the answer. This exercise required a modern-day General Marshall.

Hoople hadn't made the sale but continued. "The nation's electrical grid is at risk. Our nuclear power plants, that provide twenty percent of our electricity, are at risk. Our team, however, will focus initially on one facility, Calvert Cliffs. We know it's an active target of one of our adversaries. Even though we suspect the Russians, we're not sure. And we're far from sure how they've managed to get inside a system air-gapped from the Internet."

Rachel smiled and quietly said, "Perhaps the Stuxnet solution?"

Hoople beamed and said, "Your instant insight, Ms. Sullivan, is the reason you're heading the team. Go home, sleep well, and come in tomorrow with the confidence that's beginning to bubble through your doubts."

Chapter 11. No Exit

Scott awoke with a jolt during a rough landing at BWI, then waited by the carousel for his luggage. He'd take a taxi to Fort Meade to check in before driving home. Didn't need any more "wild," but if West Virginia still promised "wonderful," he was overdue.

♦♦♦

"You're back, thank God," the NSA receptionist said. "Let me give you a hug."

He grinned. "Is that still allowed?"

"You bet, particularly for my favorite spy. They say you escaped from a maximum-security prison."

"Yeah, broke out of solitary and scaled a twenty-foot wall when the guards were napping," Scott said. "Easier than getting into this place. I understand they've changed all the keycard codes, so I'm locked out of the upper floors without an escort."

"Let me guess," she said. "You're looking for Dr. Hoople, right?"

"Exactly."

The receptionist called, an assistant arrived, and within a few minutes Scott was sitting in Hoople's office waiting for his return. He picked up a copy of *Field and Stream* from the top of a bookcase and read about Chesapeake Bay fishing for striped bass using a Bass Kandy Delight. He'd done a little fly fishing, but the idea of casting from a moving boat in choppy waters for an elusive fish wasn't a sport that appealed.

He looked up at the sound of footsteps to see Hoople's smile and outstretched hand. "Scott, what a treat to see you back."

"And a free man, no less," Scott said.

"Already on the job, studying the fauna of the Chesapeake Bay. Trust you've learned how challenging it is to catch your prey."

"Give me a few more days to unwind, and I'll be ready. First, I have to get back to check on my home, to remind Kierkegaard I haven't forgotten him, and to thank a friend for helping spring me from a life of bread and water."

"Good, you deserve it," Hoople said. "Take as much time as you need, as long as you're back here first thing Monday morning when we formally kick off Operation Bluefish."

♦♦♦

The drive to Berkeley Springs was relaxing, traffic was light, and the foliage promised a new start. He turned off WV Route 9 to a gravel lane lined with giant oaks that led to his home. Despite the years he'd live here, he still admired its stone-cased grandeur, built early in the twentieth century by a man of means. It had been unoccupied, except for robins and rodents, for years before he bought it. The realtor said it still had good bones. New heating, wiring, and roof plus months of removing faded wallpaper brought it back to life. Kierkegaard, was still vacationing with Father Sean McManus. The house greeted him with silence.

Have I lost it? I used to love the adventure, but now the quiet of home seems so much more satisfying.

A quick survey revealed no changes. The old-fashioned kitchen, one generation beyond an icebox and a wood-burning stove, reminded him of his parents' kitchen in Pakistan. He was home with the embrace of childhood memories.

He climbed the stairs to the second floor, each groaning step reminding him of the age of his home. *A half century older than me and every bit as creaky.* The spindle bed was authentic but small for a man of his size. With the shrinkage of age, the bed would eventually fit him. He looked in the mirror opposite the bed and stared at a face with a pallor of death.

Scott traveled light, so unpacking took only a few minutes. Hanging from his neck and beneath his shirt was a flat nylon pouch for his passport. It also contained a credit card, several twenties, and the antique filigreed pendant Fredrica had sent him months before. A sign of her trust and affection. He would have returned it to reciprocate his affection if they had met in Vienna as planned—or if she had been home when he visited St. Wolfgang. Looking for her in Munich had been foolish, but a chance sighting would not have been impossible.

He walked downstairs, stepped into his study with the silver pendant clutched in his hand. Dozing on the flight back to the States, he had begun to think of it as a talisman that would bring good luck, that would reunite him with Fredrica.

The study was his favorite room. The Edward Hopper painting continued to bring him quiet pleasure. He had bought it years before in a second-hand shop. The dealer described it as a crude copy of Hopper's "Morning Sun." Scott had it authenticated. Delighted but not surprised, he learned it was an early version of Hopper's famous 1952 oil, now publicly displayed in the Columbus Museum of Art.

Scott sat opposite the painting and gazed at the stiff female figure. Hopper's wife had posed. The solitary woman sat on a bed in a stark room bathed in sun. Staring outside, lost in thought, like Scott, she was alone.

He would leave momentarily to greet Father McManus and Kierkegaard, but first he closed his eyes. He thought of his short-lived marriage to Elisabetta. He loved her still, even though she had left him for Monica. They were now living in New York running a boutique antique shop. Scott occasionally visited, pleased his former wife had found her mate.

Next, inevitably next, he remembered Sharmien—a skilled nurse who cared for him in a Pakistani military hospital. She saved his life after his vehicle plunged into a ravine off the Khyber Pass. They lost contact when his employer changed Scott's name and declared him dead to protect him from terrorists. Years later they reunited. She visited him in West Virginia. He had imagined their future together. When her niece was murdered, she abruptly returned to Pakistan where she began a campaign for women's rights. He was proud of her. He missed her.

He had abandoned his fear of spending life alone after his second visit with Fredrica in St. Wolfgang. Both in their sixties, they were ready for companionship. They fell in love. She waited for him in Vienna when he was detained in Belfast. Then she vanished. *Three strikes and I'm out.*

He opened his eyes. He'd been sleeping. The unnamed woman in the Hopper painting continued to look away. But she hadn't *run* away. He would give her a name, the woman on the wall who would listen in silence. Athena! That sounded right, a Greek goddess, no less. He stood up and looked through the boxes of antique encyclopedias he had bought at a Pittsburgh auction. There it was: Athena—the goddess of wisdom, mathematics, and strategic warfare. A perfect companion for the challenge facing his NSA team.

My team? What a conceit. I no longer know who I am. I no longer recognize the man in the mirror.

Scott glanced at his watch. Had he forgotten to reset it after returning from Austria? Or had he slept that long? What felt like several minutes must have been several hours. He had spent the time with Elisabetta, Sharmien, and Fredrica. Wide awake now, he was alone with Athena.

◆ ◆ ◆

Out the door and in his car, he drove to the rectory. Before Scott rang the doorbell, he heard Kierkegaard barking.

"Greetings, brother," Sean said. "Door's open, come in."

Scott entered. Sean remained seated. Kierkegaard yelped and turned in circles.

"Pardon my language, but what in the hell did they do to you? I gave last rites to an old guy last week who looked better than you."

"It's a long story," Scott said. "There were moments when I feared it would be even longer. Sorry you had to put up with my favorite little friend for so long."

"*Au contraire,*" Sean said. "How exactly would the Irish put it, Scott? 'Yous got it bass-ackwards?' Not sure I'd maintained my sanity without him."

"Let me guess. Sheriff Hightower has threatened you with jail, figuring a friend of mine must be up to no good. And guessing from your appearance, you've resisted by going on a hunger strike."

"Very observant. Lost ten or twelve pounds since you saw me but still have plenty to spare. A little touch of the flu killed my appetite and my energy."

"So sorry. Maybe this will help," Scott said, as he presented Sean a fifth of Bushmills and sat down in the stuffed chair next to him.

"Sixteen-year-old single malt," Sean said, reading the label. "Feeling better already."

The right words but spoken with so little conviction. There must be more to Sean's languor. Should he ask? Perhaps not.

"How've you been spending your time," he asked instead.

"Praying," the priest said. "For your safe return, of course. Mainly for God's guidance."

"Must have worked. I'm here, thankful to you and the others who rescued me from thirty years of hard time. I was facing the fate of being wheeled out of prison on my ninety-ninth birthday."

"I'll begin saving candles," Sean said, "in case the magistrate changes his mind."

Kierkegaard jumped on Scott's lap, signaling it was time to leave. Scott stood, thanked Sean for dog-sitting, and wished him a rapid recovery.

Sean rose to his feet, interrupting Scott's path to the front door. "Wait, don't leave. Sit down, I can't let you go before I unburden my soul. To put it bluntly, I'm in trouble."

"Also accused of murder?" Scott asked with a wink.

"If only it were so simple. Then I wouldn't bring others down with me. This affects the entire congregation."

Scott sat. This was no time for humor.

"I'm not at liberty to divulge names, although with your acumen as an international spy or whatever you do, you may be on it like Kierkegaard on a Big Mac."

Sean's four-footed houseguest perked up his oversized

ears at the mention of his name.

"Last Monday, two of my most devoted parishioners sought a meeting to discuss Sunday's homily. I suggested four o'clock the following day. They were both dressed in their Sunday best when they arrived."

"Your tone suggests this doesn't end well," Scott said.

Sean sighed. "I offered tea and cookies, store-bought I'm afraid, and the meeting began pleasantly. The husband arrived with a Bible, bookmarked in several places. After a few inquiries about my health, his wife leaned over and whispered to him. I couldn't hear anything except when she raised her voice and said, 'Show him.' He looked uncomfortable but didn't argue with a woman ready for battle."

Scott shifted his weight. *How could anyone be angry at this good man?*

"He held up the Bible, said it was the authoritative 'King James Version' and opened it to Matthew 25."

"It's been a long time," Scott said, "but I remember the drills we had at the seminary, practically had to memorize verses 31 to 46."

"The husband must have suspected I'd forgotten, as he insisted on reading it out loud. By the time he finished, he was practically shouting. His wife clutched his arm and nodded in agreement.

"I was about to respond when she looked up and said, 'Sheep and goats, Father, sheep and goats. Goats on the left.' She grabbed the Bible from the husband and began to read, 'Then shall he say also unto them on the left hand, depart from me, ye cursed, into everlasting fire, prepared for the devil and his angels.' She was hyperventilating, blood pressure rising, face reddening. If looks could kill, she'd have struck me dead."

"Whoa," Scott said, "I'm confused. What brought this on?"

"As soon as the husband opened the Bible to Matthew 25, I knew what was coming. I should have recognized it when they filed out of the church on Sunday, mumbled something but never made eye contact."

"What heresy did you commit this time? Offer to sponsor another Syrian refugee? Continue to meet with non-believers like Felicity?"

"Worse," Sean said, "I agreed with Pope Francis, who questioned the existence of Hell and suggested we would all be saved."

"Good for you," Scott said, "and good news for accused murderers like me."

"I'd been considering this homily for months. It began after a meeting between Francis and Eugenio Scalfari, the ninety-five-year-old editor of the Italian leftist daily, *La Repubblica.*

"I read it years ago when I lived in Rome."

"The Holy Father reportedly said, 'Hell does not exist—what exists is the disappearance of sinful souls.' Well, all hell broke loose in the Vatican. Fierce denials were issued by the bureaucracy, while Pope Francis remained silent."

"So, you and the Pope are playing with fire, so to speak," Scott said with a smile.

"Both of us on the side of the angels. Wasn't the first time he'd challenged orthodoxy. Earlier he said, 'Everything will be saved—everything,' and promised an 'immense tent, where God will welcome *all* mankind.' Quoted that to Mr. and Mrs. Doubting Thomas, but they hadn't come to listen."

"How did it end?"

"Accused me of being a heretic and announced they're

joining a congregation in Martinsburg where they can worship the true God. And with that, they were out the door. The husband came back a little later to retrieve their King James Bible. Said I had upset the wife so much she had forgotten it. He turned as he left and said, 'Thank you, Mr. McManus.' Guess he had mentally defrocked me."

"And placed you among the goats that won't be saved," Scott said. "Trust the others who showed up Sunday morning were okay with your homily. I'd say well done if you lost only two worshipers. Maybe their places will be taken by sinners who fear eternal damnation."

"Not so simple, Scott. The two who left were our major contributors. They were the difference between balancing the books and bankruptcy. Their departure will have me begging for money or closing the doors."

"It's that serious?" Scott asked.

"Including last Sunday's offerings, the church had a balance of slightly over thirty-seven hundred dollars, with a debt of four thousand dollars for the new roof. With the utility bills arriving soon, our cash assets will be exhausted. Without the annual ten-thousand-dollar contribution from the departing couple, we'll have to sponsor bingo every night of the week."

"How can I help? Sacrifice a goat in front of their home? As soon as you spoke of money, I knew exactly who they were. Shame you had to put up with their pious attitude all these years. Something good will come of this."

"It already has. Since they hadn't much of an appetite, I still have a full tin of Danish Butter Cookies you can take home to share with Kierkegaard."

Sean stood, walked to the buffet, and returned with the tin of cookies.

Scott rose and assured Sean of a brighter day ahead.

Kierkegaard pulled at his leash, eager to return home. As Scott left, he turned and said, "I'll pray for a miracle."

I want to feel his pain, but he still has the comfort of a loving God. Apart from this little dog, I am alone. Not even sure who I am.

♦♦♦

After feeding Kierkegaard, Scott returned to his study.

"Hello Athena," he said out loud, "our household is now complete."

After staring at his prized oil painting, Scott checked his email. He deleted practically everything without reading. However, when he spotted a message from his Belfast solicitor, he eagerly opened it.

"Appreciate your kind words and the funds transfer," Clare had written. "We're all square, but you should know the solicitor who's representing the bartender has shared with me evidence that may clear his client.

"Don't worry," she wrote, "you remain free as an Irish Long-tailed Tit, but this latest development will certainly flummox the prosecution. The chief inspector remains convinced you were the target. The motive remains a mystery. He may wish to question you about known enemies or recent threats. Trust you wouldn't mind another visit to Belfast for a day or two."

Return to Belfast? No way. I'd rather return to Afghanistan.

"Thanks again, Ms. Sheehan, for you research and representation," Scott wrote, "but returning is out of the question. I'm doing my best to avoid being accused of murder again, or worse, being murdered."

Kierkegaard began barking. Maybe at a stranger approaching the house or a squirrel teasing him from the windowsill. A knock on the door sent him into a tizzy, a canine adrenalin rush.

Scott opened the door, surprised to see Spencer Cobb, who had arrived with a broad smile and a wicker basket. He was not a man who generally made house calls. Nor did he appear to be a man prepared to stand before a jury. Dressed in jeans, a T-shirt emblazed with the slogan SAVE THE SHAWNEE, and steel-toed work boots, he might have wandered in from a construction site.

"Welcome home, Scott, I'm here to celebrate your freedom. And to present this hot apple pie from the missus. She took it out of the oven a few minutes ago and insisted I deliver it immediately."

"I'm flabbergasted," Scott said. "Thank you and thank Mrs. Cobb. How'd you know I'd returned?"

"Have you forgotten where you live? In a village with a population of six hundred, there isn't a thing you don't learn within minutes. The town's still buzzing about the holier-than-thou couple on the hillside who abandoned Father McManus for some uptight parish in Martinsburg. And if you haven't heard about Felicity's run-in with Sheriff Hightower, you'd be the only one."

Scott took the basket with the pie and motioned to his guest. "Come in and sit a spell. Trust it isn't too early to offer you a drink."

He laughed. "Wouldn't be too early if the sun had just risen."

Scott retreated to the kitchen, returned minutes later with a tumbler of whiskey for Cobb and two pieces of apple pie. "Best welcome home treat I've been offered in years. Doubt if I'd be here without your help in Belfast."

"You certainly look at peace, back in this grand old house. Wasn't long ago I imagined you in leg irons and an orange jump suit. I don't mind the credit, but it was Bridgette

Walsh, the young woman from the archives, who made the difference. Although you didn't have a chance to meet her in Ireland, you'll have an opportunity here in Berkeley Springs before the end of the month."

"Doubt if Mrs. Cobb will be baking pies for your friends when she learns you're inviting a young Irish woman to visit," Scott said.

"It's all business. I've lured her away from the Public Records Office to assist me in pursuing some leads in Great Britain. I'm still Of Counsel with Zimmerman and Lewinsohn in Washington, as you may recall. They've asked me to represent a whistleblower from a major American corporation with international ties. My client's prepared to file a *qui tam* complaint concerning alleged Brexit interference. I don't know shit about technology. Bridgett does. She's smart. She's clever. She's indefatigable."

"And sexy, if I recall from your description in Belfast."

"True enough," Cobb said, "although I've decided to overlook it and make her an offer anyway." He stood, glass still in his hand, lifted it to his lips and emptied it. He sat it down and shook Scott's hand. "If you have the good sense to stay put, I'll introduce you to Bridgette next week."

He patted Kierkegaard on the head and departed before Scott had a chance to ask about Felicity and Sheriff Hightower. The T-shirt with the SAVE THE SHAWNEE slogan also had a story to tell.

Time to take man's best friend for a walk. Time to wake up and smell the roses—and dozens of wildflowers in bloom along the gravel roadway to his home. Black-eyed Susans, Queen Anne's lace, and goldenrod offered color if little fragrance. The dramatic lavender Joe Pye weed was his favorite. Kierkegaard ignored them all, far more intent in remarking his territory after an absence of several weeks.

♦♦♦

Returning home, Scott found a week-old copy of *The Martinsburg Journal* folded to the Weekender section. Cobb must have left it on the hallway table. Felicity Philips was again in the news: LOCAL ARTIST CLAIMS SHAWNEE HERITAGE.

Among several photos, the one that drew Scott's attention was a close-up of Felicity and Sheriff Terry Hightower, nearly nose-to-nose, mouths open in anger. According to the story, he had reminded her the ceremony she was staging at the Berkeley Springs State Park required a permit. She had reportedly said, "F*** off, Sheriff, those are white-man's rules. This is sacred ground."

Whether sacred or not, she had taken over this historic space in the center of Berkeley Springs. A dozen or so young people were pictured performing the Green Corn Dance, described as an annual Shawnee ritual marking the first corn harvest—and absolving participants of misconduct.

Felicity claimed to be a spiritual descendent and introduced the reporter to Heidi Lonebear, a jewelry designer from Oklahoma's Shawnee Tribe. Lonebear said her work attempted to preserve Shawnee culture with new forms and techniques.

Felicity's rendering of a nineteenth century Shawnee warrior-chief, Tecumseh, was prominently displayed in the park's bandstand. Inspired by Benson Lossing's 1848 original, she said her copy "was painted with acrylics and tears in remembrance of the near genocide of the Shawnee."

The Journal reporter wrote, "Felicity's rendering of Tecumseh confirmed *her* artistic genius," but added "there was no West Virginia Shawnee at the ceremony—or anywhere in the state." Formerly considered part of the Cherokee Nation, the Shawnee were gradually pushed westward from their origins in Ohio, Pennsylvania, and West Virginia.

◆◆◆

Scott put the paper aside, walked to his study, and slumped in an overstuffed chair. He reflected on Felicity's artistry and a life marked with tragedy. She had moved to Berkeley Springs years before to escape a stalker who followed and continued to terrorize her. After her one-person gallery exhibit in New York, he broke into her hotel room and feigned a ritual suicide. Paralyzed by fear, she returned home and avoided contact with friends. Her campaign for recognition of the Shawnee was her first public appearance in months.

Scott understood Felicity's retreat to her home. He knew how it felt to be threatened, to live alone. He closed his eyes, dozed off, dreaming of Fredrica trapped with him in a lonely room. He awakened when his canine companion signaled the presence of another marauding creature. "Not on my territory," Kierkegaard barked and growled.

Scott stood, walked to a bookcase next to the window in his study, and located a yellowed paperback of Jean-Paul Sartre's *No Exit*. He had seen the play in an off-Broadway theatre several months after arriving from Pakistan. Three sinners trapped in a small room for eternity. No fire and brimstone. Instead, eternal reminders of failing, of love lost.

Scott leafed through the slim volume, stopped, and read a passage he had underlined fifty years before.

> *Just as I expected. WHY should one sleep? A sort of drowsiness steals on you, tickles you behind the ears, and you feel your eyes closing—but why sleep? You lie down on the sofa and—in a flash sleep flies away. Miles and miles away. So you rub your eyes, get up, and it starts all over again.*

He hadn't understood the play then. Now it was very clear. The afterlife would be an endless encore of one's earthly life. There would be, as Sartre wrote, *No Exit.*

Chapter 12. Intercepts and Images

Scott walked stiffly into the briefing room, stopped to receive a welcome from a former colleague, and took a seat in the back. *I don't recognize most of the faces. All youngsters. What have they heard about my Irish adventure? Or about me?*

"We're light years behind these bastards," the briefing officer said. The lights dimmed. The inevitable PowerPoint slide appeared: Courier font rendered in charcoal black on an antique white background, the customary design of the graphics guy. The first slide had the words **National Intelligence Strategy of the United States of America** above the NSA seal.

Scott had already read the report, probably the others had as well, but attendance was required. Fifty or so analysts in the darkened room looking at slides that reduced intelligence community objectives to simple bullets—and listening to the briefer read each one. Woodward, sitting next to Scott, leaned over and whispered, "Beautifully scripted for those among us whose IQ matches their age."

Scott nodded, smiled in agreement.

After thirty minutes of this intellectual pablum, Scott guessed it had cost ten thousand dollars in lost wages and the eradication of even more brain cells. The briefer, a young man who smiled more than he should have, thanked attendees for their attention. They stood up, ready to return to their offices.

"Bluefish team," Hoople said, waving his hand for attention, "before you get away, I'd like a few words."

When the others had departed, Hoople began in his no-nonsense style. "I've only one slide, and you can read it yourself." A truncated Top Secret//SI NSA report appeared on the screen: "Russian General Staff Main Intelligence Directorate actors . . . recently executed cyber espionage operations against the Calvert Cliffs Nuclear Power Plant, presumably to obtain information on its vulnerability."

"There's more," Hoople said. "I'll leave that to our team leader to discuss in detail. Meanwhile, welcome back to our veteran analyst Thomas Sebastian Scott. Also, welcome to Zachary Woodward, whose clearance has finally been restored by our hard-ass security division." Woody stood and acknowledged the welcome with an exaggerated bow.

"No longer a threat, Woody," Hoople said, "Let's keep it that way. Which means knocking off gambling with your buddy Mulligan. I'm afraid your losing streak will never end."

Woody shrugged.

"One more thing. With several key absences, we'd been running a loosey-goosey operation. Full complement here now—Scott, Woody, and Rachel augmented by three of our finest junior analysts: Marie Khan, Sam Adams, and Li Min. As you all know, the Russians have their eye on a nuclear plant a few hours' drive from Washington. Right?"

Hoople paused. No one nodded. "Good, none of you bit. We know it *looks* like the Russians, but maybe the real culprit's flying a false flag. Blame the Russies, divert our attention, and blow up the reactor when we're not looking."

Scott leaned over and whispered to Woody, "He's testing the newbies."

"How long do we have to detect the intruder?" Hoople asked. "How long to isolate the reactor from threats? I'd say somewhere between tomorrow and a few more tomorrows. That baby blows, and we'll see mass panic. Stock market tanks. Banks close. Washington shuts down."

Sam, rocking in his seat, looked at Marie and Li. They both continued to focus on Hoople.

"If the rumor hasn't preempted me, I'll conclude by announcing Rachel Sullivan as the team leader."

Scott raised his hand in the manner of a schoolboy seeking the teacher's attention.

"Yes, Mr. Scott," Hoople said, "what is it?"

Mr. Scott? Hoople's setting a tone for the three new kids. Better a little respect than to be regarded as some antique.

"I've been with this organization three decades," Scott began. "Actually, a little more. And I'm known as the guy who expresses his doubts, not only in the chief's office but in full view. I arrived here this morning with a lingering concern, afraid you might confuse seniority for skill. Dr. Hoople, you do us all proud. Rachel Sullivan has no peer for the role you've asked her to perform. Absent a half-dozen flutes and a cold bottle of Dom Perignon, I propose a toast to our chief for his wisdom and to our team leader for her brilliance."

Rachel blushed and looked away, appearing uncomfortable with the attention.

"When the team succeeds, I'll spring for the bubbly." Hoople said.

As soon as he left, Rachel began her first team meeting. "Here we are," she said, with a nervous laugh. "Not sure I'm ready for this, but Dr. Hoople insisted. Maybe I should introduce our new colleagues. Li Min, born in California, has far too many degrees for one person. Her parents wanted her to attend Julliard, believing she had the talent to become a concert pianist. She told me she was stubborn. Stubborn enough to insist on pursuing a degree in mathematics. Two degrees later, she's now recognized as an expert in artificial intelligence. And, of course, natural intelligence."

Rachel's attempt to introduce a little humor hadn't worked. No one smiled. Scott looked straight ahead, revealing nothing. Woody continued writing in a notebook, appearing inattentive.

"Also new to the agency is Sam Adams. With a name like that, I guessed he was associated with the Boston Beer Company. He corrected me, said he was a descendent of *the* Sam Adams, one of the leaders of the American Revolution. Sam's a little older than he looks, which is to say he isn't a teenager. His specialty is nanotechnology. His dissertation will be published by MIT Press next year."

Woody continued to write. Scott remained impassive. The three new members were alert, undoubtedly eager to slay some cyber dragons. Rachel remained nervous.

"Last but not least," Rachel said, "Marie Khan, whose specialty is cybercommunications, more precisely the malicious use of the Internet, including hacking and the introduction of malware. She immigrated to the United States at the ripe old age of six months and spent the rest of her life preparing for this assignment. She graduated from Carnegie Tech at sixteen. At that age I was worried about being invited to the junior prom. And if you're curious, the phone never rang."

Woody looked up. "May I add a word or two?" he asked. Without waiting for a response, he stood and began. "Welcome to our three newbies. Our recruitment division deserves an award for snagging you from academe. And you three should know that Rachel will have your back. In a pinch she'll save your career, even your life. Neither Scott nor I would be here today if it weren't for her cunning and bravery."

♦♦♦

Woody remained seated as the others filed from the room, except Marie Khan who also lingered. "Hello . . ."

"Hello to you, Marie." *Looks like the leader of the pack. Tall, coal-black hair, oversized black-framed glasses.*

"What you said about Ms. Sullivan, I mean, how did she . . ."

Hmm. A little aggressive. A lot curious. This gal's got it.

"I went off the reservation two years ago, or at least one of me did. It's no secret I've been diagnosed with Dissociative Identity Disorder. Used to be called Multiple Personality Disorder. One of my many personalities stomped out of here in anger, flew to Turkey, made its way to Iran, acted on an impulse to end the blessed life of the head of the Iranian Revolutionary Guard—and ended up back in the States in a psych ward after Rachel tracked me down."

"Is that all true?" Marie asked.

"Depends who you ask," Woodward said. "One of me would answer in the affirmative. The others might deny it. More questions?"

"Yes, I saw you writing in a notebook. Didn't mean to snoop, but it looked like Hindi, right?"

"You're correct, it looked like Hindi, but it wasn't. It's Sanskrit."

"Whoa! I'm impressed," Marie said. "No one writes in Sanskrit today. I mean almost no one. From some sacred writing? An ancient poem?"

"No, it's the lyrics from a Madonna recording called

Cyber-Raga. You'll find it on the album *Music* released nearly twenty years ago. It begins '*Ohm sri guru bjor namaha,*' which in English means 'May all be well with mankind.'"

"Now you're kidding me, Dr. Woodward. I have that album, love it, listened to it over and over. No such title as *Cyber-Raga.*"

"Oh no? Why don't you check the Japanese and Australian releases? Then we'll know who's kidding—and who's reaching conclusions before researching all the possibilities."

◆◆◆

"Coffee, Scott?" Rachel asked. "My treat, if you join me in the cafeteria." *He still looks as forlorn as he did in Belfast.*

"Where would we be without a much-deserved caffeine fix?" he replied.

Within a few minutes, they were seated in a far corner of the cafeteria, abuzz with secrets and personal indiscretions.

"I've barely slept since I reviewed the recent intercepts," Rachel said. "You'll see what I mean when you read the files. They—whoever *they* may be—have the capability to reduce the power plant to rubble. Could happen as we sit here, or never. The stakes increased overnight, as the chatter peaked. Appears to originate from you-know-where, but our techies aren't certain."

"Certain? That's a high bar."

"Yes, I know, but what if we fail? It's all on me."

"Rachel, look . . . " He paused, leaned forward, elbows on the table. "You're not alone."

"Thanks, but what if—"

"What if we fail? As Poirot tells a client in Agatha Christie's story *The Nemean Lion,* 'There is no question of failure.' In the unlikely event the power plant is compromised before we can stop it, we'll have learned enough to prevent the destruction of other, much larger facilities."

"Isn't that the coach speaking after his team loses the Super Bowl?"

"Touché. However, they're targeting a relatively small facility. Probably to send a signal, to broadcast their capabilities, or to prepare for larger prey. Maybe to increase their leverage in some future negotiations. Whatever happens, there'll be no lasting damage at Calvert Cliffs."

Rachel wanted to believe him. She could not. She tightened her grip on the coffee cup.

"Don't put all this on your shoulders. You're not alone. You have wisdom, genius, and three bright young experts to share the burden. Collectively, we can beat the pants off any rogue cyberenemy. Your role as a leader—assigning, assessing, and aggregating."

Rachel shook her head, stood, and walked to the coffee station for a refill.

As she returned and sat down, Scott continued. "Start fresh every morning with a brief meeting. Ask team members to share what they've learned in the past twenty-four hours. You'll see a pattern. Not the first day, or the second, or third. But one day your Eureka moment will arrive."

"You promise?"

"Yes, I'm counting on your intuition. You'll see it before others, before me, before Woody. That's the time your baby steps will morph into giant steps."

Rachel repressed a smile, thanked Scott with her eyes, sipped her coffee. It was lukewarm. Neither spoke. The din of the cafeteria was white noise for processing Scott's pep talk. After several minutes, she stood and straightened her shoulders. "Let's go, Mr. Scott. We have work to do."

♦♦♦

The three new team members began an impromptu meeting with Woodward. "You know the rules here?" he asked. Three heads shook in unison. "My advice—forget them. If we're constrained by some fucking bureaucratic rules, we'll all be sterilized by radiation from the melting core of a nuclear power plant."

Sam took a deep breath. The two women showed no reaction.

"No guts, no glory, as they say. McNamara used to brag about his whiz kids, the overbearing, rule-obsessed brats who brought us Vietnam. You musta' learned that old cliché to think outside the box. Forget it! We don't even know what the box is, where it is, what's in it. We got data, enough to drown us, but *mes enfants*, we don't know shit about the cyberterrorists who intend to bring us to our knees."

The three looked at each other. Marie nodded. The other two followed her lead.

Testing? They fear I'm testing. Not sure how to respond. Li's the shrewd one, laying back, waiting for the others. Not sure she's in the presence of an alleged genius or one of his repressed personalities. Perhaps the trickster?

"One more thing," Woody said. "They pay us here to make mistakes. Don't censor your instincts. After each mistake, a course correction follows. Before you can say 'Jack Ryan,' the enemy will be pissing his pants. No one else will know what you've accomplished. No public acclaim, no ticker tape parades. Maybe a secret medal, a bonus of a thousand bucks, nothing tangible except the pride you'll take in saving our democracy. Now get off your asses and get to work."

♦♦♦

6:55 AM, Tuesday. *Game time!* Rachel stood in front of an interactive whiteboard displaying a satellite photo of the Chesapeake Bay. She took a deep breath, rehearsing how she would begin. The three newbies had already been seated when she arrived. Scott came in punctually at seven. She waited a few minutes for Woody, then began without him. She made an effort to look alert. Camouflage after another sleepless night.

"Good morning," she said, with just enough brio to display confidence. "We'll begin every day like this, fifteen minutes to share what we've learned. And where we're heading. I expect you'll be attentive to a few key phrases: infrastructure penetration, industrial control systems, disaster alert, electrical grid, and of course, Calvert Cliffs." She pointed to its location on the satellite image.

Woody arrived, apologized for being late, sat next to Li Min.

"Tomorrow," Rachel said, "I expect to hear from each of you. I want your report brief and incisive." After a pause, she said, "Trenchant, yes, that's the word I was looking for. Any questions?"

No one spoke. She didn't move. Finally, Sam Adams broke the silence. "Ms. Sullivan, what if we don't have anything to report? I mean, if we haven't learned anything of interest?"

He's asking for a pass, afraid he'll fail.

"Good question," she said. "That can happen in the middle of an investigation. When you have nothing to report, say so, far better than wasting our time."

"Thank you," he said.

"We're all new at this, working as a team. So please call me Rachel."

Sam nodded, his serious face breaking into a smile.

"If that's all, let's get back to work."

Scott stood, caught her attention, and mouthed the words, "Well done."

She smiled. He was not known for flattery.

♦ ♦ ♦

His brow furrowed, Scott remained seated. *She's good, but I wonder if Hoople's asking too much?*

The team dispersed. Scott walked down the corridor connecting their offices. The junior members sat in separate cubicles in front of a trio of flat screens making notes with pencil and paper, an anomaly in a digital age. They didn't speak, sat motionless. Scott understood their anxiety, searching for something to report the next morning, something to warrant their membership on the team that would save Western civilization.

Scott reached his office, closed the door, and sat in his government-issue ergonomic chair. Rachel has the skills and the temperament to lead the team. Hoople made the right choice. *I lost my edge, driven by doubts, fixated on a woman I love.*

He reviewed a summary of recent intercepts, looking for new patterns, for disruptions, for novelty. With the agency's powerful search engine, he looked for references to the Chesapeake Bay. Bingo. He found it, detected by colleagues at Menwith Hill near the English spa town of Harrogate. Scores of recent satellite images with several locations enlarged for clarity, Calvert Cliffs among them. High-definition imagery of the plant. Also, the mothballed Russia *dacha* on the northern shore closed by the Obama administration. Neither a surprise.

Why was the tony eastern shore resort town of St. Michaels highlighted? A question to pursue. The most curious find, however, was the magnified image of a cove south of St. Michaels. Nothing except some wetland. No pier, no roads, no reason why anyone should care. But, someone did.

Scott had visited Menwith Hill a few years ago to see one of the agency's most sophisticated collection operations. What happened inside hidden to the world, but neighbors could see twenty-eight enormous white domes. They housed antennas to eavesdrop on the world, to collect digital signals, voices, pictures. The images could contain a critical clue. *What did the pictures of the cove reveal?*

His mind wandered, now picturing Fredrica. Her silence was distracting. He returned to the imagery of the bay.

"Top of the mornin' to ye, Scott," Woody said, cracking the door. "Mind if I come in and chat a bit?"

"Not at all, sit down."

"These young recruits are going to leave us in their dust. They'll have found the origin of the threat by the time we meet tomorrow. Sam may be the exception. He's an expert on nanotechnology but worries his skill set has no relation to cyberterrorism. He told me he's afraid the two young women will leave him babbling about electron tunneling and Bucky balls while they isolate the source and nature of the threat."

"It'll take a while," Scott said, "until they work as a team. May require a little mentoring from you and me."

"From you and Rachel, yes, but I'm off in a different direction. Don't be alarmed, I'm still a team player. However, we shouldn't overlook the possibility the threat is kinetic. Breaking in with digital tools is the presumed threat. The Russians or whoever expect that's where we'll look. So, let's say they leave a few clues to confirm that assumption while they attack the old-fashioned way: missiles and bombs."

Scott leaned back in his chair, eyes closed, hands behind his head. Woody waited.

"Uh-huh, I'm with you. You've been working the case several days before I returned. Any clues?"

"Yeah, but not from our data collection. From a fishing trawler or any old junk on the bay, you can have a close-up view of the power plant with its two nuclear reactors. I can confirm it's clearly visible from a broken-down old boat guided by the unsteady hand of Captain Mulligan."

"Mulligan? That obnoxious guy from that Irish pub? He's the last person I'd trust to navigate the Chesapeake."

"That night in the Irish hoosegow musta' turned you bitter, talking that way about my best drinking buddy."

"You bet," Scott said.

"Well, yes," Woody replied. "He wouldn't be your first choice for a relaxing day on the Bay. Nor mine in the future. We were adrift for hours after the engine conked out. Finally made it ashore by running into some godforsaken island on the eastern side of the Bay. Learned later we'd run out of gas."

"So, what else did you learn?" Scott asked. "Beyond validating my judgment of your buddy."

"Never claimed he was a sailor," Woody said, "but even if it was a miserable day, I saw something worth the misery. Imagine a sport-fishing boat fifty feet long, big enough for a crew and thirty passengers trying to hook a prize-winning bass."

"Okay," Scott said, "I see it now: balmy day, slight breeze, choppy waters, captain accelerating to fifteen knots, fish avoiding the bait, paying customers complaining. Is that about right?"

Woody shook his head, squinted his eyes, and said, "You just don't get it. Of course, you can drive down to Chesapeake Beach, pay seventy bucks to Captain Clyde or somebody, and join two dozen amateurs intent on catching something bigger than a sardine. By the time you'd returned to *terra firma*, you'd remember it as the seasick follies."

"You're not tempting me," Scott said with a grin.

"Patience, my friend, there's another scenario. Let's say you avoid Chesapeake Beach and other popular marinas. Instead, you head to the village of Crisfield, south of St. Michaels, drive past Somers Cove Marina, and look for Smitty's Angling Paradise."

"Still not tempted."

"There you'll meet an old guy calls himself Popeye, 'cause he has a corncob pipe permanently affixed to the corner of his mouth. He owns a forty-two-foot boat that's seen better days. You supply the gas, show him your Maryland Boater Card, and give him two hundred dollars cash. Voilà, it's yours for the day."

"And . . . "

"As I was explaining, you're planning a *ruse de guerre* by piloting to an abandoned pier several miles south of Crisfield where comrade Ivan is waiting with a SMAW, a shoulder-launched multipurpose assault weapon. With a range of five hundred meters, its design as a bunker buster allows it to do serious damage to a nuclear power plant."

"Yes, but not enough to destroy it," Scott said.

"True, but enough to cause a panic. Enough to evacuate the area. Enough to bring every journalist on the East Coast to Calvert Cliffs. Enough for the brass at Homeland Security to piss their collective pants.

"Cyberterrorism? Hell, no! While we're reading intercepts and studying images, Ivan's smuggling in a rocket launcher and hijacking a boat from Popeye the nearly-blind sailor man."

"Woody, maybe you really are a genius." *At least on your good days.*

"Or a fucking nut, but neither invalidates this scenario.

The question now is what should we do? Prevent it? Or, prepare congressional testimony explaining why we had our noses buried in cybercrap?"

Scott stood, walked to a NOAA chart of the Chesapeake on the far wall of his office, and pointed to Crisfield. "So, our terrorist of unknown nationality heads south from here, picks up his companion with the rocket launcher, and heads northwest across the bay to Calvert Cliffs. Right?"

"Exactly," Woody said.

"That invites two questions. Why hire the boat from Smitty's? And who—"

Woody interrupted and said, "Because the deranged old coot's the only person who would trust his boat to a stranger. He's so addled he won't remember who hired it."

"Okay," Scott said, rubbing his chin, "who in the agency would find this credible? We listen, look, and provide information. Without data, we have nothing except your... your story, your fantasy. Furthermore, it's not ours to act on. Find the evidence, and then we turn it over to Homeland Security for the Coast Guard to manage."

Woody nodded, walked toward the door, paused, and said, "Thanks for hearing me out. Let's wait and see what the three newbies find. In the meantime, how about joining me this weekend for a little fishing trip? I hear the rockfish are running in the waters off Crisfield."

♦♦♦

Early the next morning, drenched in sweat Rachel woke to a pulsating light. She stumbled to the bathroom, shed her sleepshirt, stepped in the shower, and vigorously scrubbed her body. *Radiation poisoning!*

As hot water replaced the jarring cold, she realized she had awakened from a nightmare. The flash was from the high-intensity LED lights on her alarm. And the heat was nothing more than a muggy summer with the AC turned off. She remained under the shower to clear her head, to begin the metamorphosis from a scared kid to a professional analyst.

She turned off the water and picked up her wet sleepshirt, white with the blue star of the Dallas Cowboys. She hated it. Must have worn it out of self-pity. A present from her New York boyfriend who knew she passionately followed the Redskins. He called it a joke. She wasn't amused, now recognized he was being passive-aggressive. *I must have sensed it before, or I wouldn't have fallen into bed with an Italian chef.*

She had worked alone after the morning meeting, stayed till near midnight. Scott had stopped by her office to offer support. Silence from the others including Hoople. For a dark moment she wondered why he had assigned three junior analysts to her team. Credentialed but inexperienced. *Would they turn out to be the Curly, Moe, and Larry of the NSA?* A test of her leadership?

She didn't know who to trust. Even herself, after that frantic moment in the shower when she felt the sting of radioactive rain. *Singin' in the rain, just singin' in the rain.*

Was she a candidate for Woody's cloud cuckoo land? She walked slowly to her closet and looked at her choices. Time to get dressed and return to work.

She gazed at the sunrise through her bedroom window. "Begin your day, Rachel. Time to begin your day."

Chapter 13. True Confessions

"I'm a dead man if I don't get off this wretched boat," Scott whimpered. *Isn't the bay usually calm? Feels like a roaring sea.*

"Next time try Dramamine, and you won't lose your breakfast," Woody said.

"Next time? Not a chance. Not ever. If I had half a brain, I'd have returned to Berkeley Springs for the weekend. Kierkegaard misses me, and Sean needs me."

A cry of help from the other side of the boat got their attention. The captain rushed to the man whose line was rapidly unwinding, threatening to pull both the rod and the angler overboard.

"Feels like a fucking shark," the guy exclaimed.

Scott leaned over the boat to complete the evacuation of his stomach. *Not only breakfast I've lost. Maybe my mind as well. Joining Woody in this hare-brained trip shows I've lost it big time.*

Woody walked toward the excitement, toward the giant shark. The captain was assisting, letting out more line, then gradually reeling it in. Over and over, he repeated the motions. The angler, who had transferred the rod to the captain, became less agitated.

Others crowded around to watch. Thirty-five minutes later, the captain landed a largemouth bass, eight pounds and six ounces.

"A noble creature," he said, "most fight I've seen this month. Stand over here, bud, while we get a picture of you and your catch, a freshwater fish with the strength of a hundred-pound shark."

The fisherman beamed with pride, thanked the captain for his assistance. Others applauded before returning to their lines, hoping to best his trophy. Scott was seated, head in his hands, quietly cursing the boat for its unyielding motion. Named *Easy Living*, Scott thought it should've been called the *Seasick Schooner*.

◆ ◆ ◆

"Lunch? Are you kidding?" Scott said two hours later. "Not in a thousand years. At least not for another day. However, in lieu of your generous offer, you can remind me again why we're here. I was halfway convinced when I agreed to join you on this fifty-foot tourist boat. Now I can't recall why."

"Not that it matters, but for the record it's forty-eight feet, bow to stern," Woody said. "We're here to do a little reconnaissance, to validate my theory that Calvert Cliffs could be easily attacked by a missile fired from a fishing boat."

"Yeah, but why would Russia or Iran or whoever risk being caught when the same damage could be done by a few bits and bytes sent over the Internet?"

"Because, my dear Mr. Scott, we would not expect it."

"Call me skeptical, but you *do* have Sun Tzu on your side."

"Beat me to it," Woody said. "We can't go wrong if we follow his advice: 'All warfare is based on deception.'"

"While we're waiting for some naïve fish to take the bait," Scott replied, "we could challenge each other with quotes from *The Art of War*. This advice apparently doesn't apply to outsmarting Chesapeake Bay fish, but offers valuable guidance to cyberwarriors: 'Let your plans be dark and impenetrable as night, and when you move, fall like a thunderbolt.'"

♦♦♦

Marie was the first to speak. Someone had to interrupt this dispiriting wake. "I feel like a feral child who's escaped to a new land. They're all nice, but . . . " She looked down, now hesitant to share her thoughts with Li and Sam. She saw them as competitors in a race to the finish.

She finished a slice of pepperoni pizza. The other two, sitting with her in the NSA cafeteria, did not respond. A quiet Saturday, few others were at work.

Silence, except the distant voice of a newscaster on CNN reporting a cyberpenetration of the Department of Homeland Security. A security expert from Brookings said the breach could set the department back years.

Sam shrugged. "That confirms it. I'm a fish out of water, a man who knows practically everything about nanotechnology and nothing about cybersecurity. If the Homeland Security network is vulnerable, what isn't? And if a nuclear power plant along the Chesapeake is vulnerable after years of operation and security lockdowns, what can we do to change it?"

"Sam, we're just getting started," Marie said, "and we're working with three pros. You saw the summary of the intercepts yesterday. It's clear someone has Calvert Cliffs in their crosshairs."

"Yeah—and you think we can stop it?"

"I'm as frightened as you, but we must . . . I'm sure we can prevent an attack."

"Uh-huh, after a week on the team, you're sure?" Sam

snorted. "Sorry, I don't mean to be sarcastic. Glad you're confident. I don't have a clue. My background's all theory with only a tenuous connection to the real world. You could tell me your toaster was compromised, and I'd believe it."

Li unexpectedly squeezed his arm. "We're a team, Sam, with a coach and a quarterback that will take us to victory. Like you, I don't know how my AI knowledge will help, but there's a reason we were recruited."

"I like your analogy," Marie said. "Scott's the coach and Rachel the quarterback. What does that make Woody?"

"Forgive my French," Sam said, "but yesterday I overheard two guys describe him as a fucking nut case."

"Perhaps a better description," Li said quietly, "would be the Leonardo Da Vinci of our team—artist, engineer, and inventor. I see him as the unorthodox team captain who calls a timeout to propose a winning play that's never been tried."

◆◆◆

Rachel paced in her apartment, alone. Not a peep from New York. Another woman? Closer, younger, perfect hearing?

He had proposed a boating trip from Annapolis but hadn't followed up. She could text him, but would not. Did not want to appear anxious. Had he been disappointed by her absence? If he lacked patience, she hadn't seen it before. A perfect ten? Maybe not.

How had a handsome man of such charm escaped marriage? Why was he attracted to her? For two decades, men had turned away when they learned she was deaf. Not him. He embraced it, understood her other senses were enhanced. Told her she had a rare intuition. Scott had often said the same. She had known it since childhood. Always been able to see below the surface, to recognize a liar, to spot a phony. Had her intuition failed her?

Monday morning would be her first test of leadership. She would ask each of the newbies what they had learned. Knowing they were being tested, they would respond by thoughtfully interpreting hard data or bullshitting to divert attention from their failure. If Scott had anything to offer, it would be succinct. Woody would scribble in his notepad, probably remain silent unless he felt compelled to correct something offered in ignorance.

She checked her phone again, a near-compulsion since her return to the States. And this time not in vain. A new message, not from New York but from Rome. Chef Roberto had written to say he missed her. "My bed," he wrote, "is lonely." Translation imperfect, but meaning clear. Rachel's spirits momentarily lifted. *La Dolce Vita!*

She would return to Rome one day, but not now. She would forget her New York lover, but not now. Memories would linger. Duty now, pleasure later.

Rachel responded to Roberto.

<So good to receive your message. What a welcome reminder of Rome. I remember more than the aroma of your freshly-brewed coffee.>

She recalled his endearing smile when she stood in the doorway of his kitchen wearing nothing but her favorite gold necklace. She walked to her bedroom, opened the top drawer of her dresser, and removed the necklace from a jewelry box. Standing in front of a full-length mirror, she put on the necklace. She unbuttoned her blouse, stepped out of her jeans. Still trim and sexy, she recalled Roberto's pleasure in admiring her naked body.

♦♦♦

Memories of Roberto had receded by the time she stood in front of her team early Monday morning. Scott and

Woody were laughing, perhaps sharing a joke. The three newbies were as serious as mourners at a funeral. Rachel could be all business, but she needed to put her team at ease.

"Marie, you're first. Do I recall you were born in Uzbekistan?"

"Yes, Ms. Sullivan."

"Rachel, if you don't mind."

"No ma'am, I don't mind. I mean, Rachel. Got it. Sorry."

"Marie, what can you tell us about Uzbek cuisine?"

"Sorry, only what I learned from my mother. I came to the States when I was six months old. Mama made a dish from rice, carrots, onions, and lamb called *palov*."

"I heard you were working here all weekend," Rachel said, "but you must have taken time to eat. Anywhere close by you could order a big dish of *palov*?"

"Oh, no, I hope not," Marie said with a nervous laugh. "I'm more of a Big Mac gal."

That broke the tension. Marie was smiling, Sam abandoned his military posture, and Li slightly dropped her shoulders. Scott nodded in appreciation of Rachel's introduction. Woody, sketching in his notebook, in a world of his own.

"Marie, what do you have to share?" Rachel asked. "What have you learned since we met on Friday?"

"As we all know, the power plant controls are not connected to the Internet, so there's no way a terrorist could remotely introduce malware."

Woody looked up and rolled his eyes.

"On the other hand," Marie continued, "the alert system is wide open, password protected from the general public but easy enough to crack. Took me less than an hour to get in, to take control of public notifications."

"I like the way you think," Rachel said. "And if the bad guys are as clever as you and break in from, say, Moscow, what damage could they do?"

"By triggering the alarm, fifty thousand people within the Emergency Evacuation Zone will be scrambling to safety—remaining in place, moving to a shelter, or driving as far away as they can. A few years ago, a false alarm in Hawaii warning of an impending missile attack was quickly corrected. But who at the power plant would be able to detect a malicious intrusion in time to avoid a mass panic?"

Woody looked up from his sketching and said, "Brava," a high compliment coming from him.

"I'm not a dietician," Rachel said, "but you better stick to those Big Macs if they fuel that kind of analysis."

Sam looked frozen, perhaps expecting he'd be next. Rachel, instead, pointed to Li. She stood, easier to be better seen and heard.

"I don't know anything," she began, standing as tall as her four-foot-eleven would allow. She paused. No one blinked. "However, I have several questions for my continuing investigation. Are the Russian-language intercepts about Calvert Cliffs really from Russia? If they were, wouldn't they be more difficult to detect? And if they are, is an attack planned or is it a diversion, the cyber equivalent of England's World War I Q-boats?"

Scott's body language gave him away. He looked impressed.

"Q-boats? Rachel said, "I'm clueless. Tell us more."

"I don't know that much, except they were designed to lure the German U-boats to the surface. I read about them in *Islands in the Stream.* Hemingway's protagonist commanded a Q-boat off the waters of Cuba. And Malcolm Lowry's tortured British consul in *Under the Volcano* had also been an officer on a Q-boat. Court-martialed, but eventually decorated, by the way."

"Fascinating," Rachel said, "and good questions. I look forward to your answers. Thanks for the history lesson. I had no idea the Q-boats played such a role in the Allied victory."

"I should have said that the Q-boats weren't actually very successful, except in fiction."

"Sam, I see you're chomping at the bit," Rachel said, attempting to engage him.

"Ms. Sullivan, sorry, I mean Rachel . . . " He paused and forced a smile. "I'm not a horse, but if I were, I'd drop that bit and run for the hills. We'd be finished in a Nano-second if I shared everything I learned about preventing an attack on Calvert Cliffs."

Rachel nodded. Best to end the meeting on a high note. Scott's smile confirmed her decision. "Time to get back to work," she said.

As others left the conference room, Woody didn't move. Pen in hand, he stared at his notebook, at the sketch he drew during the meeting.

♦♦♦

"Good morning," Rachel said, "I see you all made it here safely." She had scrambled in the dark to get ready for work.

NSA Headquarters was brightly lighted when employees arrived for work the following morning. Many had departed homes overheated and pitch dark. A freakish summer storm had left the area without electricity. A tornado had reportedly touched down at the nearby University of Maryland campus. Trees had fallen on power lines, homes, and vehicles. A transformer had been struck by lightning. Yet all was well in the NSA's self-contained cocoon.

"Power should be back in a few hours," Rachel continued. "A short preview if the Northeast goes dark for days or weeks."

"If it's still out tomorrow," Scott said, "I'm heading back to West Virginia where the electrical system has remained intact, despite even higher winds in the mountains. Says something for good engineering, perhaps for redundancy."

"You have the floor. Let's hear what you and Woody have been up to."

Scott walked to the screen and called up an image of a fishing trawler. "Woody's idea," he said. "While we're looking for cyberterrorists, they could be planning a conventional, old-fashioned attack. Imagine a few missiles shot from this innocent craft at the two Calvert Cliffs reactors. As there's no air defense, both could be knocked out—or severely damaged. The overnight crew, although trained, wouldn't know how to respond."

Scott changed the screen image. Woody stepped up and pointed, "Look at this little killer—a suicide drone. We've known for months it's been under development. Now the whole world knows. The Kalashnikov Group put it on display at a defense exhibition in Abu Dhabi. Named the KUB-UAV, it's four-feet wide, can carry six pounds of explosives. Not enough to penetrate a nuclear reactor, but certainly enough to raise hell.

"Think of it as a poor man's cruise missile, a device that any fledgling terrorist can buy on the open market. It's the aerial counterpart to the AK-47, developed decades ago by the same group. Did I mention, the Russian government owns a controlling stake in the Kalashnikov Group?"

"And?" Scott said, gesturing toward Woody.

"If a fishing boat can strike from a hundred yards, a few of these babies can do it even more efficiently. Let me correct that. Not a few, but a whole fucking swarm, controlled from who knows where."

"So," Scott said, continuing their story, "a rogue state or a couple of terrorists could control these drones, create havoc practically anywhere. And without a digital signature, we wouldn't have a clue. Gatwick was closed down for three days because of a far less lethal drone. We need more sensitive security if the only way to detect them now is by a visual sighting."

"And that," Woody said, with arms extended, "is a perfect segue to our man Sam Adams. Sam, take it away."

Rachel smiled, appreciating Woody's theatrical enthusiasm. He'd promised to help build Sam's confidence.

"I have two images to present," Sam said. "The first is an artist's rendering of the Calvert Cliffs nuclear power plant. Look at the top of the screen, and you'll see a half-dozen drones hovering, let's say a hundred meters above. And close to the shore is a motorboat aimlessly bobbing up and down. Let's call the two occupants Woody and Mulligan."

"Very funny, Mr. Adams," Woody said. "Just wait till *you* run out of gas."

Sam showed the second image and asked who could spot the difference.

Marie immediately replied, "No drones."

"Close, but not quite. The correct answer—no *visible* drones."

"Uh-huh," but why—"

"They're still there," Sam said. "Invisible. You can't see them because of cloaking. Physical objects, these drones for example, can be cloaked through a type of nanotechnology known as metamaterials. You might think of it as digital camouflage."

"They can do that now?" Marie asked. "Invisible drones?"

"Not exactly. The science isn't that far advanced. Works in the lab but not ready for prime time. But, just wait. My dissertation advisor used to quote the title of a French film, *Vous n'avez encore rien vu*, or *You Ain't Seen Nothin' Yet*."

Rachel recognized this wasn't a solution to today's problem, but it offered Sam a voice and the confidence he could productively join the team. "Great, thank you all," she said. "Let's get back to work."

◆◆◆

"Had your morning fix yet?" Rachel asked Scott as they left the conference room after concluding Wednesday's morning meeting. *I shouldn't pester him, but . . .*

"On my way," he said. "Come along, my treat."

They took the elevator to the first floor, walked in silence to the cafeteria. She ordered a cappuccino, he a double espresso. They sat on the side with a view of the open space east of the building. The rain had stopped, although dark clouds threatened an encore.

"Hats off to you, Rachel. You're a natural. Hoople saw what I've observed for years. Our adversary, the Russians or whoever, has no idea what they're up against."

"Thanks, much appreciated. I'm feeling good about work. It's my personal life that's getting in the way." *How much should I tell him? Should I keep this professional?*

"If I hadn't left the seminary after one year," Scott said, "I could hear your confession. As it is, the best I can offer is years of experience and occasional heartbreak."

Rachel sipped her cappuccino. She'd worked up the

courage to seek his advice. No one else she could trust as much.

"I'm not sure where to begin, but . . . "

"Let me guess," Scott said. "It involves your mysterious New York options trader, the man with the million-dollar smile and matching bank account. He's proposed and wants you to join him at his estate on the Riviera."

"Not exactly . . . "

"Hate to give up your suburban condo and a grueling sixteen-hour day?"

"If it were only so simple," she said, shaking her head. "He's a special guy, but I'm torn. And, uh, I fear I'm losing him. And . . . "

Scott nodded, leaned toward her.

"Maybe, you see, maybe I don't deserve him."

"I'm an expert in losing women I've loved—or still love," Scott said, biting his lip. "Not sure my advice would help."

"Fredrica? Your obsession, right? Guess I'm not alone."

"Tell me," Scott said. "Are you spending sleepless nights hoping to lure him back?"

"Yes and no. He's acting peculiar. I haven't seen him recently, but we're planning to meet soon in Annapolis. And, to put all my cards on the table, I haven't forgotten a certain Italian chef. What shall I say? He makes a scrumptious omelet."

"Got it. Say no more. You're conflicted."

"Yeah, that's for sure."

"Not sure this will help, but years ago I memorized these words from H.L. Mencken: 'To be in love is merely to be in a state of perpetual anesthesia—to mistake an ordinary young man for a Greek god.'"

◆◆◆

Rachel awoke the next morning, rested and ready to run. She popped in Scott's office when she arrived at work and thanked him for listening. "Slept soundly last night," she said.

"Good for you. Wish I could say the same."

"Dr. Hoople's joining us at our morning roundup, so it'll be a little different. He attended an inter-agency meeting yesterday that'll affect our planning. Maybe still another reason to give up sleeping."

Hoople arrived promptly at seven. "Good morning," he said, addressing the three young analysts. "Li, Sam, Marie—keeping busy? Is Rachel treating you right? Been on the team nearly two weeks, so hope you've figured out how to keep the bad guys at bay."

After a long silence, Marie spoke. "Everyone's great, sir, but with all due respect, we're just getting started."

"Of course," Hoople said, "just kidding, or should I say half-kidding. I met yesterday with the inter-agency committee on cyber terrorism. Defense, Homeland Security, Energy, CIA, and a host of others." He paused, his face revealing his concern. "The White House coordinator wants an action plan. They've all seen our daily summaries. And understand we don't know where the threat's coming from, that we're not certain it's directed at Calvert Cliffs.

"Nonetheless, a strident young man from the NSC spoke up and said the president wants an action plan. In his words, 'We're not some pussy White House like George Bush's that ignored the 9/11 warnings.' I said we would ramp up our analysis, return in a week with some options.

"The know-it-all guy looked at me and said he expected more than academic options. 'Let's make their shock-and-awe campaign look like child's play,' he said. After the meeting, I checked his credentials: campaign coordinator and video-gamer."

"Why wait a week, boss?" Woody volunteered. "Let's give 'em an action plan tomorrow. Scott and I found a small island in the Chesapeake, perfect place for a pyrotechnics display. We'll hire Zambelli Fireworks, tip off the press, and give these fuckers a show they'll never forget. Maybe we should go all out, sell seats, bring in the Beach Boys, the whole works."

"Dating yourself a little," Hoople said. "Doubt if the kids in the White House ever heard of the Beach Boys. How about Lady Gaga? In case Zambelli's tied up and Lady Gaga has other plans, we need to answer three questions: Who, where, and why? Each answer supported by compelling evidence. Give me that, and then we'll plan. And our action recommendation may be as simple as 'keep our powder dry.'"

◆◆◆

Scott returned to his office, checked his personal email. A message from Sean said Kierkegaard seemed to be homesick, but otherwise all was well. A cry for help? He would return to Berkeley Springs on the weekend. There was nothing from Fredrica. No surprise. He continued to hope.

Scott studied reports from agency colleagues, looked at raw data and fresh intercepts. If there was something new, he couldn't see it. No unique patterns to provide new insights. He skipped lunch, began to look elsewhere. The website of the Department of Energy assured the public all was well. Smiling officials dominated the site.

He found a joint report from the FBI and DHS confirming ongoing Russian cyberattacks on the energy sector.

Scores of inspector general findings revealed numerous examples of fraud, bribery, and mismanagement—but nothing concerning malicious attacks by nation states. Nothing besides the half-million attempted cyberintrusions into the U.S. electrical grid. Scott imagined the consequences if one of the half-million should succeed.

An inspector general report on a whistleblower at a nuclear power plant on the shores of Lake Ontario caught his attention. Management had allegedly been complacent about periodic shutdowns of the reactor. Although the scope of the investigation was not discussed in the report, management was held blameless. Scott read the original complaint, reread the IG's response. The reasons for the unplanned shutdowns remained a mystery. He learned the whistleblower was a nuclear engineer with impeccable credentials.

♦♦♦

Within minutes, Scott was in Rachel's office. "I've been thinking about a little trip to the shores of Lake Ontario," he said. "The team won't miss me for a few days."

"A little break?" she asked with a mischievous smile.

"Yeah, following a hunch. Might be a dead end, but there's a mystery begging for resolution. A nuclear power plant on the shores of Lake Ontario, smaller but otherwise like Calvert Cliffs. The difference? Several unplanned shutdowns."

"You don't need my permission," Rachel said, "although I'm curious. Why're you suspicious?"

"A senior nuclear engineer reported erratic behavior, repeated failures of the reactor. However, management convinced the inspector general nothing was amiss."

"You're not convinced?"

"Nor was the engineer. A few weeks later, he was killed in a freak road accident."

Chapter 14. Two Minutes to Midnight

Scott's request to meet with the director of the Lake Ontario power plant had been denied. *A cover up? Nah, likely too busy to meet with the NSA.* It took one call to the Nuclear Regulatory Commission before the director was overruled. He reluctantly agreed to a Monday morning meeting.

Scott first headed to West Virginia after work on Friday, eager to visit Sean, to assure Kierkegaard he hadn't been orphaned, and to lift a glass with Spencer Cobb. *A chance to get my head together. Stop feeling sorry for myself.*

First stop: the rectory. Kierkegaard acted predictably frisky, barking and spinning in circles to welcome home his master. Sean, too, seemed surprisingly upbeat, pumping Scott's hand and embracing him like a brother. "So good to see you. And to see you've lost the hangdog look from your last visit."

"And you, a new man," Scott said, "or at least a man exuding as much energy as my little four-legged friend. Something good has come your way."

"An anonymous contribution of ten thousand dollars, enough to stave off our debtors and keep the parish from bankruptcy."

"Ahh," Scott said, with a slight upturn of his lips, "you've been praying, and the good Lord has interceded with one of your flock to forgive your debts."

"And if I knew who bailed us out, I'd offer a special blessing for him or her every Sunday for the rest of the year. But I don't have a clue. Unless—unless it was you."

"Afraid not. Guess I've been too self-absorbed to think of it."

Sean motioned Scott to the sofa where Kierkegaard sat waiting. Scott sat.

Sean lowered himself to the easy chair opposite. "Any news from Austria?"

"*Nein*. She's remained incommunicado. Left her home in St. Wolfgang, allegedly to visit grandchildren in Munich, but still lost to me."

"Don't tell me you haven't used your technical skills to track her down."

"Did my best, but no luck. However, I'm beginning to get over my loss, to restore my sanity."

Sean stood up and walked toward the kitchen. Kierkegaard followed. Returning a few minutes later with two small plates of sweets, Sean said, "This is from the dear Muslim lady we sponsored last year. Once a month she does her best to keep me fat. Last time I saw you I'd lost a few pounds, but I'm on my way back up, courtesy of the anonymous ten grand and Nafisa's cooking."

"Pleased you're no longer shrinking. A village priest has more credibility with a little extra girth. I've always been suspicious of a skinny guy in a robe. Maybe goes back to Pharaoh's dream in Genesis where the seven ugly and gaunt cows came up from the Nile and devoured the seven sleek and fat cows."

"Not so sure I like the metaphor," Sean said, returning to his chair. "Anyway, let's get back to the search for your missing fräulein. You know, locating her might lead to even more anguish."

"What?" Scott said, shaking his head. "I'm beginning to make peace with myself, but still hope we'll be reunited. Why would you suggest otherwise?"

"I'll tell you why. Motivated in part by your ancestral search in Ireland, I did a little investigation of my own. Sent a DNA sample to one of those labs that promise to reveal your heritage."

Scott nodded. "And . . . what?"

"If they'd had a mongrel category, I'd have been a perfect fit. I have great-great-grandparents from all over Europe, including Ireland, of course. Several generations back, they even found Jewish heritage from Eastern Europe. Pretty good for an ecumenical Catholic priest?"

"God works in mysterious ways.," Scott said, smiling. "You must have been pleased."

"Yes, at first. But after I signed up for their full service, they identified other DNA providers who are related. Unnamed second cousins and so on."

"Uh-huh."

"And my daughter! You know the story, you and my confessor."

"Yes," Scott said, "I haven't forgotten a word." *Stunned when you told me you'd fathered a child when we were both in the seminary.*

"I barely knew the mother, who doesn't know me."

"But now she knows?" Scott asked. "Knows you're her father?"

"Probably not. Only if she had looked at her account since my DNA was analyzed."

"Are you going to wait? Or contact her before she

discovers you on the web?"

"I don't know. I want to call her, but don't want to cause any pain. That's why I said *your* success could lead to even more anguish. I'm afraid mine will."

◆◆◆

"Sorry I'm a little late," Cobb said as he reached Scott's table at The Country Inn. "Talking on the phone with the delightful Irish gal I met in Belfast. She wouldn't be here if you hadn't summoned me to Ireland." *And I wouldn't be here at this ungodly hour on a Saturday morning if I didn't need your assistance.*

"Summoned you? I don't recall it that way. Nonetheless, I'm in your debt for showing up and rescuing me from the clutches of an overzealous prosecutor who intended to lock me up for thirty years. I'd surely have ended up on a diet of bread and water. Irish soda bread, of course, but somewhat short of a balanced diet."

"I'd say we're even. Debt repaid with Bridgette Walsh. I mentioned last time I'd lured her away from the records office in Belfast. She's here now, working with me on a project that may change the face of Europe."

"She's here in Berkeley Springs?" Scott asked.

"No, at my former law office in Washington."

"Where you're still Of Counsel, as you continue to remind me."

"Bridgette's wise beyond her years, knows technology, British politics, and Irish history in addition to being a crackerjack researcher."

Cobb looked up to acknowledge the waitress standing by their table. She had not interrupted but appeared eager to take their order.

"I'll have whatever he's drinking," Cobb said, pointing to Scott's cup. "Has a distinctive aroma, almost like peppermint."

"Exactly right," she said. "The new chef said the old menu was tired. I'll get your coffee while you study his latest. Only place in town you'll find scrambled eggs with eggplant puree. I'm supposed to tell you it's 'eggcellent,' but frankly it tastes a little weird."

"Peppermint coffee," Cobb said. "What the hell, I'll give it a try. The brew they used to serve here tasted like they made it over a campfire in an old graniteware kettle. So vile I nearly had to wash it down with a jigger of whiskey."

As the waitress walked to the kitchen, Scott said, "You were telling me about Bridgette and your European project."

"I may need your help. I've been engaged by an Irish-American who lives the life of a British nobleman in the Virginia countryside. Horses, hounds, the works."

Scott picked up his cup and gingerly sipped the hot coffee. "How could I possibly help?"

"My client says the Brexit decision with the so-called Irish backstop will lead to violence again in Northern Ireland. He's a loyalist with close relatives in Ulster, but believes the rise of a Catholic middle class will lead to a united Ireland. He predicts the north will leave the UK."

"And your client wants to, ah, what? Stop it? Slow it down?"

"No, no. He sees an opportunity to increase his fortune. And that's where you come in."

"I'm listening," Scott said, tilting his head.

"It's all about smuggling and tariffs—livestock, butter, and whiskey. Five hundred kilometers between the two Irelands without checkpoints. Imagine a twenty-five percent tariff on Bushmills from Northern Ireland and none on Jameson from the Republic."

"Uh-huh."

"Or the opposite. Either way, the unprotected border invites the illicit movement of goods and money."

"And a return to violence among the losers," Scott said.

"Maybe, but not if . . . "

The waitress returned, fresh peppermint coffee for Cobb, a refill for Scott. "Ready to order?" she asked, in a tone suggesting it would be okay if they weren't.

"I'm an old-fashioned guy," Cobb said. "Bacon and eggs, sunny side up, toast with orange marmalade."

"Soft-boiled eggs and grits for me," Scott said. "And please tell the chef the coffee's just right—no, even better, it's terrific."

"That'll make his day."

"Then, you might say I'm passionate about coffee and would guess we're drinking freshly-ground Ethiopian arabica, infused with a few drops of pure peppermint oil."

She shrugged, smiled, picked up the menus, and walked away.

"Scott, before we get too distracted by the wonders of Ethiopian coffee beans, let me return to the Irish border. I *do* need your help. Even with Bridgette's technical expertise, she doesn't have the tools to trace the money. Just as you can guess the source of exotic coffees, I can guess your super-secret agency follows the movement of capital, including monies earned by smuggling."

"You know I can't share one iota of what my agency knows."

"I didn't mean to imply you'd share secrets. I meant to suggest you wrap up your government work and sign on with my client. With your skills, you could find information before it becomes public. Name your price, and he won't blink."

"Smuggling? Are you kidding? I'm a government snoop all the way."

"No!" Cobb said. "My client's a currency trader. Made a fortune by anticipating minute changes in the pound sterling. If he had the right information gleaned from—"

"Understood, but not for me. However, I could introduce you to a guy who knows his stuff and might be convinced to abandon his corporate sinecure if the price is right."

"Hot damn," Cobb said, his voice rising. "I borrowed the expression from an old guy who used to work at our firm. When he said it, we youngsters knew everything would be okay." *Gotta humor you to get you involved. My client doesn't need some random specialist. Those guys are a dime a dozen.*

Scott looked up as the waitress returned to their table.

"Gentlemen, looks like you're about finished. How about another hot cup of our freshly-brewed Peppermint Passion?"

"Hot damn," Scott said with a smile. "Perfect."

♦♦♦

Another day in his West Virginia home offered Scott time to prepare for his visit to the Lake Ontario power plant. He would not be welcome. His meeting would be unpleasant. Meanwhile, he enjoyed the silence of his home, interrupted occasionally by bees collecting nectar from garden flowers or Kierkegaard loudly protecting the homestead from menacing wildlife.

A text from Rachel interrupted his ruminations.

> **<Need your guidance. Alarm sounding. I'm urging patience. Others want action.>**
> **<You alone?>**
> **<Nearly. But Woody with me.>**
> **<Good enough for me. Trust your instincts.>**

Scott wished he were with her, but knew it best for her to make the decision. He trusted her judgment. With more experience in situations shrouded in ambiguity, she, too, would trust her judgment.

He sat on the front porch till dusk, Kierkegaard at his side. He reread the Inspector General's report on the Ontario whistle-blower, reviewed the press accounts of his accidental death, and looked at his still-active Facebook account. A loner, a perceived trouble-maker, and a published scholar.

Scott read his recent article, *Protecting Power Stations with Quantum-Encryption*, co-written with a scientist from the Oak Ridge National Laboratory. A paper only Woody would fully understand. Scott appreciated the theoretical solution, although brilliant, was not ready for commercial adoption. Tomorrow's innovation would be an annoyance to a plant manager responsible for stopping today's cyberattacks.

♦♦♦

Early the next morning Scott drove to BWI to catch a flight to the Greater Rochester International Airport. Waiting to board, he checked his email, looking for a message from Fredrica, now a daily habit. Nothing. He had considered asking one of the NSA techies to look for her account, to see if it was active, to confirm she was still alive. But, that would be an abuse of his authority. He would maintain his integrity.

He arrived in Rochester after a smooth flight and took a rental car to the Ontario power plant. Following a delay at the gate, confirmation of his identity, an approving beep from a magnetometer, and a wait for his escort—Scott found a seat in a conference room adjacent to the director's office. He glanced at last month's *Bulletin of the Atomic Scientists* showing the doomsday clock at two minutes to midnight. He read these ominous words: *It is now two minutes to midnight—the closest the*

Clock has ever been to Doomsday, and as close as it was in 1953, at the height of the Cold War.

The door opened, three men entered. The first introduced himself as Deputy Director Costello. Mid-fifties, overweight, gray polyester suit. From his scowl none too happy to see his visitor. He was accompanied by the chief operations officer and a young attorney.

Using his best West Virginia accent, Scott tried to sound non-threatening. "Good morning, thanks for—"

"The boss's home with a stomach flu or food poisoning," the Deputy Director said.

Scott nodded. *Food poisoning? Hmm. Anything to avoid a little chat.*

"He said you'd be here, asked me to sit in. Didn't have much notice, but when someone flies up here from Washington, I know something's up. So, I invited my colleagues to join me."

"Much appreciated."

"What can we do for you?" Costello asked. "We're all yours for the next thirty minutes before I head to town to meet with the Rotary Club. We try to keep them abreast of developments here. Some of our employees are members, including the boss. We're a big part of the local economy. Guess you know that. What was I saying? Yes, asking what can we do for you, Mr. ahh . . . "

"Scott, Thomas Sebastian Scott. I'm a consultant on cybersecurity with the NSA, the National Security Agency. I'm here regarding one of your employees who tragically died in an automobile accident." Scott showed his ID with the NSA seal and his picture.

"Pardon me for asking, Mr. Scott, but does the NSA do accident investigations? I thought you guys spied on foreign governments and collected phone calls and stuff."

The man kept looking at his watch and fiddling with his tie.

Guilty of something, Scott thought. "You're absolutely right, we don't investigate accidents. Our mission's to protect the country from our enemies: nation-states, terrorists, and others who would do us harm."

Costello cleared his throat.

"We listen to foreign phone calls, read their emails, and monitor their digital behavior. And when they try to attack our infrastructure, we work with others to stop it."

"You're right. A terrible tragedy," Costello said, glancing at his colleagues. "He'd been here forever. Everyone knew him, old Irishman named O'Shaughnessy, but known around here as Smokey. Don't know where the name came from. Big bear of a guy. Maybe 'cause he looked like Smokey the Bear. Maybe 'cause he wouldn't stop lecturing us on smoking. I mean, even years ago when everyone liked to light up. Tell you the truth, Mr. Scott, old Smokey was a piece of work."

"Meaning what?" Scott asked.

"Obsessed with rules, always finding fault. When I came here he was already a fixture, in charge of safety and security. Spent all his time writing people up for some infraction. Take sixteen minutes on a fifteen-minute break, and he'd log it."

"Not a team player?"

"Hell no! Smokey didn't have a friend. The boss finally transferred him to human resources so he couldn't make such a pest of himself. He was an absolute stickler for rules. For example, someone once saw him standing at a cross walk on a Sunday morning waiting for the light to change. Not a car in sight."

"I'm getting the picture," Scott said. "Before you leave for the Rotary luncheon, I have a few questions. In your view, any merit in his report that led to the IG investigation?"

"None. Zero. We've never had an incident here. Not in the fifty years we've been operating, not—"

Scott interrupted. "Never? What about the radioactive steam leak in 1982? Wasn't it considered an emergency?"

"1982? Give me a break, forty fucking years ago. I'm telling you, no incidents since I've been here." His colleagues nodded in agreement.

"The IG report said the whistle-blower, Smokey, claimed on several occasions personal flash drives had been observed in the operations center in violation of security regulations."

"Yeah," Costello said, "exactly the kind of trivial crap he always reported. And if you'd read the IG's conclusions, you'd have known the accusation was *not* confirmed. If I can be blunt, I'd call it unadulterated bullshit."

"I read the report," Scott said.

Costello looked at his watch, stood up, and said he regretted running out. "Appreciate you coming all the way up here from Washington, Mr. Scott. Hope you've seen we run a shipshape operation, and all the better since Smokey's no longer rattling us with his phony accusations and cockamamie theories."

"Thanks for your time. Okay to chat with your colleagues for a few more minutes?"

Costello paused. His face said no. He glanced at his colleagues. The older one nodded.

The attorney appeared nervous. No eye contact.

"Sure," Costello said, "be my guest, these guys know

their stuff."

Scott stood, shook Costello's hand, removed his jacket, and sat down.

The lawyer, sitting next to Scott, also removed his jacket.

"A little hot in here," the operations officer said. "The AC's acting up again."

"Feels like a sauna," Scott said. "How about the reactor? Has it been acting up too? Ever unexpectedly shut down?"

"Yes, but not often. It's old, kinda cranky. If it kept humming along without a problem, my staff wouldn't be necessary."

"And was there ever a time it shut down when you couldn't find the cause—and spontaneously started up again?"

"Well, yes. Down for thirty minutes or so, and then up and running before we did a damn thing. Twice, maybe three times."

Scott looked at the attorney, directed his next question to him. "How well did you know Smokey?"

"Hardly at all, sir. Not an easy guy to know."

"Have you seen the accident report? I read he died when his car ran off the road and collided with a tree."

"Yes, you're right."

"Any reason to suggest speeding or drinking?"

"Oh, no. The report showed no sign of alcohol or drugs. Drove an old Volvo, big as a tank, but apparently the brakes failed."

"Do either of you believe it?" Scott asked. He raised his eyebrows and waited for an answer.

After a long silence and an exchange of glances between the two, the operations officer replied, "I, uh, don't have the competence to make a judgment."

The attorney, following Scott's cold stare and more silence, said, "That's what the investigators concluded, sir. No one's challenged it." Sorting through a stack of papers, he looked up and said, "I have a copy of the report here for you."

Not exactly sleight of hand, but Scott surreptitiously dropped a small device in the lawyers' jacket pocket.

"Thanks," Scott said. "I have it. And thanks for your time. Please tell the boss I may have a few more questions, may return to do a little fishing—on the lake, of course."

♦♦♦

Suspicions confirmed, Scott took the next flight to BWI and drove to the Red Roof Inn, his home-away-from-home close to Fort Meade. Back in the game, it had been a good day.

He met Rachel the following morning half an hour before the seven o'clock meeting.

"You look relaxed," Scott said. "Everything under control?"

"Everything? No, but I earned my stripes in your absence. Followed my instincts and put out a fire that wasn't burning."

"Tell me more."

"The number of intercepts peaked, apparently off the charts. Key terms included infrastructure, nuclear, and bay. Nothing about Calvert Cliffs, but one of the analysts concluded it was an immediate target, recommended we issue a Hera Alert to the cooperating agencies. I remained skeptical. A false alarm would damage our credibility and undermine my authority. The analyst escalated his recommendation. He and I met with Dr. Hoople, who looked at the evidence and sided with me."

"So, you won one for the Gipper," Scott said.

"So far, but only time will tell."

Scott said it took courage to challenge the analyst's recommendation and commended her wise decision. "Waiting for certainty," he said, "is to forfeit your skills."

"Thanks, Scott, I like that."

"While you were thinking and deciding, I spent a few hours at the Ontario power plant listening. I asked a few questions and said very little, as three stooges representing the absent boss lied to me."

"Hiding something?"

"Their words, their tone, their body language insisted I not believe a word they said. A young attorney parsed his words so carefully he practically confirmed the deputy was lying."

"You uncovered the truth?" Rachel asked.

"Not exactly. Not in the few hours I spent there. However, I'm confident there's an insider threat, someone who can close down the reactor. Not sure, but I suspect he's also responsible for the death of a brilliant theorist, a certified pain-in-the-ass known as Smokey. The insider may be a disgruntled employee passed over for promotion, may be an agent for the Russians or Iranians or whoever. I don't know. I do know there's a cover-up, but not sure why."

"Maybe this will help," Rachel said, speaking faster. "Should have told you right away. I received a personal email signed God, and—"

"Well, you certainly won't need *my* advice any longer," Scott said, his face giving way to a broad smile.

"Ha! A typo, from Gold, Larry Gold, the CIA guy I met at the embassy in Rome. Looks like a god, actually, head full of curly blond hair like a Botticelli painting. He urged me to take a close look at a recent cable."

"And?"

"Classified TS/SCI, drafted by him about your favorite Russian bad guy, Viktor Sokolov."

"Let me guess," Scott said, "your friend Gold confirmed Viktor poisoned Laura."

"Even better. The cable says he's still tight with the Russian FSB and continues to work for the Italian intelligence service. He's a first-class scoundrel, a world class grifter, but provides such good intel he continues to roam free—selling everything from illicit drugs to Eastern European women."

"Nice guy," Scott said. "And he's in bed with your buddy Larry Gold?"

"Oh, no. I doubt they know each other. The station gets its Viktor info through the Italians."

"You're keeping me in suspense. What's in the cable?"

"I'll read you the key finding:

> *Source (protect) says FSB has monitored multiple false transmissions, disguised as Russian-originated, threatening American nuclear power plants. Appearing to have similar characteristics as Sony Picture hack, origin likely North Korea.*

Practically a smoking gun," Rachel said.

"Or purposefully leaked Russian disinformation to divert our attention from the real threat. No reason to doubt your man Gold or even Viktor. Every reason to continue suspecting the Russians."

Scott and Rachel walked to the conference room. The young analysts were seated at their usual places. Woody arrived early, pacing, wearing a headset. Scott wondered if he was listening to music, an audiobook, or white noise to isolate his multiple personalities. Woody took his seat at the table, still wearing the headset.

When Rachel looked his way, he traded his headset for a smile of absolute satisfaction.

"Ms. Sullivan," Woody began, "do you have any idea who among the members of Operation Bluefish would be careless enough to lose a sub-miniature transmitter, expensive government property?"

She shook her head.

"No? Well, I've been listening to a recording of a signal from New York state, from the coat pocket of a man who sounds like an attorney, talking to his wife, explaining he's in trouble, telling her Smokey was right, saying he was undoubtedly murdered."

Scott maintained his practiced look of innocence. Rachel shook her head in disbelief. The other three appeared confused.

Woody stood up, walked over to Scott, took his hand, and said, "You crafty old dog, you've done it again. Welcome home!"

Chapter 15. Belfast Calling

Head in his hands, Hoople sat at his desk waiting for Scott. He momentarily regretted convincing him to join the team. *I didn't realize how much he'd changed.*

Hoople looked up, saw Scott standing in the doorway. "Come in, have a seat."

"Thanks. Good to be back."

"Congratulations, I guess, but what the hell were you thinking? We could both be disciplined if . . . " He stood, walked from behind his desk.

"Me, sure, but without your permission, without your knowledge. You're not the least bit culpable. It's all on me."

"Might have expected it from Woody, but you? Without a warrant, you've bugged some innocent guy, an attorney no less. Not like you."

Hoople prided himself on being calm, in keeping his emotions in check. Not now.

"Alex, you're right," Scott said, shifting his weight. "Out of my lane. Hardly the first time. Put a reprimand in my file or whatever, but look at the payoff."

Hoople stopped pacing, cracked his knuckles, sat opposite Scott. "If we weren't sitting in my office, I'd say you were pretty shrewd, but I won't. I *will* say Rachel's showing her stuff. The team's really coming together."

"Absolutely," Scott said. "They barely need me. Wasn't missed last weekend, and—"

"And what?" Hoople asked.

"And won't be missed next weekend when I'll be out of touch for a few days."

Hoople stood, resumed pacing. "Don't tell me, please don't even hint you're returning to the Ontario site."

"Wouldn't think of it. I've a few things to clear up in Belfast."

"Belfast!"

"Wait," Scott said, standing and extending both hands. "I'm meeting with my solicitor, making a deposition before a magistrate, and flying back the next day."

Hoople removed his glasses and walked back to his desk. "Can't stop you if you must return, but isn't there a risk you'll be detained for more hearings? Or, God forbid, charged again for the murder of the Italian journalist?"

"Legally, they can't compel me to return without seeking extradition from an American court, but ethically, I have no choice. Civic duty has a strong hold on me. To answer your questions, I *could* be detained and I *could* be charged again. And on my way out of your office, I could slip on a banana peel and break my crown. Alex, I've led my life dealing with probabilities. You run this whole operation without any certainties. Bottom line: you can count on me to be back Monday morning, jet-lagged but otherwise ready to roll."

Scott stood, smiled, and waved as he left. Hoople shook his head and managed a faint smile. *At least he's broken out of his funk.*

◆◆◆

Scott had exaggerated a bit, but he owed his solicitor

the courtesy. She had sent a persuasive letter requesting his return. The bartender's alleged doping of Laura's drink had been dismissed on appeal. He was no longer a suspect. The initial charges against Scott had been suspended, but since he hadn't been tried, they could be reinstated. Clare had convinced the magistrate Scott's voluntary appearance would affirm his innocence. She had been candid, however, in telling him that would not be sufficient. She was working with an investigator to present an alternative theory to the magistrate.

Scott slept overnight in a plush seat in business class. *What had Laura discovered? If not Jimmy, who? Had the authorities charged someone else with poisoning Laura? Probably Viktor! Russian all the way.*

On arrival at Belfast International, he took a cab to his solicitor's office. She opened the door before he knocked, welcomed him back to Northern Ireland, and offered him coffee or tea before beginning their review.

"Coffee would be perfect, Ms. Sheehan," he said, "the stronger the better."

"We're due in front of the magistrate at three o'clock and have a full day's work to squeeze in before then. My investigator initially suspected O'Malley, your favorite genealogist, was behind the poisoning."

"O'Malley? Despicable guy, but murder? Why did—"

"Eventually cleared, although we found a compelling motive. Your great-grandfather's estate. Guess who is a potential beneficiary. Still contested, but O'Malley's a player."

"Explains why I didn't like him," Scott said.

"There's more, but for another day. Years ago, he was charged, never convicted, with planting a bomb that killed a prominent Sein Fein member."

"And you're sure he didn't try to take me out."

"No longer a suspect, although still an active Ulster loyalist."

"Had to love a guy like me who studied to be a priest."

"Mr. Scott, we have only five hours before your meeting with the magistrate. I'll present a scenario that completely absolves you."

She handed Scott a file and stepped away from her desk to brew a fresh pot of coffee. He read a summary of why the charges against the bartender had been dismissed despite the video evidence of him adulterating Laura's whiskey. The report said it was a common practice for an Irish bartender to add a few drops of water to whiskey poured neat.

"Ms. Sheehan," he said, "maybe because I had only a few hours of sleep last night, I find this water-to-whiskey explanation hard to swallow—no pun intended."

"Call me Clare, please. I understand, took time to convince me." She picked up a small book from her desk and opened it. "*McCaffrey's Bartender Manual*, circa nineteen hundred: 'Adding a few drops of water to whiskey opens up new, different, and subtle flavors that would otherwise remain hidden.'

"I'm sure I couldn't tell the difference, but whiskey drinkers swear by it. And Jimmy, our friendly bartender, showed he routinely adds a few drops from a bottle of spring water kept behind the bar."

"Spring water, huh? Jimmy wasn't dispensing fentanyl? So, who was? And how did Laura end up dead?"

"Our investigator learned from a toxicology specialist that Laura had ingested the drug within a few hours of her death, confirming she was poisoned. While drinking with you. So, absent other evidence, you're still a suspect."

"Is this the point where I should say 'faith and

begorrah' and hightail it back to the airport?" Scott asked.

"No, no, wait. My investigator, for whom you'll be paying dearly, wasn't satisfied to stop there," Clare said. "Jimmy's cleared, O'Malley had an alibi, and—"

"Clare, I don't want to be rude, but I'm sitting here staring at the bottom of my cup praying there's a punchline at the end of this sad story."

"Sorry, I'll refill your cup and proceed to act three of our little drama."

"Much appreciated," Scott said.

"As I mentioned, the toxicology report confirmed fentanyl poisoning. Our investigator also found trace amounts of heroin."

"Uh-huh."

"Furthermore, we learned Laura had spent several weeks at a rehab center in Rome before coming to Belfast."

"An addict?" Scott asked.

"Maybe, maybe recovered, maybe not. I don't know."

Scott sat up, rubbed his eyes, now wide awake from the news and the strong coffee. "So, not pure fentanyl, but heroin laced with fentanyl?"

"When she took a break to meet Viktor Sokolov," Laura said, "he supplied what he may have thought to be pure heroin, and she injected it before returning to the bar."

"Makes perfect sense," Scott said, "since he's already under suspicion for dealing in drugs."

"Exactly. All the dots are now connected except the fentanyl wrapper the police found in your room."

"Clare, it was *never* in my room. I've come to suspect one scurrilous cop named McGinty. I should say *Detective Royal McGinty*. Had me convicted from the get-go. I've a gut feeling he'd produced the so-called evidence to frame me, to advance his career."

"We're on the same page, Mr. Scott. His career was already well south of golden when he investigated Laura's death. And now it's completely bollocked. McGinty's on administrative leave pending an internal investigation of—now get this—fabricating evidence. Not yours, but good enough for me, and I'm confident it'll be enough for the magistrate."

"Clare, you're a saint."

"Not exactly, but I feel pretty good," she said. "Now paying attention, I see your cup is empty again. During my year at Columbia, I learned Americans are addicted to caffeine, so I made it especially for you. Hope I did it right?"

"What can I say? It's hot and strong enough to keep me alert."

"And flavor?" she asked. "Tell me the truth."

"I guess bollocks isn't a polite way of saying good enough, is it?" Scott said with a smile.

"No, not polite at all. More like profane. But, I get the point."

"And I've followed the point of your story, your talented investigator, and your exemplary logic. Laura died from an overdose. There was no murder—except for my great-grandfather, a hundred and twenty-five years ago. 'Hanged by the neck until dead.'"

♦♦♦

The scheduled three o'clock meeting with the magistrate began promptly. Fifteen minutes later he apologized to Scott for the inconvenience of returning to Belfast, wished him Godspeed, and concluded the meeting.

"What a surprise," Clare said as they left his chambers. "Not the conclusion itself, which I had anticipated, but I'd no idea it would take so little time."

"Delighted, of course," Scott said, "but I'm wondering why I had to be here. You presented your summary, he nodded, didn't ask me a question, and dismissed us in less time than it takes to dispute a traffic ticket."

"Mr. Scott, he *knew* you were innocent, but when the charges against Jimmy were dismissed, he had to create a record of an alternative *not* involving you. You had to be present. Look at the bright side, you've been found innocent twice and had the chance to visit Belfast again on a sunny day."

"Sorry, I didn't mean to be churlish, just curious. Can't tell you how much I appreciate your time and your splendid defense."

"Because the press continues to follow all this, my phone's been ringing endlessly. So, thank you for the rush of new clientele."

"Should we celebrate over dinner?" Scott said, as he broke into a mischievous smile. "I happen to know a good restaurant at Benedicts of Belfast."

"And a lively bar as well," she added.

"Exactly."

"Thanks for the thought, but no thanks. Two reasons. First, I've made it a practice never to socialize with clients, even when tempted. Secondly, I can't help but recall what happened to the last gal you entertained at the Benedicts Bar." She winked.

♦♦♦

Back to the Fitzgerald Hotel, where he had stayed after being booted out of Benedicts during his previous visit. A banner in the lobby announced the *Game of Thrones* celebration. George R. R. Martin, the novelist who wrote *A Song of Ice and Fire*, would be present for the screening. Scott was curious to see if the locations he and Laura had visited would be included in the presentation.

The lobby was packed when he returned from his room. Martin was already speaking, introducing the prologue of the first book in the series. Jammed in front of the elevator by the crowd, Scott couldn't see the screen. He listened to Martin as he read from the prologue of *Game of Thrones*.

> *He was an old man, past fifty, and he had seen the lordlings come and go. "Dead is dead," he said. "We have no business with the dead."*
>
> *"Are they dead?" Royce asked softly. "What proof have we?"*
>
> *"Will saw them," Gared said. "If he says they are dead, that's proof enough for me."*
>
> *Will had known they would drag him into the quarrel sooner or later. "My mother told me that dead men sing no songs."*

Pained to hear of the dead, Scott squeezed through the crowd to the front door. He thought of Laura, of her laugh, of their friendly banter on the *Game of Thrones* tour.

Was there a lesson to be learned from her death? Too early to turn in, still afternoon back home. He walked toward the Botanic Gardens, picked up his pace as he passed Benedicts Hotel. He stopped briefly in front of the university, recalling the joy he saw on the faces of the graduates in mid-June. In the quiet of the moonlit night, he fought back tears.

◆◆◆

"Welcome home, Scott," Rachel said, as he appeared in the doorway of her office. *Thank God you're back. I'd convinced myself you'd be detained again.*

"Free at last," he said with a broad smile. "What've I missed?"

"Maybe not as free as you imagine. Someone from the

FBI's been trying to reach you."

"FBI?"

"Identified himself as Agent Patterson. Promised to call back."

"Hmm."

"Also, we've another new mystery to crack. After a non-stop stream of intercepts concerning Calvert Cliffs, nothing for the past three days. Total silence! Nothing we can detect. What we had before looks like it came from the Russians, but still not definitive."

"Your Bluefish team," Scott said, "how're they coming?"

"Frustrated, except for Woody who keeps muttering about the dog that didn't bark, whatever that means."

"It's from Conan Doyle's short story, "The Adventure of Silver Blaze." The silence of the dog is the clue Holmes used to locate a missing race horse and solve the murder of its trainer."

"Hmm. Explains why Woody insists the absence of signals may be the clue we've been waiting for. I should have known better. As I hadn't read the story, I thought he was referring to *The Curious Incident of the Dog in the Night-Time* about the autistic boy who knew every prime number up to 7,057."

"I understand your confusion," Scott said. "Woody probably knows even more prime numbers. If we put that aside, his insight on the absence of Calvert Cliffs intercepts may warrant a visit to the facility. Not our business, I know, but neither was it strictly our business to visit Lake Ontario."

"I almost had my chance over the weekend," Rachel said.

"Your chance? What'd you mean?"

"Remember the invitation from my boyfriend to meet

in Annapolis for boating on the Chesapeake?"

"Mr. Wonderful, right?" he said with a smirk.

"Cut it out, Scott, but yes. He rented a sailboat and off we went, carried by the winds across the bay to St. Michaels. He tied up the boat and took me to lunch at Awful Arthur's Seafood Company. First time I ate raw oysters. Amazing. I didn't want to leave. Maybe the smell of the Bay or the frying of fresh fish that seemed so earthy, so real."

"You're here, so it looks like he finally dragged you back."

"Not until we did a little shopping," Rachel said. "Found a beautiful scarf in one of the boutiques and resisted buying so much more. Long before I would have left, he said we should return to the boat. He pointed to the clouds and said, 'Looks like a storm coming our way.' Turned out he was right, but we made it back to Annapolis well before the downpour."

"So, he finally came through."

"I'd suggested a detour to Calvert Cliffs at the southern end of the Bay. He said it would take hours and we'd be caught in the storm. He asked why I wanted to visit. When I mentioned the power plant, he shook his head and said I was full of surprises. He adjusted one of the sails and then asked again about Calvert Cliffs."

Scott winced.

"I realized I should've kept my mouth shut. However, you'd have been proud of me, Scott. I improvised, said my scientific curiosity had no bounds. I reminded him of my degree in Computation and Neural Systems from Caltech."

"Saved by the storm," Scott said. "If you had sailed by, I suspect there'd have been more questions."

"Yes, always full of questions from the time we met.

About me, my work. He seemed satisfied when I told him I was a researcher at the National Oceanic and Atmospheric Administration. Although I might have to kill him if he continues his lame greeting, 'How's the weather, honey?' I really like the guy, but he has no sense of humor."

"So, he'll be the straight man at the long-promised coming-out party," Scott quipped. "We're all anxious to meet him, size him up, see if he's good enough for you." *And I'm sure he's not.*

"You'll meet him soon enough," she said, gritting her teeth. "We better walk over to the conference room. Our team's waiting."

"And as soon as our meeting's over, I suggest you plan a visit to Calvert Cliffs and invite one of the new team members to tag along. I'll call a colleague at DOE to schedule a tour of the facility and a briefing on their security protocol."

"Got it," Scott told Rachel a few hours later. "After some resistance by the bureaucracy, they agreed to a visit. The price: sharing what we've learned from the intercepts."

♦ ♦ ♦

Rachel and Marie stopped at the power plant entrance, showed their IDs, and continued to the parking lot.

"Seemed too easy," Rachel said. *Why didn't they check the car, look in the trunk?*

They parked and walked to the entrance. Their host was waiting at the door.

"Ladies, welcome, I'm the director, Jeff Hoffmann. Delighted you're here."

"Thanks for receiving us," Rachel said.

At his suggestion, they followed from the entrance to his office. Rachel glanced at Marie and with a subtle nod offered her approval of the director.

His office overlooked the Bay. A few sailboats in the distance. Seagulls overhead. The sun reflecting off the tranquil water.

In contrast, nothing to distinguish the office. A government-issued desk, file cabinet, two straight-back chairs, and a framed poster with a sketch of Eisenhower and the words "Atoms for Peace."

"Have a seat," Hoffman said, "I've been director here for nearly a decade. The 1953 poster says it all. Atoms for Peace. Still our slogan."

Nearly seventy years ago, Rachel thought.

"Security's our highest priority, so I'm eager to hear the latest."

"Thanks for receiving us. I'm Rachel Sullivan, leading a team examining cyberthreats to nuclear reactors. And this is my colleague, Marie Khan, a specialist in cybersecurity."

"Welcome, again. We don't get many visitors from Washington."

"I understand you've seen our reports," Rachel began. "They reveal numerous foreign communications naming the Calvert Cliffs power plant."

"Yes, I've read two reports, both fairly cryptic. And neither identified the origin or the purpose of the communications."

Rachel nodded. He had done his homework.

"When I introduce you to our security team, they'll want your advice on what's expected of us. Our control systems are not connected to the Internet, so penetration is impossible."

The director turned to a white board and began to explain the security perimeter as he sketched.

"Pardon me," Marie said, "my colleague can't hear you.

I mean, not when you're looking away. She's deaf, but can read lips better than most people listen."

He turned, looked surprised, and said, "I'm impressed. Not the same thing, I know, but one of our employees here is legally blind. Not only holds his own among a very competitive group, but always excels. His other senses seem to be magnified."

Rachel laughed.

"Mr. Hoffmann," Marie said, "you've broken the code."

Smiling, looking directly at Rachel, he continued, "We're proud of our defenses against intrusion, both physical and digital."

"I've studied your plan," Rachel said. "Very impressive. What I missed, however, your defense against insider threats."

"Not published, but not ignored. My security chief can brief you in detail. She and I are the only two who know what we routinely do—and what we're prepared to do in case the threat level increases. Based on intensive and ongoing background investigations, our security chief assigns a trust score to each employee."

Marie glanced at Rachel, nodding approvingly.

"The good news," Hoffmann said, his voice revealing his pride, "practically every employee has our highest rating. This is a small town where everyone knows everyone. No secrets here. When we hire someone from outside, we keep a careful watch."

"Another question," Rachel said. "How often do you exercise your emergency evacuation plans?"

"Our brochure is circulated throughout the community, instructing people what to do in case of an emergency. The Livermore National Laboratory conducts an annual red team penetration test, which we always pass with flying colors. FEMA runs a periodic plume and ingestion exercise. We took immediate action on their recent recommendations. In short, I'm confident we're at the top of our game."

"How often have you been down in the past year?" Rachel asked.

"Except for planned maintenance, never," Hoffmann said.

"Any chance you could give us a tour?"

"Every chance, delighted to show this place off. But, don't forget, I need your guidance on what to do about those reports. I understand our enemies are talking about us. But, what to do? I don't know. Our cyberdefenses are strong, internally tested, and externally certified."

"Mr. Hoffmann," Rachel said, "we collect information and share it with our partners. But we don't have the authority or even the competence to advise you on how to improve operations. The best we can suggest: continue to be watchful and report anything suspicious or different."

"SOP," he said, standing and motioning them to follow.

Marie walked behind Rachel, but then stopped and raised her hand. "I hope I'm not out of line to say this, but your alert system is not secure. We ran some tests and found a sophisticated hacker could break your password."

"You're sure?"

She nodded.

Hoffmann rubbed his eyes. "It's never been cracked in our tests, but I assure you my security team will review and strengthen all our passwords. Thank you."

He resumed walking, showed Rachel and Marie the reactors, introduced them to the shift supervisors, and invited them to the control center. They saw several sleek consoles staffed by employees looking at screens of data and dynamic graphs.

"An emergency would trigger strobe lights and a sound like a fog horn.," Hoffman said. "The relevant screen flashes and the operator takes appropriate action, up to and including shutting down one or both of the reactors. They're all trained nuclear engineers and fully empowered to act."

"Do automatic notices go to the community—all the parties on your evacuation plan, police, fire, media, schools, and so on?" Marie asked.

"No, not before the operator has consulted with me or my deputy. We're mindful of the chaos that could follow a false alarm. After my approval, the operator sends a set of automated notices to all relevant parties, with the concurrence of a second on-duty operator. It's modeled on a two-key system the Air Force uses to launch a nuclear missile."

The tour concluded with a PowerPoint briefing by the security chief. Rachel had not visited a power plant before, so had no relevant comparison. Nonetheless, she expressed her satisfaction with the thoroughness of the briefing and the tour.

There wasn't anyone Rachel met who had failed to make a positive impression. She would report they observed a highly professional operation with a staff attentive to security and proud of their outstanding record.

As they drove north toward Fort Meade, Rachel recalled Woody's earlier observation about the location of the facility. Nothing to prevent a missile attack from an innocent-looking boat in the Bay. Or a fleet of drones.

"Woody was right," she told Marie, "the real threat is from conventional weapons."

♦♦♦

Sensing her flashing light alarm clock, Rachel awoke and sat momentarily on the edge of the bed. *Who's calling in the middle of the night?* It had been the first time in weeks she hadn't lay awake fretting about her role in Operation Bluefish.

She fumbled to turn on a light and picked up her cell phone. A new message:

<Code Blue. Come in ASAP>
<Confirm receipt. Arriving soonest>

Oh, shit. This can't be happening.

She grabbed her clothes and turned on the TV. An aerial shot of a line of vehicles extending for miles. She read the subtitles as a studio newscaster said the evacuation from Calvert Cliffs began after local authorities were alerted of a fire at the nuclear power plant.

"This cannot be happening," she said softly, as she pulled on her jeans and a sweater. Over and over she repeated the same words.

The newscaster switched to a reporter outside the ten-mile radiation zone who reported rumors of an explosion. "The traffic has come to a standstill," he said. "Some drivers have remained calm while others have panicked. A young mother with two infants in the backseat said she heard the blast was caused by terrorists."

Frozen in place, Rachel continued watching as she pulled on her boots.

Back in the studio, a Virginia Tech scientist said, "Too early to know, but examples from Three-Mile Island and Chernobyl suggest a failure of the cooling system in one of the reactors, causing an explosion and the release of radiation."

She changed the channel. Men in hazmat suits. She watched as they approached a facility identified by Kanji characters. Not Calvert Cliffs. The network was showing stock footage from the reactor meltdown at the Fukushima Daiichi nuclear power plant. *Patently dishonest. Irresponsible.*

She turned back to the first channel.

The Governor, standing in front of a police cruiser, said, "Communications have been severed at the plant, so the cause remains unknown. However, there's no reason for concern beyond the radiation zone."

Rachel breathed deeply. *Do not panic. Remain calm. Get to work.*

Fifteen minutes from Fort Meade, ten if she ignored the speed limits. She looked for her keys, found them in her purse, and sprinted to her car.

Chapter 16. Shrouded in Darkness

Move, move, move! Rachel pounded on the steering wheel of her car, idling in a line that snaked around the entrance to NSA Headquarters. The compound stood at high alert. Every vehicle searched and mirrored underneath to look for explosives. She should have come sooner. Her team would be waiting.

She texted Scott. No answer. Next, she tried Marie, who responded immediately. She hadn't heard the news, was getting ready to leave her apartment. Rachel inched forward, one car length. At that rate, she would be an hour late for her seven o'clock meeting. As thousands of innocents fled the disaster, she, too, felt the pull of fleeing. *No, not me. I will stay and fight.* She moved forward another car length, fifteen feet closer to the digital battleground.

She eventually reached the parking lot, mostly empty. Scott pulled in behind her. The two compared notes as they walked across the lot.

"I feel responsible," Rachel said. "It couldn't have been more than eight hours between my departure from Calvert Cliffs and the explosion. I intended to report that all signs pointed to a first-class operation. My alleged *instincts* apparently took the day off."

"Nonsense," Scott said. "Deception is fundamental to

warfare. You're an analyst, not a soothsayer. We collectively sensed something was amiss, but we didn't know what, didn't know when, didn't know the origin of the threat."

"But, Scott, I was there . . . "

"And several thousand of us were here monitoring traffic from all the bad guys. Guess what? We didn't catch it, either. I'll go and see what our signals guys may have found."

Rachel nodded, then turned and headed to the conference room where she found Li Min alone in front of a laptop. Not a word from Sam. No surprise that Woody hadn't arrived yet. Even in the best of times, punctuality wasn't in his vocabulary.

"Anything new, Li?" Rachel asked.

"No ma'am, nothing. Heard about the breach of the reactors on the radio as I drove in, but nothing new here. Of course, I can't get media updates on this classified computer."

Scott entered the conference room several minutes later. "The ops center director told me we're receiving contradictory information," he said. "Nothing definitive at the moment, but the Calvert Cliffs fire department has reported there's no evidence of damage. One of the networks is running with the story, resulting in even more confusion. Frightened families are still inching their vehicles away from the site."

Marie showed up, breathless and apologetic. Sam texted, promising to be there soon, delayed by a traffic jam.

Thirty minutes later, Woody arrived, unshaven and unkempt. "Those shit-for-brains guards at the gate wouldn't let me in. Had to call Hoople to come down and escort me. He agreed with the guard that I looked like a bum but assured him I was a security-cleared bum."

"Given that you're not exactly a candidate for the cover of GQ, I understand the guard's confusion," Scott said.

"Where've you been?"

"Thought you'd never ask," Woody said. "At home, on the phone with Mulligan. He was in his truck heading south for a job on Solomon's Island when he heard the first report of the reactor disaster on the news. He said the highway was practically a parking lot heading north. Not the kinda guy to allow a nuclear disaster to get in front of his curiosity, so he made a little detour and headed toward Calvert Cliffs."

Woody paused. Searched his pockets for his cell phone. "Musta left it in the car," he said. "I've a picture Mulligan sent me of the sun glistening off the reactors. But, no fire, no smoke, no evidence of a disturbance. You can see a sailboat just off the coast. To quote Mulligan's memorable words, 'Disaster my ass, so calm it looks like a painting.' Don't know if he meant Monet or Warhol."

"Hmm, suggests the network report is correct," Scott said.

"And, if true, what triggered the alarm?" Rachel asked.

"May I say something?" Li asked.

"Of course," Rachel said.

"Well, last week, Dr. Woodward, you gave me one of your skeptical looks and asked me what good was an expert in artificial intelligence in preventing an attack on a nuclear power plant. And I stumbled to try to answer."

"Roger that," Woody said.

"Then you repeated that story about the dog that didn't bark, said something was going to happen, and challenged me to figure it out."

"And?" Rachel asked.

"I don't know anything about nuclear reactors," Li said, "so I talked with Marie and learned the alerting system was connected to the Internet, unlike the reactors and control systems. So, a hacker could write code to mimic the kind of disaster that would set off the alarms. No one would—"

Rachel interrupted. "Marie and I learned the alarm is *not* sounded, authorities are *not* notified, the media are *not* informed—until the director personally approves and two operators activate the response."

"That's where a coder who knows his stuff could use AI to simulate all of that," Li said, raising her voice. "Either with code lying dormant until a predetermined time or action by a hostile nation-state or lone terrorist."

"Well done, my child," Woody said.

"I'm sure you meant that as a compliment, Dr. Woodward," Marie interjected, "but just because Li is a few inches short of five feet, she's no child. She'd never brag about it, but I happen to know she placed first in last year's Ashby Challenge, beating out guys twice her age and fifty percent bigger than she."

Rachel glared at Woody, "Nice work, Li. Maybe you're right, but too early to know. Marie, see if you can get through to Calvert Cliffs."

Within minutes, all the television networks were announcing the reported disaster as a false alarm. The director of the power plan appeared on every major channel to assure the public the reactors had not been compromised. "I apologize for the erroneous alert. It was not authorized by me. It was not activated by our staff. At this time, I cannot explain how it happened. However, we are launching an immediate investigation. Experts from the Nuclear Regulatory Commission will be here before noon to assist."

Sam Adams rushed into the conference room. "I just heard a report on NPR that it was a false alarm," he said between deep breaths. "Sorry I couldn't get here earlier."

"Understood," Rachel said. "Li just finished explaining how the alert may have been triggered. It appears the fail-safe alert protocol was compromised."

◆◆◆

The next morning, an FBI agent was waiting when Scott returned to his office after the seven o'clock meeting.

The agent thrust his ID toward Scott. "Name's Elliot Patterson. Appreciate you taking the time to see me." Buzzcut, broad shoulders, rugged face offset by a generous smile and soft eyes.

I saw his name on my schedule, but why's he here? Calvert Cliffs? This soon?

"Your timing couldn't be worse," Scott said. "On the other hand, it may be perfect."

"I've studied your Ontario report," Patterson said."

"Oh, Ontario, yes. Have a seat," Scott sat opposite, as the agent opened his briefcase and removed a sheaf of papers.

"First of all, we're interested in why you visited the power plant. A little out of the ordinary for you guys, no?"

"Yes, not our usual MO. We're investigating foreign threats to the country's electrical grid. Nuclear power plants are of special interest."

The agent looked up from his papers and nodded.

"It may be only a coincidence that the false alarm from Calvert Cliffs occurred within days after my trip to the Ontario plant. Or maybe not. So much the better the FBI's taking an interest."

"Hmm," Patterson mused, "but what prompted you to visit Ontario in the first place?"

"My interest was piqued by a whistle-blower whose report was investigated by the Energy Department's IG. The reactor had shut down and then started up again on several occasions without explanation."

"Yes, it's in your report."

Scott shifted his weight, eager to get on with the interview. "The whistle-blower, a nuclear engineer, blamed it on lax security or worse. Soon afterwards, he died in a freak automobile accident."

"Uh-huh," the agent said. "So, you went to investigate his death?"

"No, that's up to you. I went to investigate the unexplained behavior of the reactor. Why did it stop and start spontaneously on several occasions? Who was responsible? Is there an inside threat to its integrity? The same questions that will be asked during the investigation at Calvert Cliffs."

"You think the whistle-blower was murdered?"

"I don't know," Scott said. "It's a possibility. Your agency will determine that. If so, we want to know why. We want to know who caused the erratic behavior of the reactor. We want to know if a foreign power has access to the control system. We want to know if it can be shut down by an outside force, or worse, blown up. We're trying to avert a cyber-Pearl Harbor."

◆◆◆

The sky turned crimson as the sun set. The after-action report completed, Scott drove south from Fort Meade toward D.C. He reflected on the vulnerability of the two nuclear power plants—and the fifty-eight others spread among thirty states. All at risk.

He glanced at the screen on the dash when his phone rang. Cobb's name lit up.

"Hello, Spencer."

"Scott, where the hell are you? I've been calling all day."

"Long story, been out of touch. How's everything in Berkeley Springs?"

"Can't say. I'm in Washington at my old law firm, working on the Brexit issue. Something's come up that might be of interest to you. Any chance we could meet?"

"It'd be my pleasure," Scott replied. "Where and when?"

Within an hour, they were seated in the main dining room of Washington's Cosmos Club on Massachusetts Avenue. "I maintain my membership here," Cobb said, "to meet clients and friends."

"Haven't been here for years. Just passed by the rogue's gallery of notables who've been members—politicians, educators, scientists, the Washington elite."

"Not to mention the West Virginia elite," Cobb said.

Their waiter appeared. Cobb asked for a martini, dry, Bombay gin, straight up with three olives. Scott ordered the same.

"You look far too relaxed," Cobb said, "for a man who must surely know something about the Calvert Cliffs blowup."

"A false alarm, Spencer, nothing more."

'Uh-huh, nothing more. And you said that with a straight face."

Scott smiled. "And you've learned, what? How your client can exploit Brexit to become even richer?"

"Learned a lot, but Bridgette's doing the heavy lifting, now in London. As one of my former partners used to say— she's invaluable, indefatigable, and into everything."

"I'd say the same about the three women on my team."

"Bridgette learned the London Metropolitan Police have hundreds of documents showing the Russians influenced the Brexit vote through social media. One of the major British funders behind the campaign to leave the EU has numerous Russian connections as well as a Russian wife and a mysterious source of funds."

"Your client must be pleased."

"Yes, with our progress. However, what's done is done. Too late to stop the U.K. from committing political suicide."

"You may need more than one martini," Scott said.

"And you, as well, when you hear what else she's discovered."

The waiter arrived with two frosted cocktail glasses, poured the martinis from a shaker, and added three olives to each glass.

Cobb picked up his martini, looked left and right, set the glass down, and leaned toward Scott. "Bridgette's been researching Russian influence with a focus on the Russian diaspora in London. More than a few shady characters living there, many of them with great wealth, several with close contacts with the Kremlin."

"So I've heard."

"She stumbled onto something," Cobb said, "that she thought would interest my client. But it was too little, too late. On the other hand, it might be of interest to you. Maybe information even your spies don't know."

"We know everything, Spencer. We know, for example, that you're sleeping with your Irish assistant."

"Ha! If you're mind readers, then you're right. But in real life, absolutely not. Mrs. Cobb would be talking to a divorce lawyer before I returned home. Somehow, she'd know."

"You're right, we don't know everything," Scott said. He shrugged his shoulders. "I'm eager to hear what Bridgette learned nosing around London."

"Assume you're familiar with Russia's cyberespionage group called Fancy Bear. Never heard of it myself, but Bridgette knew all about it, said it's also known as APT28. She says they've targeted NATO, the White House, the German Parliament, and many others. Does that sound right?"

"Hmm, she's taught you well."

"She discovered one of their coders lives in London. Calls himself Peter, has an upscale apartment in Notting Hill. He could have been the point person behind Russia's social media attack on the anti-Brexit electorate."

"And was he?" Scott asked.

"I'm getting there," Cobb said. "She persuaded a friend from Belfast to spend a few days in London to help her investigate. Calls himself a white hat hacker, but agreed to work on the dark side for the good of the nation. He set up a device called a Stingray and began to intercept calls to and from Peter. Most were in Russian, which her hacker friend recorded for later translation. However, three of the calls were in English with someone in the United States."

"Spencer, your gal Bridgette's in trouble with the law if she gets caught intercepting calls with a Stingray."

"And we may all be in trouble if you don't follow up on the conversation between Peter and the American. A cryptic discussion about simultaneous attacks on American nuclear power plants. The last words she heard: 'Give me twenty-four hours' notice, and we'll turn off the lights.'"

◆ ◆ ◆

Another FBI agent was waiting for Scott when he arrived at his office the following morning. *Two days in a row! I should be pleased they're so efficient, but there's nothing more I know about the Ontario power plant.*

Scott sized up the agent. Mid-fifties, flabby, old style,

white shirt, dark blue tie, and polished brogans. His slight stoop and graying hair suggested he was on the cusp of mandatory retirement. He said he was directed by his supervisor, Elliot Patterson, to get more information. He presented his credentials, removed a notepad from his briefcase, and began the interview.

"You reported a suspicious death, Mr. Scott. We've reviewed the accident records and the coroner's report. Found nothing out of order. Yet you claim to have seen something the local authorities missed."

"Not exactly."

Shaking his finger at Scott, the agent said, "Let me be blunt. You were there for less than two hours, did not investigate the accident, but nonetheless concluded O'Shaughnessy had been murdered. Wouldn't you agree your report was a bit premature, even a fantasy?"

Scott wasn't prepared for this attitude. He had *not* concluded the engineer was murdered. He had reported his suspicion. He had suggested an investigation. Now he felt *he* was being investigated. If he had slept better, he would have been more patient, less defensive. He would have shown more sympathy to a man who may have been on his last assignment.

"You and I are both investigators," Scott said. "We work for the same government. I reported a suspicion of a cover-up. A suspicion, not a conclusion. What I've heard in the few minutes you've been in my office suggests you're prepared to dismiss my report."

"Wait a minute," the agent said.

"No, you wait a minute. I don't like your attitude. I don't like your suggestion I was fantasizing. And, frankly, I don't like you. As I have a meeting in a few minutes, I'll call security to escort you from the building."

"Wait, you don't understand—"

"Oh, no? You show up here unannounced, misrepresent my report, and accuse me of not understanding. We're in the middle of a crisis. Wait right here till a guard arrives."

♦ ♦ ♦

We're all on edge, but treading water. I fear we're outgunned. Rachel was writing on a whiteboard when Scott arrived. With her back to the door, she didn't hear him enter. Woody would reliably and predictably arrive at ten minutes past the hour. Rachel turned to see the three newbies engaged in animated conversation. She pointed to the whiteboard and began to summarize what the Bluefish team had learned. Her posture, her voice, her presentation—all conveyed she was in charge.

"The circle I drew has a shaded wedge representing ten percent of the pie. That's what we know about the threats directed at two nuclear power plants. The other ninety percent is what we don't know about the threats to the remaining fifty-eight stations that produce twenty percent of the nation's power."

Marie and Li were taking notes. Sam squirmed in his seat. Scott nodded. Rachel continued. "You see the line I've drawn from our little piece of the pie to the box labeled WHAT WE KNOW with two bullet points: *internet penetration* and *insider threat*. There's every reason to believe the public alerting system at Calvert Cliffs was compromised through the Internet. And there's at least a credible suspicion that the reactor at the Ontario plant has been compromised by an employee."

Woody opened the door, apologized for being late, looked at the sketch on the whiteboard, and suggested one more bullet point: *kinetic surprise*. Rachel added his contribution to the sketch.

"You're absolutely right," she said. "Our team's focus on data analysis and cyberwarfare may blind us to the conventional threat you've identified. My bad. A missile from a boat or drone, a so-called kinetic attack, warrants our attention."

Woody walked to his usual seat, sat, and closed his eyes.

"Anything else?" she asked her team. After a half minute of silence, she felt their discomfort. Before long, someone would respond. Not Scott or Woody, both waiting for one of the newbies. Li shifted her weight, looked at Marie who shrugged.

Finally, Sam spoke, softly, hesitantly. "Maybe it's just me," he began, "but what exactly is expected of us? Are we to identify all the plausible threats? Are we to show how those threats could be contained? I don't understand the boundaries. On the one hand, we're looking for patterns in the streams of intercepted data. And at the same time, the two most experienced members of our team are reporting on a fishing trip in the Chesapeake."

Woody opened his eyes, thumbs-up to Sam.

Rachel didn't respond. *Nothing. I need to encourage Sam's participation, but he's often a few degrees off center.*

Alex Hoople entered the room. "Pardon for the interruption," he said, "but you need to know what I've just learned. My counterpart from the DIA shared information from a reliable source that within seventy-two hours, the Northeast will be 'shrouded in darkness.' His words, not mine. Your task is to determine the targets and stop the attack."

Hoople turned and left.

Li spoke first. Short of breath, nearly hyperventilating, she said, "It's all on us. If we fail, I cannot live with the consequences. No Asian can forget. No one should forget.

Minutes after the bombing of Hiroshima, the acrid stench of burning bodies filled the air. One survivor spoke of a 'white, silvery flash' that began the inferno. We *must* stop it."

"Whoa," Rachel said. "We're facing a disaster, not Armageddon."

Her lips trembling, her eyes averted, Li shrunk down in her chair. "Sorry, you're right."

Rachel turned and wrote on the whiteboard WHAT WE DON'T KNOW. Below that she added two points: *Trigger Public Alarm, Destroy Electrical Grid.* "The first is easy," she said. "Calvert Cliffs proved it. The second is beyond the capability of most of our adversaries, because it would require multiple simultaneous attacks on our largest nuclear plants before the power grid would be interrupted. There's enough redundancy to maintain current operations unless several of the largest went down."

"Rachel," Scott said, "good summary. Hoople left us with an objective. You've given us our marching orders."

"If you agree," Woody said, "I'll contact a colleague at the Energy Department to identify the power plants whose destruction would bring down the electrical grid."

"Yes, the sooner the better."

"And I could work with Sam and Li," Marie said, "to come up with a protocol to isolate the alarm systems from the Internet. That would minimize the likelihood of a counterfeit public warning. Not nearly as important as preventing an attack on the reactors, but it would prevent widespread public panic."

"Let's all get moving," Rachel said. "I agree with your suggestions and like your attitude. Meet here at three o'clock to share what we've learned. And Scott, if you don't mind, let's discuss what we might do to cauterize insider threats at the critical sites."

"My pleasure," Scott said, "but first, let's walk downstairs to the cafeteria. Clear my head and get my creative juices flowing with a caffeine fix. Getting to be a habit, I know, but not my worst one."

◆◆◆

Woody was on time when the Bluefish team reconvened several hours later. He wrote the name of five nuclear power plants on the white board. "The big five," he said. "Take these out, and it's 'Goodnight, Irene,' with credit to Lead Belly and the Weavers. Sorry, kids, that was well before your time." *Sometimes I live in the country, sometimes I live in town, sometimes I have a great notion, to jump in the river and drown.*

It was crunch time for Operation Bluefish. Rachel showed it by her rigid posture and her rapid-fire speech.

Woody recalled Scott's near-death experience in a Turkish sanatorium. *Defied death looking for me, I owe him and this team no less.* He looked across the room. The three young members were wearing faces of fear. He recognized their naiveté, their vulnerability. The weight of responsibility felt suffocating.

Rachel circled the locations on the white board and turned back to her team.

"Dr. Hoople and I will be meeting early tomorrow with the inter-agency team chaired by the deputy secretary of Homeland Security. Cancel your plans for this evening. I expect we'll be here all night preparing an action plan."

Crunch time for the Bluefish team, Woody mused.

"The Energy Department's top security guy will help," Rachel continued. "He'll direct the five key sites to prepare for the three scenarios we've identified—a false alarm to terrify the public, an insider attack resulting from malware resident in the control systems, or a missile attack from enemy drones."

Rachel paused, looked across the table at her colleagues. "Any questions?"

"Yes," Li said, "how much time do we have?"

"Not nearly as much as we'd like, but with your skills and spirit, enough to get the job done." She looked at Scott.

"Simple," he said, "we write the playbook and depend on Homeland Security, Energy, and Defense to act. The alert systems at all five sites must be air-gapped from the Internet. That's the easy part. Cybersecurity forensic experts must examine, discover, and isolate any malware in the operating systems. And DOD must send anti-missile defenses to protect the sites from a kinetic attack."

"Piece of cake," Woody said, rolling his eyes. "By my count, if we get agreement tomorrow morning, we'll have roughly forty-eight hours to accomplish what would normally take forty-eight weeks."

"Implying we'll fail?" Rachel asked.

"Hell no! We'll succeed. In the words of Admiral Farragut, 'Damn the torpedoes, full speed ahead!' Or to update his advice, kill the fucking drones!"

Woody shouted with such fervor that he might have been standing on the deck of the Hartford in 1854. Rachel's face brightened. The others spontaneously cheered.

"Let's take a fifteen-minute break," Rachel said.

♦♦♦

Scott left the secure conference room, returned to his office, and reviewed the latest inter-agency information. In congressional testimony, the secretary of Homeland Security had just asserted that cyberweapons pose a greater threat to the United States than the risk of physical attacks. *Would her testimony be a* wake-up *call? Would the public understand?*

To reduce the tension, Scott took the elevator to the

ground floor, removed his personal cell phone from a lock box at the entrance, and stepped outside in the sunshine. He stopped briefly and glanced at his email. Scrolling through scores, he stopped at the subject line, Fredrica, and eagerly opened an email from Johanna Winkler.

> *I'm writing on behalf of my mother, discharged from hospital several hours ago. Now home with family in Munich, she is recovering well. She is resting now and plans to contact you tomorrow.*

His face brightened as he read it again. *But, what had happened to Fredrica when he postponed his visit to Vienna?* His joy subsided as he felt the weight of her pain.

Chapter 17. Shut your Eyes and See

Neither awake nor asleep, Scott lay in a fog of memories. Had the Joyce character on the plane been an actor or a dream? The words he heard or imagined or invented came tumbling back. *Better pass boldly into that other world, in the full glory of some passion, than fade and wither dismally with age.*

He turned over, opened his eyes. Still dark outside. Another forty winks and then—and then, another day. He closed his eyes and drifted off to sleep. He awoke hours later, rested and hopeful that the action plan developed by the Bluefish team would deter the rumored attack. Hope, however, would not overcome the inertia of bureaucracy.

The NSA would augment its monitoring and analysis of Russia and others capable of an attack. Would Homeland Security, Energy, and Defense act in time? And absent an attack, would his agency lose all credibility? A risk worth taking. The real risk: waiting for certainty.

First, before a hot shower and a cup of freshly brewed motel coffee, Scott checked his email. Nothing yet from Fredrica. Still, the anticipation of hearing from her kept his spirits high.

Scott's phone rang. "Hello, Alex."

"How fast could you get here?" Hoople asked.

"Thirty minutes, max. What's up?"

"*The Philadelphia Inquirer* has a story causing alarm. Says the National Guard's being deployed to the Limerick Nuclear Power Plant north of Philadelphia, and here I'll quote from the paper, 'to protect the facility from an enemy attack.' The reporter goes on to speculate on the consequences."

"Say no more," Scott said. "I'm on my way."

"Wait, one more thing. The Defense Department issued a statement denying the story."

"A flat-out denial?"

"Yeah, which only compounds the damage. The National Guard arrival will soon be in full view. The media will inevitably link the arrival of the troops to the recent Calvert Cliffs evacuation."

As he showered, Scott considered the consequences. *Uncertainty would be overtaken by fear.*

◆◆◆

A secure conference call had just begun in Hoople's office when Scott arrived. He recognized the voice of the DOD public affairs rep: "The public must be reassured there is no danger."

Hoople, sitting behind his desk, shook his head, raised his voice. "We've already stumbled once by denying the deployment of the National Guard troops. We must not sugar-coat the threat. We cannot say there is *no* danger."

"But, that would—"

Hoople interrupted. "We can and should say we recognize the danger, we have taken numerous steps to contain it, and we've deployed the National Guard to five facilities."

After each had contributed to the discussion, the deputy secretary of Energy summarized. "I agree," he said, "we will speak for the government on the actions underway to protect the public. We will emphasize the threat is not to the destruction of the power plants but to their temporary closing. We are taking prudent measures to ensure the Northeast power grid remains intact and fully functional."

Hoople concluded the meeting by asking all participants to refer any questions to the Energy Department. "We must," he said, "speak with one voice."

The secure conference call ended. Hoople turned to Rachel, briefed her on the call, and asked her to convene her team, share the decision, and review any late intelligence. She nodded and walked with Scott to her office.

◆◆◆

Unlike Scott, Rachel remained at the agency all night. She read the reports of the latest intercepts over and over. Had her team missed something? Why would the Russians or anyone target America's nuclear power plants? What was the motive? A one-time show of strength? The first step to war? She looked for an answer. Nothing. Not yet. Even though Scott and Woody had blessed the Bluefish plan, she knew it wasn't complete. Great powers do not act without a motive, without an endgame.

"I was petrified," she said, "all those senior people talking about a national disaster, about public fears, mass panic and—and the stupid talk of mushroom clouds. For every sensible comment, someone else spoke in total ignorance."

"True enough," Scott said, "however, wisdom prevailed."

"Yes, but it could have tipped the other way. With one wrong word or one more lie, we could have created mass panic, and it would all have fallen on Operation Bluefish, on me. Scott, I've never felt so scared."

"Scared? Of course. I never had an assignment that

didn't evoke fear. I like to think of it as an adrenalin pump. It'll drive you to your very best work."

"Maybe help me find a motive," Rachel said, forcing a smile.

◆ ◆ ◆

Agent Elliot Patterson had requested an urgent meeting.

Scott walked to the reception area to meet him. "I must apologize," Scott said, "for being so brusk with your colleague the other day."

"Not at all. He shouldn't have been here. A mix-up in scheduling."

"Well, then, we can get a fresh start. How can I help?"

"We've been working overtime," Patterson said, "in part, I must admit, to convince you we're not all dunderheads after your encounter with my soon-to-be former colleague. Your recording of the attorney was enough to get us a court order to do an investigation on Deputy Costello. Sure he was hiding something, but the guy's clean as a whistle."

"Too bad," Scott replied. "Something about the guy I didn't trust, but—"

"We didn't stop there. Costello has a brother, a local attorney who specializes in divorces. And the guy travels a lot."

"Uh-huh."

"Wanna guess where?" Patterson asked.

"Divorce attorney? Well, how about Las Vegas?"

"Nope, even better. Every other month he flies to the Cayman Islands, stays at the Grand Cayman Marriot Beach Resort for two nights, which must cost him a cool grand."

"So, the divorce business is booming," Scott said.

"Exactly," Patterson said. "He's doing so well he keeps a safe deposit box at the Cayman National Bank. High living for a man with a reported income last year of eighty-three thousand dollars."

"Thanks for letting me know," Scott said. "I'd appreciate if you'd continue to trace the source of brother Costello's funds. Could be the key to unraveling a planned foreign attack on our nuclear power plants."

◆◆◆

As Patterson left, Scott was thinking motive. He would brief Rachel in a few minutes but first would rush outside again to check his email for the promised message from Fredrica. And there it appeared: *Zwei hinreissend verdorbene Schurken.*

He recognized it could be bad news, but imagined an invitation to visit Austria again. Before confirming his hope, he tried an on-line translation of the subject line. Two ADORABLE ROGUES. Pleased by the whimsical phrase, he opened the message.

So much has happened since our planned rendezvous in Vienna. I saved the tickets to the opera Norma as a memory of what might have been. I meant to reply to your email delaying your visit a second time. Disappointed, of course, but I tried to understand. To distract myself, I signed up for The Third Man tour. As the brochure promised, we followed 'Harry Lime's footsteps through Vienna's underground sewer system.' Fascinating, until the moment I slipped, until I screamed in pain. I learned later its echo through the labyrinth of the sewer startled everyone on the tour. My next clear memory is lying in a hospital bed, a doctor by my side explaining I had a concussion and a compound fracture of my femur. It required surgery and the insertion of a titanium rod.

When I awoke, I felt no pain. The American expression, I read, is being in la-la land. And there I remained for days and weeks. I refused physical therapy, happy to stay in a perpetual state of medication with my choice of classic movies on the TV and three meals a day served in bed. It must have been the drugs, but I confess I no longer mourned your absence.

Scott stopped reading. *What could I have done different? What can I do now? She's hurting, and all because I was detained in Belfast.*

He bit his lip, continued reading.

What happened next was a turning point. I lay in bed watching this old American movie, Zwei hinreissend verdorbene Schurken, starring Michael Caine and Steve Martin, dubbed in German. Michael Caine reminded me of you, a younger you, of course, but he had that commanding presence, like you. He charmed women, like you. But he was a thief. And when he won their confidence, he robbed them. You never explained your profession. You travel all over the world, live well, and are persuasive enough to convince a widow she's the direct descendent of the Emperor of Austria and King of Hungary.

Scott's English translation of the German title was misleading. The original: *Dirty Rotten Scoundrels*. Fredrica had concluded *he* was a dirty rotten scoundrel. He continued to read.

I'm out of the hospital now, finally doing physical therapy, staying with my daughter in Munich. Looked at the movie again and realized you don't look much like Michael Caine. Any chance you might include Munich in your future travels?

Scott paused, read it again, and replied immediately: *YES! So sorry about your fall. And about my delay. Wish you a rapid recovery. I've missed you so much. I'm back in the States at work. More later. Affectionately, Scott.*

◆◆◆

Rachel looked up to see Scott standing in the doorway of her office. She motioned him in.

"The FBI has a lead," he said. "Ontario's deputy's been compromised. He's been bought. It's our lucky day."

"Lucky?" she asked, puzzled by his enthusiasm. "I see it in your face, your posture, your attitude. But if the intelligence is right, we're less than twenty-four hours before the attack. What've you learned that gives you such confidence?"

"If you're implying I may be out over my skis," Scott said, "you're right. What you see is my joy in receiving an email from my Austrian friend."

"Wow! No wonder you're upbeat." *The old Scott is back.*

"Guess I got a bit carried away. Should have been more circumspect. The FBI's on the right track, but nothing yet."

"I'd like to share your joy," Rachel said, "but I'm so anxious I can't. I know better, but fear waking up to a disaster. We don't know the source of the threat. We don't have a motive. And we don't know where it's directed. Scott, we don't know anything."

◆◆◆

Scott had planned to take an overnight trip to West Virginia, but not now, not the time to abandon Rachel and the Bluefish team. Before leaving the Red Roof Inn, he called Sean to explain, slightly distracted while looking for his car keys.

"Don't worry," Sean said, "your faithful companion's fine. Follows me everywhere, sits on my lap when I read, and keeps my spirits high. I'm considering engaging Spencer to claim adverse possession so I can keep the little mutt."

Scott laughed. "Can't blame you, but that applies only to continual possession without the consent of the owner. So, enjoy him while you can and be prepared to release him as soon as I return."

"Take your time, Scott. No need to rush back."

"If not before, I'll return for your big birthday bash week after next. Understand the parish ladies are going all out to help you celebrate."

"That was the plan," Sean said, "until Felicity got involved."

"She's not a member of the parish, is she?"

"No, but she's now appointed herself as the leader of West Virginia's disappearing Shawnee tribe. A half-dozen other Shawnees—real Shawnees—will be joining her in the Berkeley Springs park for a birthday celebration with drums, dancing, and peyote."

"Sounds like you'll be on a high," Scott said.

"Oh yeah? What do you think the bishop will say when he learns I'm going to be named an honorary chief? Felicity whispered in confidence that my Shawnee name will be Thundercloud."

"Perfect," Scott said with a laugh. "Guess you'll be trading in your clerical collar for a peace pipe?"

♦♦♦

Walking toward his car, Scott made one more call before re-engaging with the Bluefish team. Little else to do except wait. The Energy Department confirmed all nuclear power plants were on high alert. The five largest had followed the recommended protocols. The National Guard had arrived without fanfare. The troops had been augmented with specialists to shoot down drones.

Cobb answered his cell phone. "Greetings, Scott, what's up?"

"Checking in to see what you've learned about Russian interference in the Brexit vote."

"Not a damn thing. They interfered. That we already knew. Did they make a difference? Probably. Can it be demonstrated? Probably not. End of story."

"So, you've finished, sent Bridgette back to Belfast, and returned the million-dollar retainer to your client?" Scott asked.

"When exactly did you become such a wiseass? Perhaps the time I saved you from spending the rest of your life in prison? Or when I treated you to a prime steak at the Cosmos Club? Or, maybe, just to piss me off."

"All of those," Scott said, "but to get back in your good graces, I'm inviting you to join me at the Red Roof Inn for the blue-plate special. Assuming, of course, you're still in Washington."

"Still here," Cobb said, "but with my gout, I'm not able to venture beyond the city limits. Furthermore, my dietician insists I avoid chicken-fried steak. If you're a wee bit curious about Viktor, I suggest we meet at The Palm."

Scott went to Rachel's office to check in before he left for dinner and found her and Woody in an animated discussion. She, seated at her desk, twirling a pencil. He standing, pointing to the map.

"Not gonna happen," he said. "The enemy's looking for our weakness, not the five reactors surrounded with our troops and augmented with cyberspecialists."

"So, you're saying we should just relax?"

"No, no, no," Woody said emphatically. "We must remain alert, ready for a surprise. I feel it in my bones."

"Dem bones, dem bones gonna walk around," Scott said mockingly. "Have you been hanging around with your buddy Mulligan again?"

"As a matter of fact, yes. Laugh now if you wish, but just wait. Mulligan's been on a job not far from Calvert Cliffs, just off the Bay. Every day, he's seen the same old fishing trawler back and forth, up and down the Chesapeake. Not doing any serious fishing, not there, I'll assure you.

"So Mulligan says to me, 'What would the captain of that old rig be looking for?' And I say, 'Search me, Mulligan, I don't have a clue.' And then he says, 'You're maybe thinking I'm as dumb as I look.' 'No,' I say, 'ain't anyone that dumb.' He laughs and tells me if I don't show a little respect, I can do my own fucking reconnaissance."

Rachel glanced at Scott. Not the first time Woody had suggested a missile attack from an offshore boat. Or a swarm of drones. The false alarm may have been a planned diversion. Scott maintained his best poker face, waiting for Woody to conclude.

"Look," Woody said, "I'll be the first to admit this is a hunch, a theory if you like, a working hypothesis, okay? But we'd be fools not to put it to the test. If we sent the National Guard to five sites just because they're large, shouldn't we do the same for a reactor that's already scared the bejesus out of everyone?"

Scott nodded.

"I agree," Rachel said. "Nothing to lose. I'll ask Dr. Hoople to contact his liaison with DOD to invite deployment of the Guard."

♦♦♦

An easy call, Scott thought, as he drove south from Fort Meade toward The Palm, known for its great steaks and even greater egos. Frequented by politicians, lobbyists, and journalists, The Palm, dark wood and low lights, was the place to be seen. Caricatures of Washington's political and media elite graced the walls. When he arrived, Spencer Cobb waited at the bar.

"Greetings, Scott. What're you drinking?"

"Bushmills neat, Spencer. Better make it a double. Been a long day, and it's not over yet."

"Until we get a table, I'll be a little discreet in discussing Viktor. Remember, I mentioned him well before you made your first visit to Belfast."

"Yes," Scott replied, "you said he's involved with one of your clients."

"And you were, to put it mildly, less than interested in offering a little assistance, even suggesting it was such a common name that your Viktor and mine were hardly one and the same."

"What are the odds, Spencer?" Scott asked.

"Well, Bridgette confirmed they *are* one and the same. He's well known in Belfast as a con man and hustler, travels back and forth to Rome and, get this, to Moscow."

"And she's found a connection to the Brexit vote?"

"Hell, no, nothing on Brexit," Cobb replied. He looked around, then lowered his voice.

"He's into every crooked scheme you can name, including smuggling. Been arrested by the Irish cops but never convicted. She said the Irish are certain he's working for Russian intelligence but can't prove it."

Scott sipped his drink, listened without revealing that Viktor was working undercover for Italian intelligence.

"And here's the bottom line," Cobb said, "and don't ask me how Bridgette knows. He's known to American authorities but appears immune to prosecution."

"Interesting," Scott said. "Your gal Bridgette looks like a perfect candidate for MI6."

As they were invited to their table, Scott thought about the trips to the Cayman Islands by Costello's brother. Could Viktor also be his liaison from the Russians? No, Scott concluded, that wouldn't be credible even in a second-rate spy novel.

With a slight wave of the hand, Cobb acknowledged the gentleman sitting at the next table.

"Looks like—" Scott began.

"Yes, the FBI director, in person."

"And the young woman with him, I assume, is Bridgette, who he's pumping for information."

"Very funny, Scott. I give you a hot tip and get nothing but sarcasm in response. Don't blame me if your steak arrives burned to a crisp."

◆◆◆

7:00 AM. D-day for Operation Bluefish. The conference room was silent when Rachel arrived. All present. All early. All eager. Even Woody.

"Nothing," Rachel began. "Nothing on nuclear power plants, nothing on cybercrime, nothing from Russia, nothing to report. Everything about Libya, Venezuela, Brexit, and so on. But nothing for us. Our enemy is wrapped in a cocoon of silence."

Woody moved slightly, waved his hand, caught Rachel's attention. *Would he offer some insight, something she hadn't seen?*

"Everything we proposed has been completed in record time. Best cooperation I've ever seen from other agencies," he said. "You'll recall the suspicious trawler sailing up and down the coast near Calvert Cliffs."

"Good news?" Rachel asked.

"Yes and no," Woody said. "Turns out I was right. The trawler was not fishing in those waters. But otherwise I was dead wrong, not carrying enemy missiles, not conducting enemy surveillance."

Woody paused. The others looked at him expectantly.

"That old boat," he said, "is indeed part of an undercover operation, not by the bad guys, but by our very own Coast Guard—deployed to protect the Calvert Cliffs power plant."

◆◆◆

When the meeting ended, Scott watched the three young team members walk toward the elevator, to brainstorm in the cafeteria, to apply their learning to a mystery their elders had not solved. He could have joined them but not without handicapping their discussion. Instead, he went outside to clear his head. Maybe he'd come up with an idea. He found an email from Sean when he checked his phone.

Your name came up yesterday at The Country Inn when an old friend dropped by. She urged me not to invite you to my birthday celebration, said you were a spy, certain you'd be spying on the Shawnee Nation. I didn't deny it, of course, but told her it's an honorable profession. I recalled the Lord advised Moses to send out men to spy in the land of Canaan.

Failed to persuade her, but she finally said it would be okay to invite you if I promised not to share any Shawnee secrets. As I hadn't finished my coffee when she rushed off, I thought of a few words that might amuse you, particularly if you recall our freshman seminar on Genesis.

She said everyone knows you're a spy,
An allegation I could hardly deny.
Joseph's servants, remember them,
Promised they were honest men.
And as the story goes, seldom told a lie.

Felicity's nature mirrored that of the town's—full of charm, fame, energy, talent, and occasional paranoia. Scott recalled her insistence of having witnessed a ritual suicide, of fearing to return to her home, of defending a non-existent native tribe. Of course, who wouldn't be paranoid after being kidnapped, secretly videoed, and stalked for years by a crazy Russian?

Another Russian was on Scott's mind: Viktor Sokolov, tight with the Kremlin but working for Italian intelligence. Trafficking in illicit drugs and Bulgarian women. It was well past time his Italian sponsors should tighten the screws, persuade Viktor to tell all. However, Scott understood this fantasy would not stop the ticking clock. The strike could come within minutes.

♦♦♦

Rachel sat in her office alone. Quiet and calm. The data stream had stopped, but her synapses were in high gear. She didn't need data if she could find a motive. The Russians were at the top of everyone's list. She moved them to the bottom. She not only believed Viktor's earlier report to the Italians but could not envision why the Russians would strike when they were succeeding diplomatically on so many other fronts.

The Chinese? No logical motive. They were too shrewd to try a caper like this. No need to use brute force against an adversary when they were in the ascendency.

Who else? Iran? North Korea? Which had a motive? Which could gain by striking and disabling America's nuclear power plants? By shutting down the Northeast power grid? By turning off America's lights?

Rachel closed her eyes. She could not hear. She could not see. Her other senses were on high alert. A scent of ozone, maybe. Maybe her imagination. She gripped the arms of her office chair so tightly her nails nearly pierced the artificial leather.

She had experienced this same feeling before. Back in college, sitting in the office of a professor of economics. Failed the mid-term, late with her paper. Practically straight A's for four years, now threatened with failure. She didn't care about economics, admitted she hadn't studied, promised to do better. Studying to be a scientist, she believed economics wasn't logical. The stock market was fickle, she had told him.

She gripped the chair tighter, cleared her head, opened her eyes. *I see it. The motive. The threat. The enemy.*

A gentle tap on her shoulder. Startled, she jumped from her chair. Hoople backed away.

"It's nearly midnight," he said. "Go home. Get some rest. We need you wide awake and alert early tomorrow."

Chapter 18. Sunday in the Park

Quiet. Too quiet. *The calm before . . . Maybe not. Maybe we're wrong. Maybe no storm.*

Scott took a call from FBI Agent Elliot Patterson on a secure phone. "The Italians came through," Patterson began, his voice an octave higher than usual. "Everything we heard about Viktor's been confirmed. Our agents are making a high-profile arrest as we speak. We've alerted the press, so you'll see it on CNN within a few minutes."

"Great work," Scott said. "From the moment I spotted that swaggering bastard in Belfast, I knew he was trouble. Provided the drugs that killed Laura. And now what? Bribed Costello to bring down the Ontario reactor?"

"No, no. A shifty character, yes, but we're not arresting Viktor. He's on our side, a high-caliber snitch working for Italian intelligence. His story hasn't changed, but this time he's provided the evidence."

"You have my full attention," Scott said, his voice not revealing his doubt.

"Our colleagues across the river confirmed his report," Patterson said. "The threat did not originate in Russia. North Korea all the way but disguised to appear Russian."

"And Viktor's evidence has led to an arrest?" Scott

asked. He drummed his fingers on his desk.

"Along with your, uh, accidental recording of the attorney at the Ontario Power Plant. Our agent played it back for him. Said we planned to charge him as an accessory to murder. As soon as he regained his composure, he begged our agent to listen. Said he didn't know who had murdered Smokey but suspected Costello knew."

"Yeah, I bet."

"Costello's arrogance shattered like a piñata at a kid's birthday party when our agent showed his badge. He confessed to practically everything but murder. He said he'd been approached by a rep from a cybersecurity firm offering to test the integrity of their control system."

"I can hear it coming," Scott said.

"Costello said he overcame his doubts when he was shown a government certification and offered compensation. He signed an NDA, accepted a thumb drive to add monitoring software to the operating system, and began to receive monthly payments. He told us he only became suspicious when the payments arrived in the form of gold coins. Said he felt his career was at stake when Smokey filed his whistleblower report. When Smokey died in the car accident, Costello feared he'd been murdered."

"And if not Costello, who did it?" Scott asked.

"Not sure who jimmied the brakes," Patterson said, "but we know who ordered it, we know who supplied the thumb drive with the malware, we know who paid Costello in Russian gold coins. He's the man we're arresting, a prominent figure in a so-called charity sponsored by the North Korean delegation to the United Nations. Known as *Doum-ui Songil*, or as my guys say, it means Helping Hands."

"If he's the conduit, maybe the attack can be stopped.

And I'll be the first to nominate you for the Most Valuable Player award. I'm eager to watch the TV coverage of the arrest, but first I must run to a meeting of our task force."

♦♦♦

Out of breath when he arrived at the conference room, Scott caught Rachel in mid-sentence. Her eyes wide, her speech rapid, she appeared to be on an adrenalin high. " . . . although not yet public. Nothing yet from the so-called big five."

"Sorry," Scott said, "I just took a call from Patterson, the FBI guy, who told me they've identified a suspect linked to the threats—and are making an arrest in full view of the press. What did I miss?"

Before Rachel could respond, Woody spoke up, "The fucking Ontario Power Plant is down, dead, kaput."

"But," Rachel said, "it's not yet public knowledge. Our worst-case scenario, mass panic, could be minutes away if the story leaks. It's an irony that the government's protection of the five major sites may be the trigger for the scenario we're trying to avoid."

Li raised her hand. "May I say something."

Rachel nodded, appeared impatient.

"Marie and Sam and I were here at six o'clock, down in the cafeteria trying to make sense of all this. Sam suggested it could be a prank, home grown by hackers here in the States. Marie wondered why we weren't considering other nations. Belarus, for example, might be acting as a proxy for Russia. And I keep worrying about us, about our team. What happens to the three of us if we fail?"

"We will *not* fail," Rachel said, "although I commend you for your initiative, for stretching our boundaries."

"No time for wringing our hands," Woody said, "not when the cyberattack is apparently underway, not when the

FBI's arresting a suspect, not when Rachel is poised to share her analysis."

"Thanks, Woody," Rachel said, "I'll make this brief. I've been puzzling over a motive, something I learned from Scott when we first worked together. Our man in Italy, Larry Gold, filed a report from Viktor Sokolov pointing the finger at the North Koreans."

"Pardon me for interrupting," Scott said, "but the FBI's confirmed his story. Learned that on the call a few minutes ago."

"Perfect," Rachel said. "Although North Korea has limited resources, it has a motive." She hesitated, looked around the room, waited for someone to connect the dots. Scott did not venture a guess. He waited. Woody squirmed in his chair. *Is he restraining his impulse to show off?*

"The motive," Rachel said, "is money." She stopped speaking, waited, and looked from one colleague to another.

Sam was the first to break the silence. "Money?" His voice was faint and uncertain.

"Think Bangladesh," she said. "North Korea showed its cyberprowess in 2014 when it hacked Sony Pictures, at a cost of some fifteen million dollars to Sony. Two years later, North Korea stole eighty-one million dollars from the Bank of Bangladesh through a cyberheist, fortunately thwarted by the Federal Reserve Bank of New York before the planned billion-dollar transfer was completed. They have the means and the motive if they can manipulate—"

The door to the conference room opened. Hoople entered, slammed the door behind him, and strode to the front.

"Twitter's killing us," he said. "Someone reported the Ontario reactor was attacked. Also, the Limerick nuclear power plant. We confirmed nothing amiss at Limerick, but that hasn't stopped the rumors."

"Will the Energy Department make a statement, correct the rumor?" Rachel asked.

"That's the plan," Hoople said, "but with the story half-true, I expect the rumors will go viral on social media."

"Dr. Hoople, I'm Marie Khan. May I add something?"

"Of course. Go ahead."

"Thank you. Just want to say, it's not the words that do the most damage. It's pictures and videos."

"Marie's right," Rachel said. "If someone posts pictures, even fake pictures, of a nuclear reactor on fire, we'll face a public meltdown. No pun intended."

◆◆◆

Hoople returned to the operations center to be briefed on media reaction. *All it takes is one network, one false report, one phony image to cause mass panic.*

"What do we know?" he asked the shift supervisor.

"The cable networks initially ignored the social media rumors," she replied, "but CNN is now reporting the arrest of a man described as 'a lynchpin of cyberterrorism.'"

Hoople watched as a man in handcuffs was escorted to a police van. The reporter identified him as Stanford Cooke. The story that followed quoted an Energy Department official denying rumors about the Ontario and Limerick reactors. "The Ontario reactor has been temporarily shut down to prevent compromise," he said. "And operations at Limerick have not been affected."

The operations center piped in a radio commentator who began to link the stories.

I have to tell you, your government's engaged in a massive cover-up. The feds arrest a guy in New York and charge him with cyberterrorism. And within seconds, the Energy Department confirms the Ontario nuclear reactor is on the fritz, claims everything's hunky-dory at a power plant within spitting distance of Philadelphia. And its nuclear reactors are surrounded with armed soldiers! Are you listening, Philadelphia? Are you thinking Three Mile Island?

Hoople stood, raised his hands, and shook his head. "This big-mouthed clown's doing his best to encourage mass panic."

♦♦♦

Rachel continued her team meeting. "North Korea's dead broke but proud and skilled in cyberterrorism. It's fair to assume it doesn't have the resources to cause serious damage to our nuclear power plants."

She paused, looked for reaction. Nothing. *They trust me, but what if I'm wrong?*

Rachel took a deep breath and continued. "On the other hand, Pyongyang could create the perception of damage, of a full-blown disaster. And that, in turn, would create fear and lead to a stock market crash."

Scott spoke first. "Good. I like your reasoning, and I see where you're heading."

"Shit, Rachel, now you tell us," Woody added. "I should've shorted my vast holdings in General Electric or whoever owns those reactors. Just kidding! Any money I might have invested's already been lost to Mulligan in my campaign to wipe him out with Texas Hold 'Em."

"Good luck, Woody," Rachel said, managing a smile.

"If the market reacts," Sam asked, "that would mean my very first contribution to the government retirement fund would crater, right?"

"Not exactly, depends on your allocation. Worse case

would be a fund that invests primarily in the companies that own the sixty nuclear power plants."

"I don't invest in anything," Li said, "still paying off college debts. And I don't understand anything about stocks, certainly don't understand how the North Koreans would profit."

"Let's say you knew what was coming," Rachel said. "You could short the stock of the corporations that would be affected and make a killing."

Pleased to see Scott nodding, Rachel continued. "Put it this way, Li, you're the finance minister of North Korea, short of hard currency. You find a willing American confederate to invest on your behalf by betting against these stocks, start a panic, watch them plummet, and take your earnings and run. Would make the Bangladesh heist look like child's play. Could be billions of dollars at stake."

Woody stood, applauded Rachel and with a flair, bellowed, "By Jove, I think she's got it." The others joined in applause.

She blushed, thanked everyone, and suggested a break. "We've been in this secure room for nearly two hours, without natural sunlight or network news. Let's get a hot cup and check the late news."

♦♦♦

As Woody returned to his office, Rachel walked with the others to the cafeteria. *They agreed with me, even Woody.*

The cafeteria appeared normal, people chatting, some standing in line to order a late breakfast. The TV sets in each corner displayed network talk shows, one showing a Discovery Channel documentary on how scientists photographed a black hole.

Rachel sat at a table with Scott, as the others went for

coffee. Although pleased that panic had not begun, her confidence was flagging. Shaking her head, she said, "The applause was premature."

"You're due more than applause," Scott replied. "First, the FBI has concluded North Korea *is* behind the threat. Theory confirmed. Second, the seventy-two-hour deadline has passed without an attack. No panic. Operation Bluefish—a success."

"So far," Rachel said, "but I recall Woody's reminder of the dog that didn't bark."

"And I recall Woody's alarm about the suspicious trawler in the Chesapeake, that he eventually learned was operated by the Coast Guard. Even our resident genius can be wrong."

"Surprised he didn't join us for coffee," Rachel said.

"Woody never fails to surprise," Scott said, rising from the table. "I'll be back—with a half dozen cream-filled donuts. Promise." He smiled and walked toward the pastries.

Rachel's mind drifted to the email she'd received that morning from Chef Roberto. "Cara Rachel, maybe plan visit Italy during *Ferragosto*. Rome almost closed, also my restaurant. Much time for drinking good wine and making parties."

She'd reply later, after sending a short email to her New York boyfriend to ask if he still planned to visit Washington this weekend.

Just as the other three returned with coffee, Woody joined the table with a smile that previewed his news. "Talked with my buddy at Energy. The secretary's holding a press conference to assure the country the threat's been contained. He'll say the intelligence community's identified North Korea as the perpetrator. And he'll identify two Americans who've been arrested and charged with felony crimes—the deputy director of the Ontario Power Plant and the executive VP of a North Korean charity known as *Doum-ui Songil.*"

"Just like that?" Sam asked. "It's all over?"

"No, not exactly," Woody replied, "but it's the beginning of the end. Panic's been averted, in part because of the TV coverage of the FBI arresting the North Korean charity guy. Wait till you see the clip. Couldn't have been better staged by Hollywood. Six or eight agents in flak jackets standing by as two tough-looking guys escort him out of an office building on Rockefeller Plaza. He's struggling, resisting, swearing, with a look on his face that says guilty. Why, a jury could practically convict him on his appearance alone."

"Shouldn't we move closer to the TV," Rachel suggested, "to see if CNN covers the secretary's press conference? Let's hope he'll defuse any remaining rumors."

"That would be the first time," Woody said, "for *this* administration to stop a rumor."

◆◆◆

Returning with a box of donuts, Scott joined the team in front of the TV. He passed the box to Rachel. *She's biting her nails, revealing her skepticism, while the others look ready to party.*

"Thanks, not now," she said, "I'm focusing on the news."

The first story featured hundreds of Central American women and children waiting in Tijuana to enter the United States as refugees. It included an interview with a woman who claimed her husband had been murdered and feared she would be next.

"A good sign," Scott said. "They didn't lead with the threat of a nuclear meltdown."

The Bluefish team, anxiety etched on their faces, watched two more stories: a plane crash in the Philippines and a coup in Sudan, before the Energy secretary appeared. Brief and authoritative, he commended the several agencies that had cooperated to avoid a disaster.

> *The intelligence community sounded the alarm in time to close down the operation directed by North Korea. The American population was never in danger, although stockholders could have lost a small fortune. Our colleagues in Treasury learned that one hedge fund alone could have profited by several billion dollars, most of which would have ended up in North Korea.*

Scott tapped Rachel on the shoulder to get her attention and said she'd called it exactly right. She smiled and looked back at the screen. CNN was showing footage from early in the day, a man in handcuffs struggling and cursing as he was led to a police van. BLEEP " . . . ing scum, dim-witted fascist pigs," he shouted.

"Oh my god, it can't be!" Rachel screamed. She closed her eyes, covered her face with her hands and began to sob. Her colleagues were stunned.

"What is it?" Woody asked.

Scott did not speak. He understood. He understood Rachel's life had just been upended.

◆◆◆

The next morning, Hoople paced behind his desk, waiting for the team to arrive. *Three veterans and three budding geniuses pulled it off.*

He glanced at his watch, then walked to the conference room to greet them.

The three young members, nearly giddy in their excitement, arrived first. Scott and Woody walked in together minutes before seven. Scott's limp had all but disappeared. Marie whispered to Sam that she had never seen Woody wearing a tie before. Waiting for Rachel, they took turns recalling their fears of failure and the relief of success.

"Congratulations," Hoople said. "A nearly perfect day, time for a quiet celebration. No public acclaim, but recognition throughout the agency that Operation Bluefish has succeeded beyond expectations. If this had been an Olympic event, I'd be awarding gold medals."

He looked across the room. No Rachel.

"Sleeping in and well deserved," he joked, "we'll catch up with Rachel a little later. I'm here to thank you for keeping us safe, for defeating the enemy, and for being the best team ever assembled since Lou Gehrig retired from the Yankees in 1939. And you three—Li, Marie, Sam—the academy's loss is our gain. Well done. Woody, thanks for keeping us honest. And Scott, we couldn't have done it without you. However, next time you're in an Irish bar, you may wish to drink alone."

◆ ◆ ◆

Rachel was home, still in bed, still wide awake after many hours. *What a fool I've been!* The temporary joy of success had been punctured when she saw her boyfriend in handcuffs, brawling with the police, exposed as a thief. Worse, a traitor and a terrorist. Not a financial analyst for Goldman Sachs as he claimed but a hedge fund manager for a little-known company called the Crossfire Capital Group. Months before, his explanation of leveraging, short-selling, and derivatives had left her cold. Now she understood the North Korean investment could have multiplied a hundredfold.

He targeted me, compromised my position with the NSA. The Utah ski trip and his weekend visits purported to show he cared. The boating trip on the Chesapeake seemed innocent enough, but now she recalled his probing questions about her work. Should she have recognized his affection as fraudulent, his interest as manipulative? Her fabled intuition had failed her.

Dr. Hoople had told her there would be an internal investigation. "They'll treat you like a suspect," he said. He told her it wasn't a reflection on her and advised her not to worry. It was like a doctor telling a patient she would be treated for a suspected brain tumor, but not to worry.

She lay in bed questioning her judgment, pondering her future. She was not a quitter, but the temptation arose. She sat up, stood, walked to the window, and opened the drapes. She squinted at the sunlight flooding her bedroom. She had never before wallowed in self-pity. She wouldn't begin now.

Freshly showered and coiffed, dressed to impress, and thoroughly caffeinated after twenty-four ounces of black coffee, she ignored the receptionist and walked directly to Hoople's office.

"Good morning, boss," she said. "Rachel Sullivan reporting for duty."

♦♦♦

A week later Rachel accepted Scott's invitation to join him in West Virginia for Father Sean's birthday party. *A party? The last thing I need. Still, it might be a distraction.*

She accompanied him as he drove from Fort Meade to Berkeley Springs. After miles of silence, Scott asked how she was doing.

"Me? What can I say? He was the first guy who cared. I mean the first guy who *pretended* to care. And I believed every word."

"Rachel, you could not have—"

Her voice breaking, she continued, "He betrayed me, my profession, my nation. How could he?"

At the steering wheel, Scott briefly turned his head and patted her shoulder.

Arriving in town, he stopped in front of The Country Inn. "I've booked a room here for you."

"What?" She raised her voice "No, I'm not staying here. I don't want to be alone. Can't I stay at your home?"

"Sorry, I didn't realize . . . You're very welcome to stay at my home, not stylish but fairly comfortable."

"I know you're a gentleman," she said, "and I don't care what people think. What will they think when they learn I was sleeping with the Benedict Arnold of our day?"

"They? If *they* come to know or even suspect, they'll gossip for a day and then move on. The rest of us will praise your role as team leader and admire your grit in picking yourself up and returning to work."

"Thanks. And you're right about work. Hoople said I'd be cleared within a week."

Scott drove her to his home, pointed to the guest room, and said he'd return shortly after retrieving Kierkegaard from Sean.

♦♦♦

Rachel lay down, fell asleep, dreamed, and awoke when Scott and Kierkegaard returned. She was greeted with raucous barking as she descended the stairs.

"Not to worry," Scott said, "his bark is worse . . . "

"Yes, I know, worse than his bite. I've just been dreaming about a two-legged creature who was the opposite, bite far more treacherous than his bark." *Still can't believe I was so deceived.*

"Let's talk," Scott said, walking toward his study.

She followed and sat on an antique Windsor armchair beneath his prized Edward Hopper painting.

He sat opposite her. "I'm going to yield to temptation and share some news I've promised to keep to myself."

"It was his evil twin," Rachel said, "not my phony boyfriend?" She smiled, the first time today.

"Don't we wish? Still, there's news that may warrant another smile. Operation Bluefish will receive the Director's Award for Valor." Two thumbs up.

"You must have made the nomination, called in a few chips."

"I would have, but our newbies beat me to it," Scott said. "The nomination's signed by Li, Marie, and Sam. The director immediately approved it. First time it's been awarded in more than two years. It will be presented to you at the White House."

"I should be gracious, but I don't deserve it."

"Deserve it?" Scott ran his hands through his hair. The agency is bursting with pride—all because of you."

"Nice of you to say, but—"

"Rachel, there's only one person who doesn't believe in you." He pointed. "You! Hoople knows, Woody knows, I know, we all know. Please join us in celebrating what you've accomplished."

"Scott, I have to confess, I still don't understand who killed Smokey, the Ontario engineer. Even if Stan's a traitor, he's not a murderer."

"Doubt if he personally jimmied the brakes, but he's responsible. Smokey was killed when he discovered the link between Costello and Stan, somehow learned the deputy director was receiving a monthly payoff."

"And Viktor Sokolov?" Rachel asked, "innocent?"

"Innocent? Hardly. A first-class scoundrel, dirty and rotten, but he provided the clue to identify the soon-to-be-convicted felon, Stanford Cooke."

"I can't believe I was so bloody wrong," Rachel said,

her voice breaking.

"If it's any consolation, I was wrong on several counts in Belfast. I thought for the longest time that Viktor had murdered Laura. Then I thought it was orchestrated out of some cockamamie religious conviction by a vengeful old genealogist named O'Malley. My next suspect was a crooked cop, Royal McGinty. It took my solicitor, Clare Sheehan, to set things straight. She eventually demonstrated Laura had died of a drug overdose."

"But your antenna for sensing bad guys didn't fail you. Viktor, O'Malley, McGinty—all three should be in jail."

"Let's hope. McGinty's out on bail but will certainly be convicted. And Clare told me O'Malley will soon be charged with transporting guns across the border. Ten to twenty years if convicted."

"And Viktor? Working for Italian intelligence but otherwise . . . "

"Otherwise a crook? So it would appear, but he's been protected by the Italians with the acquiescence of MI6 and likely the CIA."

"Selling drugs, trafficking women!" Rachel replied. "And they gave him a free pass?"

"His Italian handler insisted he's just been playing a role to get close to the real crooks."

"Some role," she said, leaping to her feet. "What about the fentanyl that killed Laura?"

Scott stood, opened his phone, found a picture of Laura and handed it to Rachel. "There she is, sitting next to me at Benedicts, hours before she died." He took a deep breath.

"And Viktor's still a free man?"

"Not for long. The Irish magistrate has issued a warrant for his arrest—for selling Laura the drugs that killed her."

She raised her hands, turned and stared at the lone figure in the painting, and turned back to Scott. "You knew it, you knew it all along,"

"Suspected, yes, but . . . "

Rachel waited for Scott to continue.

"When Viktor provided the intelligence on the North Koreans, I wanted to believe he was simply an undercover agent playing a role—until the Irish warrant was followed by a Justice Department request for his extradition to the States."

"Now you've lost me," Rachel said.

"They've charged him with illegal currency transactions, allegedly worth millions on behalf of a prominent American politician."

Rachel shook her head. "I never cast an eye on Viktor, never saw the evidence, but never doubted the fucker was guilty."

"Sounds like Woody's expanded your vocabulary."

"The least of what I've learned in the past month," she said, following Scott to the kitchen.

"Kierkegaard's been whining, reminding me it's his lunchtime."

As Scott opened a can of Alpo, Rachel mentally cataloged what she had learned. "Still missing something," she said. "O'Malley? Why did you suspect him?"

"Suspect him? No evidence. I just didn't like him. Didn't like his manner. Didn't like his gloating about my great-grandfather."

Scott stopped to feed Kierkegaard.

"After O'Malley gleefully reported my namesake had been hanged for murder, a pickup team of Spencer Cobb, Bridgette Walsh, and Clare Sheehan proved he was wrongly convicted. And I just learned that a British court has awarded me the princely sum of ten thousand pounds because of his wrongful conviction and death. It will go anonymously to Father Sean to repair the roof of the church."

"So, *you* made the contribution?" Rachel asked.

"Not the original ten thousand dollars. That came from Cobb, who hinted he'd mitigated his guilt for overcharging a rich client by forwarding it to the parish."

"The two of you've been working miracles," Rachel said.

"And it might not be the last. Won't know for years, but my great-grandfather's homestead might just revert to me—and to hundreds of unknown second and third cousins in Northern Ireland. Doubt if my share would cover another night at Benedicts of Belfast."

♦♦♦

"Testing, testing." The Honorable Spencer Cobb, as he was known in West Virginia, stood at the edge of the bandstand in the center of Berkeley Springs State Park. A young man adjusted an amplifier to eliminate the squealing feedback from the microphone.

"Is that better? Yes? Thanks for coming out to honor Father McManus on his birthday. Since he wouldn't divulge his age, I said I'd report he's older than Moses. He insisted that'd be a sacrilege, so let's just say he's ageless. The church ladies asked me to MC this shindig, so I'll begin by stating the rules. A few friends promised to say some good words about Father Sean. Not gonna put them under oath, but I expect the truth, the whole truth, or at least something resembling the truth."

A couple hundred people, members of the parish and other townspeople who knew Father McManus, were assembled around the bandstand. They applauded as Cobb introduced the first speaker, Thomas Sebastian Scott.

"Thank you," Scott said. "I first met Sean when we were seminary students together. He was my best friend. Still is. He wasn't the best student in our class. Nor was he the best behaved. But he had the biggest heart and the best smile. Still does. Sean, I'll keep this brief, because there's a long line of well-wishers behind me. I promise to be at your side to celebrate many more."

More applause. More introductions. More speeches. Sean beamed.

"Our next speaker needs no introduction. Felicity Philips—everyone's best friend, the town's pride and joy, world renowned artist, and an honorary member of the Shawnee tribe."

"You know me," she said, "you know I don't belong to the church, don't go to Mass, but Father McManus has a special place in his heart for sinners. His counsel has helped me through some rough patches."

Sean's smile broadened.

"My Shawnee friends are here from Oklahoma," she said, pointing to the men and women standing under a tall oak. "Let's give them a big hand. This morning, as the sun rose, they performed an ancient ritual to honor Father McManus and bestowed on him the Shawnee name of Chief Thundercloud."

More applause.

A perfect day for celebration. The canopy of century-old trees protected revelers from the sun, the cherrywood scent from the barbeque pit whetted their appetite, and the strangers approaching the bandstand piqued their curiosity.

"I have a special treat for you," Cobb said. "Three young women visiting our little town for the first time. This smiling redhead, Bridgett Walsh, is visiting from Belfast. With a little luck and a formality called a green card, she may soon be joining our community as my associate, technically a paralegal. She's always one step ahead of me and full of surprises, not the least of which is my discovery a few hours ago that her many talents include music. She's borrowed an old fiddle from our little museum and promised to entertain us later with some Irish music including my favorite, "Molly Malone"."

She waved and smiled as the crowd applauded.

"Standing next to her is Rachel Sullivan, an associate of Scott's. She's here from Washington, relaxing a little after quietly saving our nation from terrorists. No kidding, folks, but I can't say another word except to urge you to welcome her."

More applause. When Rachel didn't acknowledge, Cobb recognized she was too far from him to have read his lips. Bridgett nudged her, repeated his words. Rachel raised her hand and waved.

"Finally, straight from Johnstown, please welcome Professor Cecelia MacDonald. Since I barely know her, Father McManus has agreed to explain why she's here to celebrate his birthday."

After extended applause, Sean joined Cobb on the bandstand. The crowd had increased as a few curious tourists joined the festivities.

"Thank you, Spencer. Thank you all for being here and for your service to the community. Many of you, members of our parish, are aware we've been facing a financial crisis. My prayers were answered when some anonymous soul made a very generous contribution. And then a second miracle this very morning. Another major contribution from a second anonymous donor. We'll not only repair the roof but also expand our pre-school program. God bless."

His beatific smile led to more applause.

"This is more than a special birthday," he said, "because

I've witnessed a miracle from God."

The crowd was silent as he stopped, bit his lower lip, tried to hold back tears.

"When I was a seminary student, a young unwed mother gave birth to a baby girl who was adopted by loving parents. She grew up to become the wonderful woman who Spencer introduced as Cecelia MacDonald. Through the miracle of DNA testing, several months ago I learned the name of her father. Last week, she also discovered his name. When Cecelia arrived here in Berkeley Springs last evening, she addressed me—as father—and then we both cried. She embraced me, and I told her it was the happiest day of my life."

Cobb, surprised by Sean's candor, watched one couple turn and walk away with a look of disapproval. Many others rushed forward to shake Sean's hand and meet his daughter.

♦♦♦

The festival was nearly over. Most visitors had departed. Father McManus and Cecelia were seen walking toward the rectory. Spencer Cobb assured Bridgette her green card would come through and urged her to look around the town that might become her temporary American home.

Scott walked with Rachel across the park to The Country Inn and ordered two Guinness draft ales. *Deceived and betrayed, now the healing would begin.*

"I needed that," Rachel said. "I cried too, realized that miracles still occur, even when you have to wait half a lifetime. And I'm beginning to think you may be right. When I saw strangers applauding at the ceremony, I decided to leave my doubts behind. I'm moving on."

"Good for you, Rachel, and not a moment too soon. You're the best!"

"Thanks. A few hours ago, I sent a text to Roberto. He

responded immediately. Then I booked a flight and expect him to greet me at Rome's Fiumicino Airport a week from today."

"That should give us both time to wrap up a few loose ends at the agency. I may even see you at BWI before you board your flight. By coincidence, I'm flying non-stop to Munich the same day. Fredrica promised to get tickets for *Cosi fan Tutte*, thereby ensuring a happy ending."

THE END

Acknowledgements

For her support, patience, editing, and good humor—I thank my wife, MaryAnn Fulton. She read the manuscript chapter-by-chapter, offering her candid advice and council while taking occasional breaks as grandmother-in-residence at the home of our daughter and son-in-law in Ridgewood, New Jersey. However, our five-year-old granddaughter, Hadley Emilia Walsh, and her two-year-old sister, Philippa Kingsley Walsh, showed little interest in reading the manuscript.

I thank Norma Williamson for her superb copyediting and stylistic guidance. I recognize and highly value the encouragement and criticism generously offered by Jody Olsen as I was writing the novel. I appreciate the discerning advice from Warren Obluck, who reviewed the near-final manuscript and offered valuable suggestions. Thanks to Sue Rohan for her comprehensive review and exacting editorial oversight. And thanks to Paul Converti for his exacting review and correction of the proof copy of the manuscript.

Finally, I am deeply indebted to the other four members of the Doomers writing group: John Gregory Betancourt, Megan Plyler, Carla Coupe, and Karen Diegmueller. Professional novelists and editors, they mentored me as I revised the novel. To the extent you enjoy it, much of the credit goes to them for patiently coaching me, for insisting my characters move as well as speak, and for prodding me to introduce internal thoughts and reactions from my characters.

About the Author

Barry Fulton writes the Thomas Sebastian Scott Espionage Mystery series: *Behind the Seventh Veil, The Lady is Bugged,* and *Flame: Hackers, Artists, Lovers, and Spies.* He is a member of the Washington Institute of Foreign Affairs, the Public Diplomacy Council, DACOR, and Sisters in Crime—and a former board member of the Salzburg Global Seminar. A retired diplomat, Air Force officer, and university professor, he has been posted to NATO headquarters, Italy, Japan, Pakistan, and Turkey. He lives in Chevy Chase, Maryland, with his wife, MaryAnn, and spends weekends in a cabin in West Virginia.

Made in the USA
Middletown, DE
12 April 2022

63794878R00182